The Fame Game

NJ Moss

Print ISBN: 978-1-917214-32-2

For Krystle

Prologue

David

David was scared. He didn't want to admit it, but he was terrified right down to his core. He'd never had a knife pressed against his throat. He'd never thought he might die. Obviously, everybody died. But he'd never, ever dreamed that it would be like this. He wasn't even forty.

"Explain."

David licked his lips, then he said, "It was just a game."

"A game? A *game?*" More pressure with the knife. "If you don't explain what the *hell* you thought you were doing, I swear to God, I'll bleed you out right here. I don't care anymore. Too much has happened, too much has gone wrong for me to care. And all because of *you.*"

David was almost certain he could feel blood dripping down his neck.

"I wanted to... make a point," he said, hating the fact he'd paused, hating how desperate he felt.

"What point? I'm really, honestly curious."

More pressure from the knife. David was finding it difficult to speak. Urine was trickling down his leg. "People will do anything for fame."

A laugh. "*That's* your point? *That's* why you blackmailed a married woman? Why you threatened to expose an affair? Why you ruined so many lives? Because 'people will do anything for fame'? Do you realise how obvious that is? You might as well tell me you did it to prove the sky is blue."

"It was... more than that."

"I'm curious. Tell me."

David licked his lips. "I don't agree that people, in general, will do anything for fame."

"You're the one who bloody said it."

Because he had a knife to his throat! "A *lot* of people will," he went on. "But Vicky? A happily married woman with two children? I wanted to see how far a *normal* person would go. But I didn't expect any of this. How could I? Do you honestly believe I wanted any of this to happen?"

"You secretly recorded your sexual encounter with a married woman. You then used the video to blackmail her for the most pathetic reason I can think of. Do you think I should let you go, David? Do you honestly think you deserve that?"

Suddenly, David was on the floor, a knee on his belly, the knife tip pushed directly against his Adam's apple.

Chapter 1

Vicky

Walking through town, Vicky felt naked. David had threatened her with a sex tape. Apparently, he had secretly recorded her in some dingy hotel room over a decade ago, but he'd refused to show it to her. Either way, he could expose the historic affair if he really wanted to. He'd tell Seb, and then Vicky would be forced to lie... but what if David had found somebody who'd seen them kissing, or checking into a hotel, or... worse?

When her mobile rang, she sat on a bench, head rushing. It was Nat, her seventeen-year-old daughter. "Mum, are you going to be home soon? I'm meeting Mia and Grandma isn't here yet."

Vicky's mother and Nat were helping to take care of Vicky's youngest child, Max, during the summer holidays. Vicky swallowed, feeling like her daughter somehow knew about the affair too, feeling exposed. "I'm on my way."

"Can you get me some foundation? The one I like?"

Nat's voice got tight as if she expected a back-and-forth like usual, but Vicky felt too drained. "Sure."

"Oh – thanks."

"Bye. Love you."

"Love you, Mum."

Vicky put her phone in her bag and looked around the high street. The sun beamed down and the air was thick with clouds of vape smoke, and more than half the people were staring down at their phones. Vicky never normally paid attention to stuff like that, but David's sick challenge – no, his blackmail – had made her suddenly hyperaware of the technology all around her.

David had always fancied himself as an intellectual. In hindsight, David's so-called intellect had been a bunch of clichés spoken in a husky voice designed to make him *seem* clever. But this was just sick... and exactly the sort of thing David enjoyed doing.

"I'm a troll," he told her once, toward the end of their two-month-long affair. When she'd asked what he meant, he said with his easy smile, *"People don't have proper control of their emotions. It's too easy to trigger them. I go to certain pages and comment certain things, and people massively overreact."*

He'd been grinning, bragging, but his tone had changed when she'd sat up and said, "What sort of pages?"

It was like she was seeing him for the first time.

But then he'd clammed up. The next time they'd met, Vicky had pressed the issue. Finally, he'd admitted to going to missing persons Facebook pages and pretending to be the missing person. He didn't see anything wrong with it. That was when Vicky knew – though she should have already – she'd made a serious mistake.

She'd spent the last ten years trying to make up for it, but she hadn't told her husband. She'd thought this was in the *past*, for Christ's sake!

David's blackmail was typically David, typically sadistic and typically pointless. He'd sat in his flat, his hair markedly thinner and greyer, his belly bigger, glasses now instead of contacts, and told her with a wet smile that made her wonder if he was drunk. "It's simple, Vicky. I want to test the system. If a regular person – which you, angel, clearly are – were to try their best to chase online fame, how effective could they be?"

He told her she had to get a TikTok video with a million views. Or he'd tell her husband about the affair.

"Do you think this is clever?" she'd asked, trying to hold back tears.

"I think you can bleat all you want. But you're going to do it. Or your kids will know their dad's dick wasn't good enough."

Vicky had almost swung for him, but the prick had been smirking. That was what he wanted. She went to the nearest café and got a double espresso, trying to get her mind to work. He'd given her three weeks, she reflected, as the coffee scorched her throat. Three weeks to become famous. It sounded like a joke.

Chapter 2

Alek

He roamed the streets and saw past the cigarette butts, the children with their drug-filled knapsacks slung across their chests, doing wheelies on their bikes, the elderly with hope in their eyes or hopelessness weighing down their sagging wrinkled features like there was something physical piercing through. He saw through it all, into the past, and he wished everybody else could too. He saw an overweight person casually throwing away food, and he had to resist the urge to scoop up an iced bun and stuff it into his mouth.

Aleksander was not a poor man, but his grandfather Maksym spoke to him continuously. *'We would wait outside in the alleyways; we would suck what little gristle was left on chicken bones; we would eat apple cores, if we were lucky; the countryside was quiet in a way you cannot understand. There was no wildlife. People said it had all been hunted in the early days. But I know the truth, dear child – even the rodents had succumbed to grief.'*

People gave Alek strange looks, most likely because he was not dressed in a tracksuit or a T-shirt with a stupid slogan or symbol painted across the front.

He walked down the high street, into the park. It was summer, and he could smell rotting flesh. He could smell poorly managed earth. He could smell suffering horses and the metal of tractors without engines, brought for the photographers, for the badges of progress.

When he heard the girls laughing, he turned and smiled. How old were they? Perhaps sixteen, seventeen, dressed in a way that would invite no good attention. *'They are harlots, dear child. They are lost women.'* Tight-fitting leggings, shirts that showed their developing bodies. It sickened and confused Alek. Why would their parents let them dress this way?

"Is something funny?"

"Weren't talking to you, mate," the leader called over. She was the most well-fed of the group.

"But you were laughing at me."

There were four of them in total, but only the leader had the courage to look Alek in the eye. The rest looked to the leader, seeming to take some strange solace in her bright pink shirt and her proud belly and the green vape she constantly sucked on.

"So what?" she almost yelled, becoming absurdly aggressive absurdly quickly.

"I would like to know why," Alek said.

"Char, let's go..." One of the other girls tugged on her hand.

People were often discomfited by the way Alek spoke. He didn't understand it. He was calm, especially when wearing his Modern Face.

"We don't gotta go *anywhere*," Char said proudly, before enveloping her face in another cloud of vapour.

Alek reached into his pocket and took out several notes. The girls' eyes all widened.

"Want to make some money?" Alek said. They were by no means alone in the park; it was summer, almost full, but people ignored them. Nobody wanted to deal with a strangely dressed man – their opinion, Alek guessed – nor these wasted souls.

"You a nonce or something?"

"I'm a virgin, in fact," Alek told them, which got them all laughing in a thoroughly depressing manner. Like many people in today's lost world, they were proud of their prematurely shattered innocence.

"How old are you?" Char cackled.

"Thirty-one."

"And you're a *virgin*, mate?"

"Yep. I don't want you for that. I want to ask you two questions, that's all. If you get both right, I'll give you..." He counted the notes. "Eighty pounds."

"Really?"

"Char, come on..."

But the girl approached until she was almost at Alek's bench. "What questions?"

"Simple. Question one, can you tell me what the Holocaust is?"

"Are you joking? That's it?"

"Can you?"

"Hitler and that, what he did to the Jews and that. In the war. World War Two. Killed them and that."

"And that," Alek said, nodding, smiling, "is correct. Question number two. Can you tell me what the Holodomor is?"

"The holo-what?"

"The Holodomor," he repeated.

"Uh..." Char sucked on her vape so hard it was like she thought the answer was contained inside. "Uh... something in history, right?"

"*All* things are in history."

"Uh..."

Alek sighed, tucking the notes away. "That's a shame. It's probably best you get back to your friends."

"Wait – can I ask the others?"

"You shouldn't need to," Alek said, his Modern Face slipping just a bit. "Good day."

"But—"

"Fuck off."

That was his Famine Face coming out. Maksym sent a shiver of approval through Alek. *'Only the strong survived.'*

The girl looked like nobody had ever talked to her in that way. Her mouth fell open in a cartoonish manner, and then her whole body vibrated. "What?"

"I said..." Alek grinned. "Fuck, and then I believe I followed it up with, off."

"My brother'll break your neck, mate!"

"Then I suppose you better go and get him."

Char ran back to her group, none of whom had any idea what it truly meant to be intimidating, or interesting, or noteworthy in any respect. They chattered in their small circle, Char talking into her phone, summoning her brother. They kept looking over at Alek as though expecting him to flee. He lit a cigarette and smoked it slowly.

Ten minutes later, the brother appeared, wearing a shirt that marked him as the employee of a mobile phone shop. He was a broad, rough-looking man, with the sort of facial hair that somehow made him look poor. Not that Alek was judging.

"You the one who thinks you're tough, mate?" he said, standing over Alek's bench.

Alek rose, smiled at the man. Alek was not small; Alek was not weak. It was one of Maksym's disappointments that Alek refused to starve himself. But that was inauthentic. One day, if he managed to complete his project, he would experience it for real.

The phone shop man didn't look very tough anymore. He was probably accustomed to his mere presence being enough. "Your sister doesn't know what the Holodomor is."

"Who gives a fuck?"

"Do you?"

"That's not the point, mate."

"It *is* the point," Alek snapped. "Before the Holocaust, there was the Holodomor, the purposeful starving to death of millions of people. The only ones who grew fat were the ravens. They plucked eyeballs out of heads. Stalin took the land, the spirit, the identity – humanity was lost... Do you think that matters?"

The phone shop man took a few steps back. Alek hadn't meant to raise his voice, but this idiot's attitude was insulting. Did he expect Alek to be *afraid* of him?

"Just leave little girls alone, psycho."

"I thought you were going to assault me."

"Wuh-what?"

"When you marched over here, so filled with bravado, I thought a fight was afoot. Well, are you? Or are you going to just stand there?"

"He's mental, Char," the man said, turning away and then leading the girls from the park.

Alek left soon after, since he knew that in this modern age, *he* would probably get into trouble for trying to educate the morons. He went to the supermarket and bought eighty pounds worth of food – a trolley full of tinned goods, rice, pasta, sauces, biscuits, and a few perishables – and then dumped it all in the donations box.

Afterwards, he went home, smoked more cigarettes, and took his small wooden box from its secret place behind the display cabinet. He rattled it as he stared at the black-and-white photo of Maksym on the wall. He kept rattling, and then

Maksym's lips moved. His voice was quieter, more ghostly, than usual, but that was because the old photo distorted it.

"You... are... the... only... one... who... can... save... me..."

"I know."

"You... can... save... us... all..."

Alek rattled the box. He didn't want to admit the next bit. "I'm frightened of what I'll have to do."

"You've... done... so... much... already..."

"But..." Alek swallowed. "I'll have to do much, much more."

Maksym's lips curved into a frown, then the voice stopped. No matter how much Alek shook the box, it wouldn't return.

Chapter 3

Vicky

Vicky was sitting in the kitchen with her best friend, Michelle. The sound of Max and his friend jumping on the trampoline filtered through the window, and the scent of strong coffee drifted up Vicky's nostrils and all through her body, almost making her feel sick. Footsteps thumped upstairs; Nat and her friend were practising a dance for social media.

Michelle leaned forward, lowering her voice. "Do you think he really has a video?"

"It doesn't matter," Vicky replied. "If he tells Seb..." Vicky stopped when the trampoline noises cut off, but then she heard them start up again. She glanced through the open patio doors and saw Max and his friend playfully wrestling. "If I don't go along with his insane plan, he could just tell Seb. I wouldn't be able to lie. Keeping it a secret is one thing, but lying?"

Vicky felt raw as she moved her finger around the edge of her mug. She had become used to being happy; the affair, more than a decade ago, was like a hazy nightmare. She'd regretted it the moment it ended – actually, even before. But would that mean anything to her husband?

"I'll lose everything," she whispered, fighting off tears,

annoyed with herself. "Maybe Nat will be okay. She's had both her parents for seventeen years. But Max? Will he? I don't want to be divorced. Why did I do it? For God's *sake*, what's wrong with me?"

Michelle tried to touch her arm in a gesture of support, but Vicky leaned away. She didn't deserve any sympathy. She didn't want to cry, which she knew she would if she let Michelle hug her.

Sensing what was required of her, Michelle said, "Remember when we first met, and you were trying for Nat?"

They'd met in their late teens. Vicky had been in university for art criticism, and Michelle had been studying fashion. Since then, they'd both moved back to their seaside hometown and begun jobs in a call centre, not really using their degrees, but making a living, at least.

Michelle had thought Vicky was crazy for trying for a baby. But when Vicky met Seb, they both knew: this was it. They wanted a life together. They'd both wanted kids ever since *they'd* been kids.

"*Hellooooo?*"

That got a smile out of Vicky. "I remember."

"Remember how you attacked the problem? All the research? All the experimenting?"

"What does this have to do—"

"*That's* what you need to do now, Vicky. Just play his stupid game. I'll help you. We'll download the app and look at trending videos, then just make a bunch and we'll see. There's a chance, at least."

"I don't even know how to use the bloody thing," Vicky snapped.

"Then *learn*," Michelle said, just as fiercely.

Vicky nodded, knowing Michelle was right. Then her phone vibrated on the table. It was Seb.

> Hey, beautiful. Fancy a curry for dinner? I've had a day.

Vicky couldn't help it. There was something in the simplicity of the text that just went right to her tear ducts. She tried to push the pain away, but a warm tear was sliding down her cheek. This time, when Michelle touched her arm, Vicky didn't pull away.

"Take a few moments," Michelle said. "Let yourself feel hopeless. Let yourself feel sad. Then get your head on and *attack*. I can help you too, remember. I've been doing the social media stuff for my cousin's brewery, and that's doing well. I'll just need to keep it quiet."

"Can't muddy your brand with mean old me."

Michelle smiled tightly.

By the time Max came in to ask if he and his friend could play their computer game, Vicky had got herself under control.

<h1 style="text-align:center">Chapter 4</h1>

———————

<h2 style="text-align:center">Alek</h2>

Alek peeled his eyes open, looking at the ceiling, a shimmery image of Maksym's face watching him. Normally, Alek would try to exist in this in-between place of wakefulness and sleep; it often allowed him to communicate with Maksym far more easily. But the knocking jolted him into the full, unpleasant light of reality.

He jumped to his feet and went to the front window, looking down at the stone-covered entranceway, to find Liuba standing there with a bag-for-life clutched in each hand. She must've heard the window open. She looked up. "Were you sleeping?" she said, concern in her voice.

Alek firmly implemented his Modern Face, beaming, laughing. "At this hour? Don't be ridiculous, Liuba."

He was pretty sure she narrowed her eyes, so he disappeared into the house, reminding himself to call her Michelle. Their parents had given them Ukrainian middle names, and it was only Alek – or Alex Aleksander Bodar – who routinely used it as his first. It was their way of keeping a hint of home while abandoning their traditional naming system.

"Liuba?" she said, raising an eyebrow when he opened the door.

Alek grinned, doing a quick mental check. Had he hidden everything that needed to be hidden? Were there any signs of his project waiting around to betray him?

"I just like seeing the look on your face." He smiled. "But honestly, you should be prouder of your heritage."

"Just help me with the bags, numb nuts."

Alek took the bags and led her into the kitchen. Because of his sister's frequent visits, he was forced to keep the majority of the house in some kind of order. The cellar, once an entertainment room, was his only refuge; he'd told Liuba he was going to have it renovated, so he'd sealed it off, covered everything in dust sheets. It was unfortunate, the need to lie. *"The honest died first,"* Maksym said then, to alleviate some of the guilt.

As they walked into the kitchen, Alek spotted her eyeing his medication boxes. He was always diligent about keeping them at the correct number of pills. But he despised how they made him feel; the bonds they weakened; the voices they quietened. The pills were like a red plague corrupting his soul, closing him off from the rest of the world, filling his mind with fake photographs of the reality *they* wanted him to see.

Alek began unpacking the shopping. "You don't have to do this, you're aware?"

"I'm *aware* that you'd starve if it wasn't for me."

Alek laughed, since he was Modern Faced, but this was a grotesque thing for her to say, especially considering what their ancestors had experienced. But Liuba despised when he stated basic facts about the past.

"Anyway," she went on, as she busied herself at the coffee machine, "if I didn't visit you, who would, huh?"

Alek didn't need visitors. He had his project; he had his jaunts around town. He had Maksym.

"Have you seen the news?" he asked.

Liuba gritted her teeth, just for a moment.

"Do we have to talk about that?"

"It's a simple question..."

"If you care that much, Alex, why don't you host some refugees? How many bedrooms in this old house?"

Alek winced. It was a fair, and annoying, point. If it hadn't been for the project, then he would have filled their parents' old house with Ukrainians.

Liuba made a that-settles-that face.

"How's work?" Alek asked, as she handed him a steaming mug of coffee.

They sat at the kitchen bar, which overlooked the wild garden.

She laughed. "You always ask that even though you don't care."

"That's because I'm a polite, functioning member of society."

She laughed again, a wonderful sound; it always had been, ever since they were kids. "Work is work. Sometimes exciting, sometimes miserable, mostly just existing."

"Then why do it?"

"Why don't I live on Mum and Dad's money, you mean?"

Alek shrugged. "Not all work involves financial reimbursement. Some of the *best* work, actually, has nothing to do with money."

"Such as?" Liuba said.

He knew how she saw him. It was useful for her to believe he spent his days lounging around, taking meds, doing nothing but eating and occasionally working out, or going for walks. But sometimes, it bothered him. She thought he was wasting his days when in reality, he was doing something more important than everybody in this town – in this country – combined. *"And don't you ever forget it,"* Maksym said, approvingly.

When Alek didn't reply, Liuba blew on her coffee. "You should clean the garden up, Alex. Or hire somebody to do it at least."

"Why? It's not like it's bothering anybody."

"Mum would hate to see it like this."

Mum and Dad were dead, but Alek wasn't about to throw that in her face. It came back to the basic facts thing. He'd never phrase it like this with his sister, but she needed reality to be wrapped in soft, inoffensive material for it to make sense.

"What are your plans for today?" she said.

"I'm going to get started on the garden."

"Really?"

"Yes. You're right. Mum wouldn't have liked to see it this way. And it will give me a project, something to focus on."

"Ha, ha, a project. Very nice." Alek concealed a secret smile with a sip of coffee. He already *had* a project, of course.

Soon, it was time for Liuba to leave. She hugged him how she always did, with a hint of desperation, like she was willing him to still be there the next time she visited. Before Alek had found his purpose, he'd done some silly, self-destructive things. Then they'd put him on all these numbing agents, obliterating his mind. But now, he was free. The only sick part was he couldn't tell Liuba about it.

"I love you," she said.

"I love you too."

He kissed her on the cheek.

When she was gone, he went straight to the cellar, pulled aside the board he'd laid across the door, then opened it and walked down the stairs. The cellar was broken into sections; it had been his father's carpentry workshop once upon a time. Now, there was a small kitchenette, a cubby room with a toilet and sink inside, a mattress with crumpled, dirty sheets all wrinkled across the middle, and a man with a heavy chain around his ankle, secured to the wall.

The man was crusty with dirt. He reeked, and Alek knew he'd have to wash him soon, lest the smell travel up the stairs and into the house proper. He'd painstakingly soundproofed the walls, but he hadn't smell-proofed them. His captive was around forty years old. He had long, greasy silver hair. He was a heroin addict, a sex offender, a purveyor of children.

And he was missing a hand. The wound was healing terribly; Alek was no doctor. The bandage was yellow and ugly. The man ran at Alek, the chain pulling taut and yanking him backwards with a loud clang.

"That was very intelligent," Alek said.

"You piece of shit," the man raved.

"Oh, Ollie," Alek said, shaking his head.

"You animal."

"I'm the animal? You confessed all your worst sins to a complete stranger. Worse, you did it with a smile on your face, all because he gifted you some cheap cider."

Alek had encountered a problem when deciding to graduate from animal bones to human ones. Just as with the animal bones, he'd wanted to ensure he wasn't crossing any significant moral boundaries. 'There's no place for morality in the soundless lifeless dark of hell,' Maksym had said, but Alek disagreed. Despite everything, he wanted to be a good person.

So, for the animal bones, he'd searched for roadkill, or bought wholesale beasties from the butchers. But when it came time for humans, a question: how to do it and keep his soul intact? So, he'd donned his hobo garb and gone roaming, drinking, talking, searching.

Finally, he'd found Ollie, a proud predator.

"Please," Ollie whispered, whimpering, his clothes reeking of shit and piss and despair.

"You bragged about being with a thirteen-year-old girl, sir," Alek said. "There's no space for 'please' after that."

"I didn't... I didn't..."

"You didn't what? Mean to assault her? Mean to ruin her life?" Alek sighed. "In any case, this isn't about what you've done. It's about what you're going to do."

When Alek turned and walked into the kitchenette, Ollie began to scream. He knew which drawer Alek was going to; he knew what tools were inside. Maksym sent a shiver of warm glee through Alek, but Alek felt no pleasure on his own accord. He couldn't begrudge his grandfather, though. His life had made him callous. How could it not?

'The next cut will kill him,' Maksym said. 'Best to just go all the way, Alek. More bones with that method, anyway.'

"True, true."

"Psycho!" Ollie yapped. "Talking to yourself like a freak."

Alek took out a long, sharp blade. This was one of the reasons he didn't like barbers; he knew the damage cutting tools could do, and with what ease.

"Does antagonising me seem like a very intelligent thing to do?" Alek asked.

Ollie screamed some more, then raised his one good hand like he was going to fight. But Alek was a large man; he was a strong man. And, more than that, he had the fury of his voiceless ancestors roaring in his heart.

Chapter 5

Vicky

For the next two weeks, Vicky lived a double life. One night, Seb wrapped his arm around her, nuzzled his face into the back of her head so that she could feel his breath, and said, "Are we okay?"

She'd said, "I love you, Seb. Of course we are."

"Good," he'd replied, then, just a few minutes later, began to snore.

Each night, this was when Vicky came to life. She'd wait for the snoring to deepen, and then quietly climb out of bed and move through the house until she was at the very back, in the study. This was the best room for what she had to do, nightly, on repeat: humiliate herself. Michelle had become her researcher, looking up the latest trends, attempting to guide Vicky in the right direction.

Michelle even helped Vicky learn how to use the apps. It turned out that her brother Alek was quite active on certain forums online, and so she'd taught him a lot about using a variety of tools for that purpose. He'd even gone through stages of creating his own videos a few years ago. *'He's so clever. He remembers everything, Vicky. Show him once and he never forgets.'* Luckily, Michelle was happy to show, via screenshots or quiet video calls, Vicky something several times if she didn't get it. She wasn't that clever.

Vicky had first tried a video in which she'd narrated over some photos of Nat and Max when they were little. She wanted to get some feel-good vibes going, with emotional music in the background. She spoke passionately, about the love she'd felt instantly. *'It was like having a piece of me returned to myself.'* She was pretty sure she'd stolen that from an author. Something Berry. But it was true too, so she didn't beat herself up too much.

Anyway, it didn't matter. The video got eight views. She tried that twice more, and then switched to a motivational story about a half marathon she'd run last year. It got twelve views. Michelle said there were lots of videos of people giving 'hot takes' while doing their make-up, so Vicky went to an AI platform online and searched 'divisive political opinions'. She made videos on both sides, using two accounts, a left- and a right-wing one.

The left-wing one got five hundred views, and it taught her something; she had to shock. She had to *grip*. This sentiment was hammered home even more when David, the little weasel, sent her a Facebook message. *Tick tock...* followed by a clock emoji. She hadn't blocked him, because she was worried he'd reach out to somebody else instead. But she always deleted his messages instantly upon reading them.

Another message came through as soon as she'd deleted the first. *What do you think happens if you fail, hmm?*

She just could just see him there in his dirty flat, reeking of drugs and cigarettes, that proud, unearned smile on his superior face. Vicky still found it difficult to believe she had ever fantasised over this man, and maybe that was because she hadn't, not really. She'd fantasised about Seb being more emotionally available, more physically affectionate, less distracted. It had made her weak and blind.

Send me the video then, she'd replied, something she rarely did with him. *Of us. The secret one you took.*

You mean the one of you in fishnet stockings, begging for it to be harder?

Vicky cringed with something akin to PTSD. Not only did she feel like she was living a secret life, but it was like her mind had split into two as well. Perhaps it was the constant staring at cameras; there was trauma attached to that, something ugly from her childhood. It hurt, almost physically at times, to look at cameras. But she was doing this for her family; she couldn't think of a better reason to stuff her emotions somewhere deep and dark until it was a more appropriate time to deal with them.

Maybe I'll send them to your hubby, he went on.

What are you getting out of this? Why are you torturing me?

He didn't reply. Vicky deleted the message and continued with her split life. A couple of times, she was almost caught by Seb, but she heard him and quickly rushed into the kitchen, pretending she couldn't sleep and was making some chamomile tea. His sympathy was the worst, the real concern in his eyes. They were more in love now than she'd dreamed they could've been during that rough patch ten years ago.

"I'm here," he said, pulling her into a hug and kissing the top of her head. "Always."

Vicky kept working, trying various niches, basically switching her mind off and letting it happen on autopilot: meal prep with some very amateur timelapse stuff; an attempt to turn an old picture frame into abstract art; some basic cleaning tips; a thrifted clothes haul, which really consisted of clothes taken from her wardrobe; a fitness challenge she had no intention of completing; various political rants, all of which performed better than anything else; a video in which she pretended to be a

Ukrainian under fire, her hair purposefully messy, a black smudge of ink across her face meant to imitate debris; eating a hot chilli and trying not to scream so she'd wake the whole house; reviewing their coffee machine, or attempting it, since it was difficult without actually turning it on; she even tried a Q&A with questions she'd written herself.

Later, she'd wonder how she'd recorded *that* video so thoughtlessly. It certainly wasn't one that Michelle had OKed... but she had implemented all of the tips that she had given her. It had come in the midst of a flurry of sleepless activity, none of which she was proud of, all of which had felt insanely surreal. She had been staring with bloodshot eyes at her phone, trying to become *internet famous*, because of some stoner she'd once taken a deranged, sick comfort in.

But how had she done *that* without thinking? Pretended to be a victim of war?

Two weeks and one day after the blackmail began, Vicky's life changed. Seb had already left for work when Nat rushed into the bedroom, her face red, looking like she'd just sprinted a mile. In one hand, she had her phone. In the other, her tablet. She stared at Vicky almost like she hated her.

"Mum, what the hell? What the *hell*?" She sounded like she might cry. "*Mum?*"

"What?" Vicky said, swallowing as fear twisted through her.

"That video!" she yelled. "Mum, it's all over the internet. There's even a newspaper article online about it; it'll probably be in the actual newspaper today! It has two million views. Jesus, Mum!"

Vicky almost smiled. Two million was twice what she'd needed. All she had to do now was get through whatever minor controversy this caused. She could even delete the video once David had seen how many views it got. And if he decided to keep trying to blackmail her, then... She hardly wanted to think it, but she'd have to tell him no. She couldn't do this forever, not with Nat looking at her with borderline hatred in her eyes.

Nat walked to the edge of the bed, sat down, and seemed so grown up as she gave Vicky a searching look. "What's going on?"

"I was just experimenting," Vicky said, knowing how stupid it sounded. But it wasn't like she could tell the truth.

"Experimenting," Nat repeated, but then her mobile started ringing. "It's Mia." Nat quickly answered, her speech speeding up into teenage babble. "Yeah, I saw. Yeah, literally, like a hundred messages. No joke. I know. Yeah. I know. I know. Yeah. It's mental."

Vicky listened to her daughter talk, knowing there would be some stress, but also knowing that very soon, life could go on as normal. She'd be able to bury the affair like she always had. This life could end. The disconnection she'd experienced every night staring at the camera lens, thinking of *before*, could end.

"I'm sorry," Vicky said, causing Nat to abruptly cut herself off. "Nat, you're right. Maybe I had a midlife crisis. I'll delete the vid—" She almost said *videos*, plural, but she didn't want Nat to learn about any of the others. "Video."

Nat just huffed and left the room. Vicky quickly went to her TikTok account. She was stunned to see it right there, the view counter, *exploding*... with all her other videos slowing creeping up too. Weirdly, as she deleted the other videos – she didn't need them now, and didn't want them out there – she felt... not bad, exactly. But almost like, well, wasn't it a waste? Look at all those numbers going up and up and...

But that was just madness. This was over; it hadn't been easy, but it was done. A few local newspaper articles, some passing outrage or interest, and then Vicky would never have to think about social media again.

Michelle had texted her:

> Well done. I'm just sorry it had to be THIS video.

Michelle was of Ukrainian descent. Vicky hadn't even considered that. She'd made literally hundreds of videos within the past two weeks. But was that an acceptable excuse?

Chapter 6

Alek

Something terrible had happened, and Alek knew who was responsible. His grandfather's voice had vanished, the moment Alek watched Vicky's video. One moment he was there like usual, and the next – after Alek had learned of the video through the local newspaper – there was nothing, just the echoing silence of a hopeless skull, just the desperate dream to find him again.

Alek watched the video over and over, trying to make sense of it. Sitting up in bed, he must've replayed the damn thing at least a hundred times. He had never paid too much attention to his sister's friend before, but now he felt like he could draw her from memory.

He went to the comments, relieved to find many of them were disgusted, but there were others, people arguing that she was merely shedding light on a difficult topic.

This is absolutely heartless! She isn't even Ukrainian!
Wow, talk about ignorant. Who even is this person?
Guys, relax. She's just trying to help.
Help what? Herself!
It was grotesque on a visceral level, but that wasn't Alek's

main concern. Where the hell was his grandfather? What about their plan? Alek had gone too far to back out now. He put his phone in a drawer, thinking maybe Maksym didn't want to speak while the video was playing, but it didn't work. So Alek went downstairs into his study, and tried to read. Often, when he read, Maksym would make comments about the text.

But it didn't work. Everything was too silent. There was nothing. Alek was alone. He'd have to do something about it, find a way to make this right.

He couldn't let Vicky get away with this. When Liuba rang him and said that her friend, Vicky, was arranging a barbeque, Alek understood immediately what Maksym wanted. He was working through Vicky.

"I think she just wants to get back to normal," Liuba said cautiously, as though she knew how truly grotesque her friend was. But Alek had to play the game. Or try to, at least.

"I understand," he replied, and Liuba gave a sigh of relief, clearly anticipating some meltdown from him. "That sounds lovely."

The party was already too loud. There was something ugly about the noises of this Modern-Faced world without Maksym there to make it all more understandable. Alek had the ability to reshape reality through the conduit of history, so he could see that these people had existed countless times before – their mannerisms, their hopes, their dreams.

Liuba looked at him, winced, clearly understanding this was a mistake. Then she painted a bright, pretty smile onto her face and grabbed his hand. "Don't look so grumpy," she said, squeezing his hand. "It's a *party*."

Alek didn't want to upset her, so he bared his teeth in a decent smile. "And I'm *excited*."

She laughed, and Alek almost did, but then *she* appeared. Vicky, looking flustered, wearing an apron, her hair all in disarray. Nothing like that video – nothing like the weird words she spat out, which took Alek's grandfather away. Vicky stopped, stared at Alek. Alek realised he was murdering her in his mind. He forced another smile.

"Vicky, you remember Alek, right?"

"Yes." She forced a smile too, oh-so civilised. "It's nice to see you again. It feels like it's been years."

"I think the last thing I dragged him to was the work Christmas party, what, three years ago?"

Alek shrugged. "Yes, maybe. Around that."

His mind superimposed the video over Vicky in stunningly impressive colour and accuracy. It was like he was projecting her sins onto her face. He even heard the music.

"Are you hungry?" Vicky asked now, turning toward the hallway, all the doors open so there was a straight shot to the sunny garden, with a few kids bouncing on the trampoline.

Liuba nudged Alek. "You're staring at her."

"Am I?"

"Is this about the video?"

Alek flashed a smile. "What video?"

They went into the garden with the others. Sebastian, Vicky's husband, was standing at the grill. There was something weak about him, though Alek wasn't sure what it was, exactly. He flipped burgers, waved when he saw Alek looking, though they'd only spoken a few times over the years. Alek waved back.

When he turned to Liuba, she was staring, her eyes all glossy, like she was a proud mum at the playground watching her stunted son finally make a friend. Alek resisted the urge to snap at her.

"She didn't mean anything by it," Liuba said quietly, close to Alek's ear.

He sighed, shaking his head. He didn't need to constantly be talking about it; it was the last thing Liuba should've reasonably wanted. She didn't even know the full extent of it, the connection between Maksym and the upload. Not here. Liuba deserved a fun party.

"I know," Alek told her.

"It was a stupid bet with a mate."

"I said I know."

She sighed. "I'm going to get a drink. Want anything?"

"Water."

Liuba went into the kitchen. Alek leaned against the wall, his arms folded, watching as three boys and one girl competed to see who could jump the highest on the trampoline. Other people were milling about in groups, more kids running around. A teenage girl approached Alek, a plastic cup in one hand and her mobile phone in the other. She had Vicky's sincere eyes.

"Uh, sorry," she said. "Alek, right?"

"Yes. And you're Natasha. I saw you once when you were much younger."

For some reason, this made a shiver move through her. There was so much noise in the garden. Crackling meat and screaming children and the *scree-scree-scree* of the trampoline like a rotted corpse being torn to pieces.

"Uh, yeah." She laughed for no reason. "Sorry, it's just, do you mind not sitting on that?"

Alek looked down. Without realising it, he'd been sitting on the green hose box. Now that he paid attention, he also noted Sebastian looking over with fatherly and home-owner concern. Alek studied the box; his weight had seemingly partially dislodged one of the fixtures.

"Ah," he said, nodding at Natasha. "You're right. I've broken it."

Sebastian approached with a slight awkwardness, which bothered Alek for some reason. He was shuffling, rubbing his hands together. Somehow, Alek knew he could spit in this man's face and there would be no consequences other than mumbling and stuttering and threats of police.

"I'm sorry, Sebastian," Alek said. "I sat on this box and now it's partially broken."

Sebastian leaned over, then smiled, waved a hand. "Don't worry about it."

Alek went for his jacket pocket, his chequebook, which he kept mostly because it made him feel connected to the past. "I can write a cheque... or bank transfer?"

"What? No, no, seriously." Sebastian laughed. "Don't *worry*."

"What's funny?" Alek asked.

Natasha looked at her dad in a strange, accusatory way. It was as though she had previously warned him about Alek... perhaps because of the Ukrainian connection through the video?

"Just... don't worry about the hose," Sebastian said.

"But you laughed."

Liuba appeared with two plastic cups, a confused smile on her face. "What's going on?"

"I've damaged their property," Alek said.

"No, really, it's nothing."

"This is your home," Alek told Sebastian. "Your home."

Liuba actually took the melodramatically drastic measure of putting both plastic cups down and taking one of Alek's arms with both of her hands. She dragged him away from Sebastian and Natasha, muttering unwarranted apologies until she'd trapped Alek in a quiet corner of the garden.

"Stop being so intense and weird," she snapped. "You're freaking everybody out."

They had every reason to freak out with an amoral woman like Vicky in their midst. With over five million views, with local newspaper reports about them, shouldn't people have *cared*? But the virality was already fading; her fifteen minutes were draining to sludge, taking Maksym along for the ride.

But Alek couldn't have this. Liuba would get too hands-on otherwise, with her questions and her monitoring and her daily visits. He smiled, touched her arm. "I'm sorry. I think I need a drink."

"Is that a good idea?" she asked softly.

"I can have one drink. Just to relax me."

Liuba looked uncertain, but she nodded. Alek went into the house, resisting the impulse to wince when he saw Vicky talking to an elderly woman in the kitchen. Vicky was standing there in her apron like she was a wasting-away mother in the icy heart of December without even a root to gnaw on and with an unmarkable evil rotting in the corner of the tiny room.

Alek walked by them, tuning out their conversation, or trying to. He grabbed a beer from the fridge and cracked it open.

"I think it was very moving," the elderly lady was saying, as Alek rushed for the door. "You brought *awareness*. Being offended over that, it's just... well, excuse me, but absurd!"

"I'm absurd," Alek whispered under his breath, taking a big sip of beer. Immediately, he felt it rush around his head. He'd never been the biggest drinker.

He smiled at Liuba as he joined her on some patio chairs.

"What did you say to her?" Liuba said.

Alek took another sip. He quite liked the taste of the beverage. "Nothing. I just got my drink."

"Oh. Okay. Good."

"You're worrying too much."

She gave him a look. It bothered Alek, but he just sipped more beer. She was communicating the entire history of their lives with a little head nod. When they were younger, Alek had sometimes ruined friendships, or made mockeries of parties, or humiliated his sister, all without knowing he was doing it or meaning to. Liuba became a flustered girl as she looked at him.

He leaned over, kissed her on the forehead. "Please relax."

"That's what I'm trying to tell *you*."

"I'm with my wonderful sister. I have a lovely cold beverage on a warm sunny day. I may even go on the trampoline soon. I'm doing just fine."

That got a smile out of her, and she took a sip of her own drink.

Chapter 7

Vicky

"Are you sure that's a good idea?" Seb asked, leaning against the kitchen counter and looking out of the window.

They were all gathered around the trampoline, clapping and cheering as Alek threw himself up and down, waving his arms wildly. Michelle stood nearby, the same tight note in her posture which had been there all night.

"He's drunk," Seb said.

"He'll be fine. It's his choice."

Vicky preferred to have him on the trampoline than glaring at her. Shame stung every inch of her body each time somebody complimented her. They were proud of something she'd hated doing. But there was a small piece, a tiny one... Everybody gasped as Alek spun over, almost landing on his head. But at the final moment, he shifted and hit his back instead, then stumbled up and climbed off the trampoline.

Vicky hoped he'd stay out there. His obvious judgement was almost too much to handle. The challenge was over – the game was done. She just wanted to move on.

Seb touched Vicky's arm. "Are you doing all right?"

She hugged him tightly, closing her eyes, savouring the

moment. She could hate the video all she wanted, but without it, she wouldn't have this. But what if David lied? What if he'd use the video against her again, anyway? She couldn't let herself think like that.

"I'm doing fine now," she said into his chest.

He trailed his hand through her hair. Soon, his parents were in the kitchen with them, and they all started chatting about conservatories and house extensions. Around five or ten minutes passed, and then Michelle and Alek walked into the kitchen. Alek's height and general demeanour had a way of putting people on edge.

Vicky reminded herself he was ill.

"So, what's the topic of conversation?" he said, marching over to the kitchen and pulling the fridge door open aggressively.

"Alek—"

He grabbed a beer, turned, cut Michelle off. "Liuba, my angel, it's a party."

Alek leaned against the kitchen counter, drinking his beer. He looked huge as he threw his head back and started necking the beer. Michelle tutted, which made Alek put his beer down. He folded his arms and smiled around the assembled crowd.

He grinned at Sebastian. "This has been a lovely party, sir."

Sebastian returned the smile, but Vicky could tell he felt awkward. He didn't even like it when his assistants at work called him *sir*. "You're welcome."

"All the free beer a man can drink. I guess TikTok really is lucrative, huh?"

"Alek," Michelle snapped.

"It's fine," Vicky said, mostly just to keep things civil. Contained in the kitchen, with the rest of the party having a good time outside, they could at least limit the damage. She turned to Alek. "I didn't make any money off the video."

"Hmm," Alek said. "But you should have. It was quite the performance. Oscar-worthy, some might say."

"Thank you," Vicky said stiffly.

"Have you acted before?"

"Only in a school play."

"And I bet you were great!" Sebastian's dad said loudly, with a forced smile, basically trying to give Alek the subtle British *leave off it, mate…*

"Only in a school play," Alek repeated, drumming his fingers against the counter. "Only…" He drummed them. "In…" And again, seeming to work up to some sort of chant.

Michelle put her drink down and walked toward her brother. "Right, that's it. You're drunk. I'm taking you home."

"Drunk, me?" he said, putting his hand on his chest and swooning to the side. "How could you say such a thing, sweet sister? How could you think such a thing?"

Seb gave Vicky a look. She didn't know what to do; neither of them had experience of dealing with somebody who was severely mentally ill. Sure, they got anxious, had their ups and downs, but Alek's intensity and aura was different, somehow.

"Come on."

She pulled on her brother's arm, but he didn't move it. He just kept it there and tilted his head at her. For a confusing second, Vicky thought he was going to hit her.

"But I haven't made *my* video yet." Alek winked at Vicky and Seb moved closer to her, which somehow made it worse. Alek straightened up and glared, as though he thought there was going to be a fight.

"Stop it," Michelle snapped, sounding on the verge of tears.

"I'm not doing anything wrong," Alek said.

"I hate you when you're like this."

Alek stared down at her, blinking, looking hurt, his eyes glistening. Michelle let out a sob. "For fuck's sake, let's just *go.*"

Vicky's mother-in-law tutted when Michelle swore, and that really annoyed Vicky. They were clearly watching some heart-wrenching family drama unfold, but all she cared about was the words.

"But wait..." Alek danced away from her, laughing, slipping his hand into his pocket and taking out his phone. "You're forgetting about *my* video."

He laughed again, turning on the camera and speaking into his phone. He spun so they were all in shot. Michelle stood with her hands at her sides, glaring at her brother. She looked at Vicky with another apologetic look.

"Ladies and gents," Alek said, speaking into the phone. "My name is Aleksandr Bodar. My grandfather was Maksym Bodar, and he survived the Holodomor, a Ukrainian tragedy. And look who I've got here with me!"

"Listen, mate," Seb said, but Alek just went right on. Seb was soft and loving and loyal. But he wasn't tough; Vicky had never needed him to be. Except during the affair, when she'd taken David's aggressive wannabe philosophical ranting for some kind of toughness.

"Vicky underscore thirty-seven, in the flesh." Alek cackled, sounding truly insane now. It was a cruel thing to think; it made Vicky feel bigoted. But he did. "She's currently kicking me out of her house!"

"Oh, God, Alek," Michelle said, tugging on him.

"It's the truth, isn't it, Vicky?" Alek ranted. "You're happy to use my history to benefit your social media *career*, but you won't even let me finish my meal!"

"It's not your meal we're worried about," Seb snapped, a little louder this time. "It's all that booze."

"All that booze," Alek repeated, sounding confused. "I've had half a drink."

"Just get out," Seb snapped.

"It's because I challenged her about the video," Alek told the camera. "I said I felt thoroughly disrespected because she'd humiliated my heritage, my grandfather. She's not a good person. Hashtag..." He laughed again, wilder this time. "Vile Vicky!"

"*Enough*," Michelle yelled, grabbing his shirt and doing her best to drag him toward the door. "You're going too far now. We're going. Right. Now."

"For telling the truth," Alek shouted into the camera.

Vicky felt as if she'd been slapped in the face, even though she agreed with him. The front door slammed. Seb was standing at the entrance to the hallway, staring, as if getting ready for Alek to turn back. But what could they do? Vicky realised she was shaking.

"Mummy?" She turned to find Max standing there with one of his friends. Max's cheeky look changed to concern when he saw Vicky's face.

Vicky smiled, pushing away the panic pulsing in her. She'd been on edge ever since the blackmail, and this obviously wasn't helping. Would he upload that video? Things had started to settle down...

"What is it, sweetness?"

"Can we go on the trampoline again now? Or is that man still going on it, Mummy?"

She ruffled his hair. "It's all yours."

He and his friend rushed back outside. Vicky's phone vibrated. It was Michelle.

> I don't even know where to start. I'm so, so, SO sorry. I told him not to drink.

> It's okay. It's not your fault. It's not his fault. He's ill.

Michelle replied, and Vicky could feel her rage through the text.

> He has to start taking some responsibility. It's like he thinks he can use it to do whatever he wants.

Vicky leaned against the kitchen counter. Seb was next to her, his hand on her arm. He had an almost guilty look in his eyes, like he thought he should've done more. Vicky leaned over and kissed him on the cheek. He was perfect the way he was.

She almost didn't want to send the next message. Michelle probably had her hands full with him. But she had to know.

> Is he going to delete the video?

Chapter 8

Alek

"You absolutely humiliated me." Liuba was crying quietly as she spoke, sitting outside their parents' house. His baby sister was shaking all over, but trying to contain it. Alek felt like there was a pit where his heart was supposed to be.

"I'm sorry," he said.

"What the *fuck* is the matter with you?"

Alek rubbed his head. "I shouldn't drink on these pills." *Yes*, he imagined Maksym saying, *it's those pills you haven't taken in months...* If only he'd still been there with him, instead of – Where? Somewhere? Someplace? Banished by the bitch.

"Don't blame it all on that," Michelle said.

"It's in the guidelines for the medication," he told her. "That's not an unreasonable explanation."

"So, this is all just the booze, then? You clearly have a problem with Vicky."

"You should too," Alek said, but he found it difficult to look at her because she was still making those awful crying noises.

"She's my friend. And it was a *bet*, okay?"

"A bet," Alek repeated. "Right."

"Delete that video," Liuba said. "Then get out of my car. I don't even want to look at you."

Alek sighed, took out his phone.

"And show me," she snapped.

He smiled at her sadly. Her cheeks were glistening. Her aura was wild rage. If he'd tried to touch her now, to wipe her tears from her cheeks, she probably would have slapped him. He showed her the phone screen as he deleted the video.

When he climbed from the car, she screeched away, kicking up dust like it was some goddamn Western. Instead of going home, Alek walked down the street, taking out his phone. He went to the recycling bin and restored the video to his main catalogue.

At the newsagent, he got four beers. Mr Charba smiled. "Having a party?"

Alek smiled right back. "Yeah, should be a good one."

They always had nice small talk. Alek went home and started drinking some more. He went into his study and fired up the computer. Alek was a big man; Alek was a strong man; Alek was an intelligent man. He often went on the forums to see video clips of the war, to read first-hand accounts. He even had a modest account of his own, where he'd ask insightful questions and share his own connection to the country.

Some people said he should fight. Alek couldn't tell them the truth; he *was* fighting. But now, he had something they could help with. He'd finished one beer before even rewatching the video, somehow. With his second cracked open, he focused on the video, staring at the outrage on his face.

There he was, taking a stand, willing to forgo the social niceties and the veil of civility and to speak the truth, *the* truth, without any shame or equivocation.

He posted on the forum, opening a new topic. *Have any of you seen the viral trend about people pretending to be in the*

Ukrainian war as a way to 'empathise'? See attached video then share thoughts below.

He uploaded the video, then stood and moved around the study, smelling the familiar comforting mustiness, the dust, the oldness of the house. After another refreshing sip of beer, he grabbed his phone and dropped into one of the more comfortable armchairs in the house.

Liuba answered the second call. "Stop ringing me!" She hung up.

Alek sighed and rang her back. She answered with a snappy, *"What?"*

"I want you to know I love you," he said.

"You're slurring your words," she snapped, her voice getting tight. "Oh, Alek, it's not *that*, is it?"

Alek told her, "This isn't my last call. Calm down."

"So you're okay?"

"I'm fine, just—"

She hung up again. Alek didn't even get angry. He just accepted her unreasonableness in as relaxed a way as a man could reasonably be expected to. He cocked his head back and drank some more beer.

Five minutes later, when he rang her again, she answered and shouted down the phone. On the next call, she sounded like she was panting. "What? God. *What?*"

"Whatever happens, I love you," he said.

"What are you talking about? Stop trying to freak me out."

"I didn't delete the video," he told her, which was more than he'd planned to. "I took it out of the recycling bin."

"What. The. Fuck? Alek!"

He sipped more beer. "There are things I can't explain."

"I'm turning around. I'm coming over."

"Why?" he said. "I won't let you in. I'm not a danger to

myself or anybody else. I'm not doing anything illegal. In fact, Liuba, I'm going to go to sleep soon. I'm very tired."

"What are you going to do with the video?"

"Whatever I want. Whatever has to be done."

"You sound..."

"What? Crazy?"

"No, just... Alek, please. Vicky's my best friend."

"Just what? You can say it. I sound mental. I sound deranged. But I'm not. I just have a plan."

"Please don't do anything with that video."

"I won't."

"I'm coming by first thing in the morning. You have to *promise* me, Alek. You have to swear."

Alek hung up the phone, then texted her.

I'm falling asleep already. I love you.

She texted back several times, but Alek switched his phone to silent and put it face down on the table. He got his remaining two beers and kept them close by, then he just kept drinking. If she came over, he'd ignore the door. The more he drank, the less everything seemed to matter. He was able to simply melt into his chair. He wondered if Maksym would finally speak up; maybe this entire thing had somehow been a misunderstanding, or just a miss of some other kind.

He melted deeper, smiling, a distant part of him wondering if he *should* delete the video. But what was he supposed to do? Let her win? Stop fighting? Let Maksym go?

"Do you know what a blood eagle is?" Alek asked the little rat bastard, the snivelling freak who was blubbering all over himself: the sort of man who gave and deserved no respect.

The man was tattooed in the most general way possible, a cliché seeking identity, with his tribals swirling up his arms and his stupid face. He was snorting and dribbling as Alek walked slowly around him, occasionally trailing the knife across his skin, causing a shiver that brought Alek no pleasure, he told himself, just justice, just order, just the way things were meant to be.

"Please."

"How is that an answer to my question," Alek said, making it a statement.

"What did I do?"

Alek sighed, walked in front of him. Oh, Maksym, where art thou? "You don't remember spitting at that woman?"

"Wuh-what?"

Alek lunged and brought the knife in a precise, accurate, beautiful arc which ended at the man's shoulder. He felt the blade puncture the skin as though the sharpness was a part of him. When the man screamed, Alek headbutted him and then shoved a hand over his mouth, catching the cowardly expression of pain.

"Would you like me to ask you again?" Alek said.

The man seriously thought now; the low-IQ cogs were visibly turning in his disused mind. "Oh, I know, I know!" he bleated, as though he thought Alek would be proud.

"Explain. Then we'll return to my original question."

"I didn't mean—I just..."

"An elderly lady was sitting at the bus stop. You were pacing and moaning and drinking beers in the middle of the day. When she asked you – politely, you fuck – to give her some space, you spat at her feet. An elderly lady. What makes you think you have *the right to do that? Have you never been punched in the face before?"*

Alek withdrew the blade from the man's arm, which caused a torrent of blood; he'd nicked an artery, clearly. Already the man, hanging abattoir-meat-like, was beginning to slouch and become lifeless. "I'm going to carve your back open, my friend, and then I am going to use my considerable strength to make wings from the cages of your ribs."

The man's voice became weaker, more pathetic. "Puh-puh-puh..."

Alek began to draw on the man's skin with the sharp knife.

"Why the fuck are you camping on A, you retard?" David yelled into his headset, as he pushed on the B flag. He was almost at diamond rank on *Iron Battalion*, a popular first-person shooter. There David was, sweating hard to make his team win, and this bloke refused to leave the first flag, which was already secured. "*Fuck!*"

He almost smashed his controller when, suddenly, a grenade appeared from seemingly nowhere and took his last respawn. Now he was forced to watch as the last remaining player – the one glued to point A – just sat there, staring at the doorway he was guarding.

"Push B," David snapped. "Jesus Christ – push B. We're going to lose either way!"

But the moron just walked up and down in front of the flag, and then, snipe, dropped like a sack of shit. When he died, big letters appeared on the screen. *You Lose.* David saw his rank drop by three points, knocking him back down to eighty-seven, meaning he was still not diamond and would have to work hard to regain his rank.

"Jeez, buddy," the idiot said. "Relax."

"Relax?" David's hands were shaking. "Relax? Why don't you learn to play the fucking game?"

"I gave my kid a go. Get a life, bro."

"You gave your kid a go on a *ranked* match!"

"Get a fucking life!"

David threw his controller at the wall. Dammit. He was all too familiar with that noise. For fuck's sake. He stood up, and he thought about cleaning his sofa. It was a bloody state. But he needed to focus. Maybe something would come from *the other thing*. At least that would be some fun. Like the game, but in real life. That slut and her so-called happy family and that look on her whore face when she learned just how powerless she was.

But he'd thought blackmailing and tricking Vicky would've brought more pleasure than it had. He'd been so excited when sending those original messages, the little nudges, the risky steps into her world. Now, he was numb. Always numb.

With David's controller broken, and his headset therefore disconnected from the console, he heard a child's voice say through the TV speaker, "Daddy, why was that man shouting at me?"

David went into the kitchen and began rolling a cigarette. Now they were going to try and make *him* feel bad for *trying to win the fucking game*. Idiots.

Chapter 9

Vicky

It had been a long day, and all Vicky wanted to do was sleep. She was lying in bed, her eyes falling closed as she stared at a book, trying not to think about what had happened; she wasn't reading, just staring blankly at the page. There was a sick twist in her belly every time she thought about the scene in the kitchen. But Michelle had told Vicky that her brother had deleted the video. That was *something*, at least.

After Alek stormed out, they had tried to go on with the party as normal. But a few people had seen what had happened. It was like the atmosphere was poisoned. Even Seb started getting short with Vicky, and he was still being distant with her this evening. Now that her affair had reared its ugly head, she felt like she had no right to challenge him on anything. It was a vicious, ugly feeling.

He walked in from the en suite wearing boxers and a T-shirt. He scowled as he glanced at her, then fixed a fake smile to his face. But Vicky had seen it. She knew something between them was wrong. He wouldn't want to argue, though. The next day, Sunday, was his only real day off this week. He was probably thinking about golf with his mates in the morning, then heading to the gym.

When he got into bed, she cuddled up next to him. She always felt a little guilty when she did this, ever since she'd had the affair. But the years had let the intensity of the feeling fade. Not anymore. All the stuff with David and that horrible video had brought it back to the surface. She needed his contact though, her husband's closeness.

He rolled over, not brushing her hand away, exactly, but not holding it either. More like nudging it with his wrist. She wanted to ask if they were okay, but she didn't want an argument.

Finally, she wavered. She could tell Seb wasn't sleeping. "I'm sorry," she told him, kissing the back if his neck, sick to her stomach because he couldn't know what she was really apologising for. *Not ever.* "Seb."

"It's fine," he said tightly. "I'm trying to go to sleep."

"I know I never should've made that stupid video."

He sighed again, said nothing. She probably should've just left him alone. But she wanted him to understand that she'd never wanted to do it, without having to tell him why.

"I feel pathetic for posting it," she said. "For thinking it was a good idea."

"It's fine," he said, tighter this time.

"But it isn't. I've upset you."

"It's not you," he said. "It's him. It's today. I just want to wake up tomorrow, have a good day, and forget all about it. All right? Is that too much to ask?"

He turned off the lamp. Vicky rolled onto her back, folded her arms and tried not to say anything else. She wanted to stay up for hours, solve it like a puzzle, piece it all together. She wanted to get to the heart of it without ever addressing what had really happened.

"Stop thinking," he said.

"I'm not."

"You are. I can hear it. I swear, we're fine."

"But how do you feel about it all?" she asked. "Don't you have an opinion?"

"Vicky, please, come on."

"Come on, what?"

He groaned. "I just wish you'd never made the video, that's all."

"So do I."

"But..." He paused; she thought he wasn't going to go on. "I don't know."

"What don't you know?"

Sometimes, it was like drawing blood from a stone with Seb. It was like he thought she was too precious or too terrifying or a weird mixture of both, to just say it bluntly. Was that her fault? Had she been too dramatic, too many times?

"Today, when Alek took out his camera."

"What about it?" She wanted to shout at him to grow some balls and get on with it. It was a mean, horrible thought, one she'd never share, buried deep down where she could ignore it. But it was there; it was one of the reasons she'd cheated on him all those years ago.

"You were smiling," he said. "And you adjusted your hair."

"Did I? I don't think so."

"You did," he said confidently. "It was like, the second you saw that camera, you wanted to look your best. In case it went viral."

"Is that really what you think I want?" she snapped. "To be on *camera*?"

She realised his mistake. Or was she using it, her past, the horrible thing with the camera and the pervert and the boo-hoo blah-blah-blah, the nastiness of it all? She didn't want to think about it, ever. But it was a part of her. It had happened. She *did* hate cameras because of... the terror, the pain, the ugliness, the hate, the yellow fingernails and the chapped-lip grinning.

"Vicky, I didn't mean—"

"I'm going for a cigarette."

"Since when?"

"I have a ciggy once a week. Hidden in the same drawer as the binbags. So obviously, *you've* never found them."

She sat up and put on her slippers, leaving the bedroom. Seb just sighed and stayed in bed. They had been together too long to let this spin into something serious. They'd only ever screamed and thrown things a handful of times. That was good going for nearly twenty years, Vicky thought. She got the cigarettes from the drawer and went into the garden, right to the back. It was her usual spot, near the tree.

She went to the other side of the tree and leaned against it, looking at the fence, into the dark. The security light was switched on, but with the tree blocking it, it was still dark here. She lit the cigarette, hated it as she smoked it. It was gross. But it gave her a headrush, which distracted her from her life for a second. Even the sick taste was a welcome distraction.

She took another drag, then a shock moved through her when she heard their garden fence shifting. A squeaking noise made her turn towards it. The fence was shaking as if somebody was climbing it. Vicky threw her cigarette into the grass and got behind the tree. Fear gripped her and she didn't know if she should scream.

A man dropped into the garden. She heard his breathing, deep and somehow angry, like he was looking for a reason to hurt somebody. She waited, adrenalin surging through her. She wouldn't let anybody get to the kids.

The man stalked past her, dressed all in black. He had a mask over his head, a balaclava, like a bank robber. He wore leather gloves, a black hoodie, black trousers of some kind. He walked toward the house. Vicky got herself ready, crouching down, knowing she'd just have to go, do it, not think. Run at him and – do something. Hurt him, somehow.

But then he stopped near the trampoline. He reached into his pocket and brought something out, tilted his head, was looking down at whatever it was weirdly. With the security light shining down on him, she tried to get a better look. But he was standing facing the house, the object in his hand, looking like a religious fanatic studying a holy object.

Then he tossed it into the trampoline bed and moved back toward the fence. She held her breath, moved around the tree, tried to be quiet as she attempted to keep the trunk between them. But maybe she let out a breath or something. Or shuddered. Or he just sensed her.

He turned, his eyes seeming bright staring out from the mask. She couldn't be sure, but she thought he smiled, from the way the fabric shifted. When he spoke, his voice was very deep and gravelly, almost like he was ill. "Show anybody else, I slit your throat."

Then he vaulted over the fence. Vicky collapsed against the tree, shuddering, her breath feeling like it was trying to assault her. Her lungs were exploding. She wasn't sure how long she sat there then, the grass feeling wet through her trousers. She coughed, then retched, a dry heave which tasted of tobacco.

Finally, she was able to climb to her feet. Now that it was over, she found the event becoming blurry, almost surreal. Her head hurt so badly. She walked to the trampoline.

Show anybody else...

and leaned right over, toward the middle.

...I slit your throat.

The item was a small brown envelope. Vicky forced herself to grab it. Something rattled around inside. She poured the contents onto the trampoline, staring at them numbly: dozens and dozens of tiny bones, like chicken bones, or something else, a rat maybe. She didn't want to think about it. Was it some kind of statement? Was it David? Had the man been short, tall? She couldn't remember. *How* couldn't she remember? It had only just happened!

Had it been Alek? Had the man been as big as Alek? It was so annoying. Her heart was beating too hard, the panic cutting off her memory.

What was there to do, really? Maybe it *had* been Alek. Maybe this had some crazy logic behind it, and if she told someone, and he somehow found out, he'd make good on his promise. Or maybe it was somebody else... What could she do? Some would call it cowardly, putting the bones back in the envelope, then putting the envelope in the bin, then tying the binbag.

"What're you doing?" Seb said out the window, almost making her scream.

She made sure her voice was steady. "I just saw a rat. I'm making sure the bin's covered."

"A rat? Inside? Outside?"

"Outside, near the back of the garden."

"Christ, that's just what we need."

He closed the window, and Vicky tried not to think about how easy it had been to lie to him.

Chapter 10

Alek

When Alek woke, he thought he would hear his grandfather. But it was just the sound of himself groaning. The voice sounded like him, like Alek, but it was like he had just emerged from being underwater. He groaned deeper, as if he was in pain, then slowly realised that he was. His groggy mind told him that his side was tweaking strangely.

Sitting up, he rubbed his eyes, becoming fully awake. Harsh sunlight glared through the tall windows. The light shimmered and danced across the walls, taunting him; those motes of dust had more idea about how Alek had got to bed than he did. Beer cans were strewn across the bedroom floor.

Alek never drank. Or rarely, at least. It was that place, that woman. Slowly, he remembered the video... storming out, coming home, falling asleep downstairs, and then... He held his side as he walked down the stairs, hoping to alleviate the feeling of pressure.

His phone was on charge next to the front door. So, he'd stumbled to bed... but had the presence of mind to put his phone on charge first? *This* was exactly the reason he hated alcohol. He'd been weak last night. Dammit. Eleven missed calls and twenty-two texts from Liuba.

The texts ranged from soft and understanding to outright rage and resentment. Clearly, she'd had more alcohol last night too, because the texts went on until 3am. Alek hiccoughed, then covered his mouth and ran into the kitchen. He vomited into the bin, his belly wrenching. His vision wavered, he felt dizzy, then he stopped, almost smiling. *The forum!*

He'd forgotten about it. He hurried into the study, taking a glass of water with him. He probably shouldn't have been excited about this, but it was an interesting idea, and Alek strongly suspected Maksym would've agreed.

Suddenly, there was a pounding at the front door. Alek finished his water, then went to answer it. He'd have to check the forum later. The hangover was making his sister's silhouette shimmer in the door frame. Alek opened it, finding a red-eyed and tired-looking Liuba glaring at him. "Morning," he said, trying to smile.

"Are you joking?" she hissed.

"Aren't you happy to see me?" Alek tried to smile... then Liuba swung at him, tried to slap him in the face. Even hungover, it was easy enough to step out of the way. But still. "Don't make it violent, Liuba. Please. What's wrong with you?"

"What's wrong with *me*?"

"I don't feel good about yesterday, but I'm not supposed to drink on my tablets. You know that." He gestured inside. "Are you coming in, or shall we argue on the doorstep?"

"Stop being so reasonable," she snapped, marching into the house, past the sealed off cellar door. Maksym would often be happy to see her walk right by that door, unaware. But it didn't bring Alek any pleasure.

In the kitchen, Liuba put the kettle on to boil and started making a coffee.

"None for me?" he said.

"Stop it," she said.

"Did you get drunk last night?"

"Obviously. It's the only way I can stomach texting you."

"Shame I wasn't around to humour you."

"Why? Where did you go?"

"Awake, I meant," he said, shaking his head. "I passed out."

She narrowed her eyes. "What about that stuff with the video? You said you got it out of the recycling bin." *Ping-ping-ping*, Liuba's hand was shaking as she spooned the coffee into the mug.

"Why are you shaking so much?" he asked.

"Because I'm tired and hungover and you're stressing me out, okay?"

Alek sighed, sat at the bar, put his forehead in his hand. His head was splitting right down the middle, but *he* was trying to be polite, at least.

"I didn't delete the video," he said. "I posted it to a forum for comment."

"For comment from *who*?"

"Just some online friends," he told her.

"What *friends*?"

"You don't have to sound so surprised that I have friends."

She threw the spoon into the sink with so much force it almost bounced out right away. "Stop acting like I've forgiven you. *You're* in the wrong here, Alek."

"I drank too much," he said. "Crucify me. Slit my wrists. I'm *sorry*. Do you want to know about the forum, then? I can show you."

He stood up, walked out of the kitchen. He couldn't stand the sight of her staring at him with so much shame and sadness in her eyes. It made him feel like a cruel bully, like he'd just kicked in her hearth, found her limited store of grain and punished her by... He almost heard him. Grandfather.

In the study, he went to the forum and logged in. By the time he was loading up his post, Liuba had walked in, blowing on her coffee.

"How do you delete it?" she said.

"Hold on."

He scrolled down. The hangover drained away. He had 112 replies. For a post on a fairly niche forum – the *war* wasn't niche, but this little corner of the internet was – it was quite impressive. As he scanned the replies, he fed on the outrage.

"Stop smiling," Liuba snapped. "This is awful. Look what they're saying about Vicky!"

"Attention seeker. Selfish. No empathy. I don't see the problem."

"That one said she's a stupid fat bitch!"

"Oh, of course you pick the one troll. You're always going to have trolls."

He clicked over to page two, kept scrolling. It was mainly people talking about how unfair it was, the fact that Vicky had gained virality through such a callous move. Many people were also saying that Alek should upload the video to a bigger platform.

"You're not doing that," Liuba said. "Just delete this post, then delete the video, and we're done."

"Let me at least read all the comments. This is a lot of replies." He really *was* smiling; he couldn't help it. "The most one of my posts has ever got is, I think, fifty-one. And that was only because I was talking about Granddad's diaries."

"What about them?" Liuba asked, no clue she'd only read the ones Alek approved for her. Her soft and beautiful soul wouldn't be able to take the other ones; there were few, in fact, who could bleakly and in long stints stare at the truth.

"Just sharing his experience. People think I should write a book. But I wouldn't use his story for that."

Alek kept scrolling, then paused when he saw that somebody had embedded a video in their comment.

Hey, Alek_Remember_Their_Names, I've taken the liberty of uploading your video to TikTok. I hope you understand that this is a public platform, and any video you post can be downloaded. I know... dick move! But I just felt like this HAD to be seen. It's only been up for three hours, and it's already got five thousand likes and one thousand comments!

Alek shook his head. "They stole my video!"

"Alek, what the...? Can you delete that? The TikTok one?"

"How old are you, Liuba?" he said. "You obviously know I can't. It's his account. She downloaded my video and posted it to *his* account."

"What are the views on now?" Liuba said.

Alek clicked the video, which took him to TikTok. It now had 17,000 likes and 3,000 comments.

"Is this going viral?" Liuba asked, her voice shaking. She put her coffee down heavily. The liquid swilled over the edge and right onto his desk, but Alek didn't say anything. She was clearly upset, and he knew it would only make it worse. Though it did annoy him; it also annoyed him that he knew his sister would never give him credit for this video on any level. It was morally repugnant to her; *he* was morally repugnant. And he could see in her eyes that she was thinking those depressing nihilistic thoughts, about medication and illness and history and... and nonsense. Absurdly irrelevant drivel.

"*Alex?*"

"It seems to be going viral," he said, pointing out the obvious.

"You have to stop it. Delete it!"

"How?" Alek said. "It's not my account."

"Message the person on the forum, then," she said, reaching for the mouse.

Alek lifted it up to move it away from her. "I'm not so sure about that."

His heart broke a little at the tears in her eyes as she glared at him, her hands shaking. She looked like she was ready to scream. Alek actually expected her to, any second. "What. The fuck. Are you *talking* about?"

"I don't necessarily think deleting the video is a good idea."

"Why? Do you want to be famous now?"

"It's not about me. It's about the cause. She made light of it. She *used* it."

"She was being blackmailed!" Liuba snapped. "Fuck you, for making me break a promise. Her ex was blackmailing her, okay? She had no choice."

"With what? What ex?" Alek said, only mildly interested. The reason didn't matter to him, though he did find it curious somebody would do something so senseless. "She's been married for years."

Liuba stared at him, as if he should be seeing something obvious. He'd never liked that look. It made him feel like he was under the spotlight for something. Then it hit him. Ah. "It was an affair."

"Please," Liuba begged. "Just, please. She's my friend."

"So this ex blackmailed her into making a video about the war?" Alek asked. "That seems so specific. So strange." He was wondering if she was lying to him somehow; he didn't like how unreal this seemed.

"No, just to become famous. He's *nuts*, all right?"

Alek smiled; she usually hated terms like that. She gave him the middle finger and went on, "I don't know why he did it. He had his own reasons. The point is, she didn't *want* to do it."

"But he didn't tell her to make that specific video?"

"She just jumped on a trend!"

Liuba trembled some more, being very emotional. But Alek wasn't as crazy as she sometimes liked to pretend. He used *reason* and *logic*. She just wailed into an emotional storm as if that would solve everything. "She tried whatever she could."

"I'm sorry that your friend is a bad person. I'm sorry she'd use a tragedy for her own gain. I'm sorry that's who she is."

"Delete it," she said. "You're being mental."

He stood up, keeping the wireless mouse in his hand. Modern technology saved him from her yanking on the cord; she'd probably garotte him with it. He paced the room, tossing the mouse from hand to hand. "Go on, then. Let's hear your little speech. You look like you've got one prepared."

"You're being so vicious and *ugly*."

"Haven't you?" he said, tossing the mouse with good accuracy and rhythm from one hand to the other.

"I know you."

"Obviously you know me."

"You're acting weird. You seem a little hyper. I don't know why you care about this video so much."

Alek gritted his teeth, then forcibly relaxed himself. He didn't want to get angry with her. "This has nothing to do with my diagnosis of schizophrenia."

"*My diagnosis of schizophrenia,*" she repeated. "Why are you saying it like that? You don't think you're schizophrenic, anymore?"

Alek knew that there were certain parameters within which he had to operate, and that powerful people liked to clamp down on those who dreamed outside the limits. He knew that other people were jealous; nasty thoughts bled from a person's skull as though split open from a cold steel-booted kick. "I obviously know I'm schizophrenic," he told her, but it hurt to say it. "It will never stop, even with the medication; that just helps me to tame the psychosis."

He parroted his idiot nurse's words at his sister. It was easy enough to repeat whatever the morons wanted him to say.

"Are you still taking your—"

"Are you joking?" he cut in. "Why do you think I was so *drunk* last night?"

That seemed to soften her up a bit. He'd become so quickly drunk because he rarely touched the poisonous shit, but Liuba was in her mental health nurse mood so he fed her what she needed to hear. Thankfully, it seemed to be working.

"Will you please just delete it?"

"I can't do it," he told her.

Liuba threw her arms in the air as though she thought Mum and Dad were watching; it was the same exact gesture he remembered from thousands of moments. She was imploring them to make him stop whatever he happened to be doing which she deemed to be wrong.

"I don't get it. If you want to make a video about the war or whatever, do that. But that's just... It's cheap, Alek. It's like *TMZ* trash. It's beneath you."

Ah, sweet sister. That almost got him. On one level, she was right. Of course, Alek would have much preferred to write a ten-thousand-word thesis about the connections, on both a social and international scale, between the current conflict and the Holodomor. But who would read it? Ten people? Twenty? Thirty?

Alek wished he could just tell Liuba about Maksym, about what her fucked-up friend had done to their grandfather. But her mind was too small to understand things like that.

"Don't be like them, Alek, chasing their fifteen minutes of fame. You're not that pathetic. You're not that desperate."

"I would agree with you," he said. "If we were talking about a man uploading this merely to become famous... but we're not. We're talking about righting a wrong."

"I told you—"

"It doesn't matter if she has excuses," he snapped, his voice getting louder than he'd intended. Liuba did an annoying thing; she sort of cowered and cringed back, like she thought he was going to leap on her, beat her to death with the mouse. "She still did it; she didn't have to choose *this*. And, honestly, I'm surprised you aren't angrier."

"You need to listen to me—"

"She's your friend. She knows your heritage. Didn't she stop to think to herself, *Hmm, my best friend is Ukrainian, maybe I won't do something so callous?* No?" He was almost shouting, which annoyed him, and she went to the other side of the room near the bookshelf. "I know what she really thought." Alek made his voice female and high-pitched. "*Michelle will let me walk all over her. I cancel half the plans I make with her, anyway. It doesn't matter if I spit in her face one more time.*"

"You're such a vicious *prick*."

Alek shrugged. "Insult me all you want, but you know it's the truth. It should be me and you against her, not the other way around. It's actually a little disgusting that you're even asking me to delete it."

Alek didn't enjoy, exactly, the hesitation on his sister's face. But it was far better than how she'd ranted before. But she looked sad and lost as she sat down, pulling her sleeves up, biting her lip.

"Disgusting," she repeated.

"I went a little far," he muttered. "But surely you can see my point. You're supposed to be her best friend."

"Not everything's as simple as you're trying to make it."

"Be that as it may, you've not exactly disagreed with me. Are we done fighting?"

"Have a conversation with her," Liuba snapped. "At least let her tell *her* side of the story."

"Why?" he said. "I don't see any reason to do that. It gives me no tactical advantage."

"Tactical advantage in *what*? Is this your war, is it, Aleksan*dr*? Your big moment to shine. Some TikTok tabloid bullshit."

"You can be as antagonistic as you want, Liuba. But the fact of the matter is, there's no way, either through force or persuasion, to get me to delete this video."

"Stop calling me that," she hissed, being petty now.

"It's a lovely name, though. A beautiful name."

She looked around the room, as though searching for another argument, or another choice. When she realised she didn't have any, she walked toward the door. "You're going to speak with her about this. She might want to take legal action, Alek. And I really am worried about your mental health."

She stood at the door half turned away, half facing him also, so she didn't have to look him in the eye. She looked so weak... but almost like a bully, like she was stacking up all her reasons so she could beat him over the head with them.

"There's nothing wrong with my mental health," he called after her. Maybe he was being the petty one now. He raised his voice, even though it hurt his head. "I'm not the one in a toxic friendship!"

She slammed the door. Alek watched her drive away, kicking up gravel. Then he went outside and closed the gate, bolted it. Let her ring or press the bell if she wanted to be let in. He went inside and scrolled the comments in the video.

Who is this guy?

This is the hero we need!

Yeah, you tell her!

He savoured the glory they were throwing at him, even if he

knew they shouldn't. On the forum, he selected the user *Paragon_of_Truth* and went to their profile. As well as uploading Alek's video, he was heavily active on the forum. He had posted three thousand times and been with the forum four years.

Alek sent a message. *Hello, friend. I'd like to discuss the ownership of the video you have uploaded. I have a proposal, which I think will be of great interest to you.*

Chapter 11

Vicky

"Mummy, what would you do if drawings could come to life?" Max asked, sitting cross-legged on the living room floor, his notepad resting on his knees. The house had a lazy Sunday feeling. Sebastian was out playing golf; Natasha was upstairs, watching a film and having a nap.

Vicky nestled deeper into the sofa. She had to try and relax. Be present for her family. "I think if that happened, you'd rule the world."

He giggled. "*Mummy*."

"You would. All those drawings, you'd have a whole army."

He laughed again, then Vicky's mobile vibrated. She felt the familiar motherly guilt as she checked it. It was Michelle, asking if it was convenient to speak. She sighed.

"Mummy, are you upset?"

Vicky smiled any bad or awkward feelings away. Or did her best to, anyway. "No, honey."

"I'm not *honey*, Mum." He laughed and turned back to his drawing.

Vicky tried to keep her face composed as she typed out a response.

Max turned on his games console and started playing on the TV, sitting right in front of it. Shamefully, Vicky was glad to let him. It meant she didn't have to hide the emotions on her face.

That was, until Natasha came down, sitting on the sofa and putting her feet on the coffee table.

"Gross," Max said, looking over.

Natasha rolled her eyes – a trademark she was perfecting lately. "I might go out in a bit."

"Where to?" Vicky asked.

"Just a mate's."

"Is it a boy?" Max said, laughing.

"Ew, no."

"A girl?"

"No," she snapped. "I'm going to die alone."

"I really wish you wouldn't say things like that," Vicky said.

"Which one is it? Have boyfriends? Don't?"

"There's a big difference between taking things slow and *dying alone*."

Natasha took out her phone and started scrolling. She played the videos out loud. Most of them were of people dancing. Others were motivational. With each swipe, Vicky winced. *Her* version of the video was down, but she constantly worried about somebody uploading it again.

Suddenly, her phone rang. It was the number she'd saved as *Workmate Sarah's Old Phone.*

"Is it Daddy?" Max said, as Vicky stood up.

"It's work," she told him. "Are you at the next level yet?"

He laughed like that was the funniest thing ever.

"There aren't any levels in this game," Natasha said, without looking up.

Vicky went into the kitchen, answering the phone. "What?" she snapped.

"Oh, how lovely," he said with heavy sarcasm.

"We're done. We agreed." Her hand rose to her mouth instinctively, like she was going to start biting her nails. But she caught herself, lowered it. "I gave you what you wanted. Just because it was way easier than you thought it would be, it doesn't mean you have the right to—"

"Oh, just calm down," he said, in that weirdly persuasive tone he had often used with her almost a decade earlier. A tone that could get her to do anything. "I'm not ringing about that. Do you think I wanted to keep hold of that video *that* badly? No, sweetheart – don't flatter yourself."

"Fuck you."

Before she could hang up, he quickly said, "Don't. You'll want to hear this."

She leaned against the kitchen counter, somehow resisting the urge to throw something. "What?"

"You're going to get another taste of that sweet, succulent fame real soon, baby."

"Don't call me that," she hissed.

"Some psycho from your party uploaded a video of an argument. It's pretty funny. But I'm actually quite offended I didn't get an invite."

"He uploaded it," she said, feeling like she'd been punched in the gut.

"It's getting *serious* attention."

Her head was swimming. She felt like she might fall off balance at any moment. "Text me the link." She forced her breathing to come slowly, forced her nerves to stop fraying, or tried to. Then Natasha's voice rose from the other room. "*Mum! Mum! There's a new video of you!*"

She hung up the phone and almost ran through the house. Natasha was standing up, Max at her side, both of them staring down at the phone. She tried to snatch it away, but Natasha said, "We've already seen it. It's on a loop."

Her hand dropped.

"Vile Vicky," Max said, his little voice sounding broken. He was on the verge of tears. He turned to her, stared, eyes all glassy as if he thought she could somehow make it all better. "Mummy?"

"Just ignore it," she said, bringing him into a hug and glaring at Natasha over his head.

"He was going to see it eventually," Natasha said. "It's almost at a million views already. People are using the hashtag. Everybody is giving their opinions."

"Everybody? Not the newspapers again?"

Natasha laughed. "No, like other creators and stuff. Look." Natasha played a video. A young, stylish woman was sitting in what looked like a studio, blue paint flecks on her face. "Was he rude? Yes. Was he hostile? You bet your *ass*. But did he have a point? Damn. Not only did he *have* a point, it was so good, hurt that evil woman so much, it made her kick him the hell out of there."

"That's just one," Natasha said, swallowing as she pocketed her phone.

"Mummy, where are you going?" Max said when she rubbed his head then turned away.

"Don't be such a baby," Natasha snapped.

"You apologise to your brother, right now!"

She glared at Vicky, but then spat out a barely audible *'sorry'*. Vicky didn't push any further. She knew how close Natasha was to really exploding. She was doing her best to hide it, but only just.

Vicky went into the hallway and called Michelle.

"He's uploaded it," she said.

"I... I know," Michelle muttered.

"Since when?"

"Uh, he just told me." Vicky knew she was lying. But she

didn't want to argue with her.

"I need to speak to him."

"I just talked to him, actually. Says he's had second thoughts. He doesn't want to meet. He's said everything he wants to say to you, apparently. I'm sorry."

"Sorry? Mate, come on. I need your help here. Can't you make him delete it? He isn't..." She hesitated, lowered her voice, as if that would make it any better. "He's not *well*, is he? He's not in his right mind."

"He's got an illness," Michelle said defensively. "But he's certain about this. He's on strong medication; he never should've been drinking in the first place. I'm just so sorry. I hate this. It's all my fault."

"No," Vicky said automatically. But it was. Why did she have to invite him?

"What can I do?" she said. "I mean... I'm sorry, but I might have to ring the police. Surely he can't record a video in my house, and just post it like that? There are privacy laws!"

"I told him you might do that," she said.

"Yeah? And what did he say?"

"I don't think he cares."

"What?"

Natasha walked into the kitchen, and sat at the bar. Vicky waved her away, but Natasha just gave her a deadpan look and turned back to her phone.

"If you went down the legal route, I'm just saying, he could probably play that game longer than you. You know my parents had money. I know I sound like an arse right now."

"It's not your fault you were born rich," Vicky told her, again automatically. It was something she'd said many times. But though she wouldn't admit it, it bothered her right now. "It wouldn't matter anyway. It would be a criminal charge."

"You'd have to prove it," Natasha interjected.

"Nat."

"You'd have to prove to the police it's worth going after," Natasha said. "There was a case about it in my Law class." Despite the fact Vicky wanted her to have nothing to do with this, she couldn't ignore how alert and involved Natasha looked. How grown up, almost, though it hurt her to even think that.

"What would prove that?" Vicky asked. "Sorry, Michelle."

"It's fine. You can put me on speaker if you want."

Vicky wondered if she'd look back on this as crossing a line. But Natasha was already involved. She needed all the help she could get.

"I'm just saying," Natasha went on. "He's definitely messed up on privacy laws. He's in our house. But in this one case, right?" She adjusted her bracelets, getting even more invested. "The video was a fight between a husband and a wife. The wife, she used the video in some big online essay about feminism and, uh, abuse, I think. Anyway, because the video was considered to be of, what was it called? Public interest. Yeah."

"But this isn't—"

"It could be," Natasha cut in, and Vicky wasn't even annoyed. She looked like a little lawyer in the making. "What if he pays some fancy pants lawyers to say it's all about the war?"

"But it's in our *home*," Vicky said.

"All I know is, he'd fight it," Michelle said. "He's stubborn. He's always wanted to be special. His illness didn't exactly help."

"If I go to the police, will he have to remove the video? Or will there be a case first?"

"I don't know."

"Hang on. I'm on Google." Vicky paused while she read. "It says here that there could be a temporary removal, pending the case. Or that you might have to wait until after the case."

"It's out there now anyway." Natasha sighed, fiddling with her bracelet. "It's already been downloaded loads of times."

"Already?" Vicky said.

Natasha nodded matter-of-factly. "One time, this YouTuber I like got her video taken down. Within, like, an hour, there were thirty uploads of the same video."

"Why do people waste their time doing that?"

Natasha shrugged. "People are weird on the internet."

"Alek was making a big deal about the angle too," Michelle said. "He had it on selfie mode the entire time. Everybody else is in the background. He's the focus. He doesn't show any identifying factors of your property. Our dad used to call him *smart Alek* for a reason. Not just because he was cheeky."

Somehow, Vicky knew her friend was smiling, reminiscing about her brother. The weird connection between the three of them made this more than awkward.

"I'll let you know what I decide to do, hon," Vicky said. "I've got to go."

"Okay. Speak soon. And I'm so—"

Natasha gave Vicky a look when she hung up. "What?" she said.

"Did you cut her off on purpose?"

Vicky had to nod; Natasha knew already. She laughed. "I don't think you'll beat him by going to the police, Mum."

"How, then?" she said. "This is your world."

"My world?" She did that annoying teenage thing of repeating what Vicky had said as though it was the stupidest thing ever.

"Your world. TikTok and filters and selfies, and all that crap."

"I know what I would do," she said. "If this is a war, right, you've got to fight back. If you want people to stop hating you—"

"People *hate* me?" she said. "They don't even know me."

"They don't need to. They know this version of you. This facsimile."

Vicky blinked. "You're going to have to educate me, sweetheart."

Natasha smiled. "It means version. Or copy. I think." She shrugged.

"You're so clever," Vicky said.

That got an eye roll. "You should do it, though. Make a video. Make *your version* of the story into *the* story."

"I'm not sure there's anything I can say. It was bad enough before. This has just made it worse."

"You can tell them *your* story." Natasha swallowed, looked down. "Mum, I looked up what happened. With that bloke and his videos."

Vicky kept as emotionless as possible. It was a long time ago, she reminded herself. "A local pervert. He told us he was a professional photographer. He got quite a few of us, actually. I still don't like cameras."

"You can use it, Mum," Natasha said.

"My childhood?"

Natasha nodded, looking like she was sickened by herself, but also excited at the same time. Devious; that was it. "You can use it to beat that dickhead, Mum. You just can't get in your feelings about it."

In your feelings. Meaning she had to be cold. She had to be able to take a few knocks, some pain. So she had to be a mother, then. She was ready. Was she really going to listen to her teenage daughter, though?

"Tell me your idea."

Chapter 12

Alek

Alek paced, the phone on loudspeaker. To combat the ugly effects of the hangover, he had consumed a so-called energy drink in an almost fluorescent can, which had sent electric jolts of adrenaline pulsing through him. He was talking with a solicitor he had hired online for a consultation, which was costing him ten pounds per minute.

"Let's assume, worst-case scenario," Alek said, "she goes to the police, and they think she has a strong case. The video was on her property—"

"That's suspect, for one," Mr Hurney cut in.

Alek couldn't help but smile. "Her home is suspect?"

"But can we *tell* that it's her home in the video? Are there any identifying features?"

"There were witnesses."

"But does the *video itself* violate her privacy, Mr Bodar? There are plenty of avenues for us to explore. For example, has anybody donated to any charitable funds as a result of watching your social commentary video?"

Mr Hurney had done that a couple of times now, called it a *social commentary* video. Alek would be lying if he said he didn't like it. He'd started this for Maksym, and his grandfather would always come first, but there could be aspects of enjoyment along the way.

"Would it help?"

"I couldn't comment on that, Mr Bodar," he said. "That's merely an example of how we might argue that this video is for the public benefit. And with an issue as contentious as this sad, sad war..." *Sad, sad* sounded very, very forced. "...one can never be sure how the public will take drastic legal action."

"I think I'm starting to see how this works," Alek said, spinning around in his computer chair, hitting *F5* to refresh his laptop screen, then spinning around again. "The video has just hit one million views."

"That's amazing. Congratulations!"

Alek grinned, no fool; Mr Hurney's friendliness was a transaction, but that was okay. It was *still* a good achievement. "Let's say, worst-case scenario, this goes to a trial. Assuming money is no object, how long would you be able to keep the video online for?"

"I highly doubt it would get this far," Mr Hurney says.

"Don't talk yourself out of extra hours," Alek joked, and Mr Hurney laughed way too hard. "How long?"

"It's impossible to give a firm answer, but I would be confident in saying your video, and your important message, will remain online."

"That's quite firm," Alek pointed out.

"But there's a small chance, if she has the right team and the police are particularly sympathetic – again, with the Ukrainian angle, this would be fightable – but what I'm saying is, yes, there's a chance she could win."

The Ukrainian angle. Alek momentarily imagined slitting Hurney's throat, though he actually wasn't sure what he looked like. He'd seen his photo on the page, but remembering the specifics was difficult.

"That's good to know," Alek said.

"We've got you covered, Mr Bodar. We shouldn't give her the chance to censor you and the vital message you have for the world, and she has no right to affect your social media career…"

"My career?"

"It was my understanding that you're an aspiring activist? I'm not sure where I heard that. But I thought you, yourself, were going to join or even establish some group, perhaps a charitable foundation, based on your presence online."

"Hmm," Alek said. "Maybe. I know what you're getting at, but it sounds like a lot of work."

"What work? A few minutes recording a video?"

"I'll think about it," he said. "Thank you, Mr Hurney."

"Thank you, Mr Bodar. Call me anytime."

Alek hung up, remembering an argument his father and Makysm had had when they were both still alive. Alek was young, sitting near the fire, as Maksym grumbled that Artem no longer understood what money meant. *'It means I'm successful…'*

'No. It means people lie to your face. They laugh at your jokes. It means you are the one now, son, the one who comes late at night and raids the cupboards, who burns the hay out of spite, who rapes the mothers and sisters and wives, who gloats about it to their loved ones. You!'

And then he'd started screaming and raging. This was towards the end of his life. Alek hadn't known him properly until they'd met again later, when the whispers in his diary had turned to savage certainty. Alek went to the computer, researched the page.

Over one million views. Comments still flooding in. He scrolled through them. Then… what the hell? Many of the comments were referring to another video. *Wow, I hope you guys are proud of yourselves! This ISN'T as simple as you think!!!*

That reply had thousands of likes, more coming in each time he refreshed the page. In the comments, some people were still using *#VileVicky*, but others were now commenting things like, *Vicky Stapleton's video about this is really good. Go to her channel!*

Alek searched her name. He wasn't supposed to care about any sort of social media war, but this was really, really pissing him off. Her channel had one video, already at fifty thousand views. *One* video on her channel – all the others gone, all the ugly fame-chasing ones, the sick desecration of history.

He clicked it. Vicky was sitting in cold lighting, maybe in the kitchen. She looked tired. Her eyes were dark and puffy, as if she'd been crying. Was it make-up? She looked genuine; she looked devastated. Alek gritted his teeth. The bitch. Was this an act? If so, then the fucking *bitch*. He didn't enjoy thinking this way about a woman. His mother had always told him women were meeker than men in many ways, and they needed men, because men could crush them any time they wanted. Alek wasn't so sure about that; Maksym's diary told stories of hardy, root-like women who wouldn't quit. But in any case, he usually reserved this level of violent hatred for men.

But— "Fuck that fucking *bitch*."

Before Vicky started talking, she sniffled and touched her face, looking broken. It was so damn convincing. "I'm guessing many of you have seen the video Alek uploaded," she said. "I guess now a lot of you have plenty of reason to hate me even more than you already do." She sniffled, touched her cheek. "Up until now, I've tried to just let this blow over. As much as you might find it hard to believe, I *really* don't like cameras."

Oh, that was good. That was Hollywood, right there. She

did a laugh, eye roll, smile, sad sound all at the same time, like she was laugh-crying at the irony of life and inviting the viewer to join in.

"There's no simple way to say this. When I was a teenager, a local man tricked a few of us into going into his house... and, well, let's just say—" A voice crack, looking down, a splash of shame. "Cameras were involved. He did things... He was arrested. His name was Barry Jenkins, if you want to look him up."

From behind the camera, a small, loving voice, "I'll put the article on the screen, Mum."

It appeared, fading in. *Military Veteran Arrested: 'I have no regrets...* The paper was a tabloid, the photo was of a scary-looking house and a camera lens in the background. The first lines of the article made it clear that sexual abuse had occurred.

It was a fine touch, the addition of the daughter, the love they clearly shared. The image of the article faded away. Vicky went on, "Recently, I think..." More sniffles. "I had... I was a little poorly."

Suddenly, the girl came into frame, her mascara smeared, hair messy, like she'd been crying. Like Alek had devastated them all. Oh, this was so, so good. He was almost proud of her.

The girl put her hand on her mother. "You had a mental breakdown, Mum."

Vicky sniffled, the liar. "Yeah, yeah." As in, *I know, I need to face the truth, thank you for nudging me, beautiful daughter.* "I thought the only way I could have some sort of confidence is to use the camera. Oh, I don't know what I was thinking."

"It's childhood trauma, Mum," the teenage girl said, the main demographic on TikTok, giving credence to this woman, a frontline trooper in the public favour war. She looked at the camera. "She was trying to get over her trauma through fame.

She regrets it. She doesn't *hate* anyone. And *that* man scared us all in our own home—"

"Nat—"

"It's true," she snapped. "And he knows it. He knows you, and about your past. His sister's been your friend for years, for God's sake. He took advantage of you."

The video ended on that note, abruptly, so that the final line would echo around the viewer's head. There was something so skilfully done about it. Alek laughed, then he was blinking and staring at the bookshelf, and he realised he'd punched in an old Dickens hardback. His knuckles were bleeding.

He went back to the computer, refreshed. The *numbers* weren't important. Her connection to Makysm was. But her views were going up fast. She'd hit the mental health angle. The trauma angle. She'd included somebody from the primary demographic of the platform. She'd *humanised* herself. She'd declared war.

Alek checked the comments. Almost all of them were positive.

He gritted his teeth, shaking his head. He didn't honestly care about the comparative number of views, or her general popularity levels. Maybe, okay, a little. But a *seriously* little bit. But it was because of Maksym that he couldn't let her win.

He grabbed his phone, then went to the upstairs study, opened the drawer with all of Maksym's journals in it. This was when Alek had truly met his grandfather, when these words had bled into his mind. He flicked through them, wondering...

There were some he would never be able to share online. There was one in particular that even Maksym was ashamed about. Alek knew all of his grandfather's diary entries from memory, he'd read them so many times...

How does a man admit that he consumed another man? Is there any polite way to do it? Is there any decent path? I think, however I state it, and however empathetic the audience, many people will judge and hate me on a fundamental level. I believe God, or nature, made it that way, and for good reason. But, if you can see past that, then listen.

It was a difficult thing, detaching the meaty morsel in my hand from the person it had belonged to. That is what I would like to think. It was difficult. But hunger is such a demon, that I didn't even have to imagine it to be something else. My belly rumbled at the mere thought of something meaty and stringy between my teeth, even if it was my fellow man. I never had to cross the line, to kill and eat, like others, but perhaps that was merely the timeline of history saving me. Perhaps, if famine-genocide had continued for another month or two, I would have been a hunter too.

In my heightened state, the sad truth is, it tasted like succulent pig meat. The man was a friend of mine. I didn't have the strength to bury him. I consumed him, and then I sat, sleeping and waiting to die, in my hovel of a hut, the so-called paradise for which I had been forsaken. Then my dear brother returned home. He had been scavenging in the city. He was half dead himself. But he had enough morsels to sustain me.

When I finally become lucid, I saw that he'd removed my friend's remains. He didn't say anything about it until the end, two weeks later, as he was dying. Then he said, "Maksym, my sweet brother. I know what you did with our friend." I tried to argue, but he said, "I know, and I forgive you, and I give you permission..."

We cried together, two near-corpses in a single bed. I held him as he died. And then... Well, he was my brother. And he had given me his permission. And I was starving. And no man can know what humanity is, what strangulation truly feels like, until he has felt a primal howl deep in his swelling gut to find something, now, or die. Now. Die. Now. Die. Eat. Die. Eat.

Alek slumped into a sitting position, almost feeling drunk again. Sometimes, when he remembered the diary entries, it was like he could hear Maksym's voice. But it was just a cruel trick. He kept searching through the journals. He definitely couldn't use *that* one.

Once he'd selected an appropriate entry, he returned to the study. But there was a problem; he didn't own the original TikTok account, the one which had amassed so many views for the video. It belonged to another person. The account belonged to somebody called *InquisitiveInquisitor1982*. Alek saw they were online, and quickly sent a private message.

Hello, friend. Thanks for your effort in uploading the video. I am keen to upload another one. Could you possibly send me the details for the TikTok account?

He started writing a reply immediately. Alek had seen Inquisitor on the forum a few times, now that he thought about it. He was extremely active, probably seeing himself as something of a warrior, an *activist*.

I'm not sure that's the best option for me, Inquisitor typed.

Alek gritted his teeth, smiled tightly. He was not an alien to the internet. He had, in fact, taken a keen interest in it. Once, a few years prior, he had routinely used the dark web. Not for the evilness which others might; he had been purchasing Adderall and sometimes speed, because it had made him feel so alive and productive. But in hindsight, all he'd done was sit around the house reading old books for long stints at a time. He was better, clear-headed. More productive. But the point was, Alek knew what IP addresses were. He knew there were ways, unless Inquisitor was using an app to block it, to find Inquisitor's location.

I think we should discuss the best direction to take the account in, Inquisitor went on.

The video is mine. We're not a team. You have no say in the direction of anything. Send me the details.

Just relax. We need to think of this logically. We need a strategy.

"We, we, we," Alek said, shaking his head, closing the browser to the regular internet and opening Tor, the private browser, which would allow him to access the dark side of the internet. He began the laborious process of searching for a market, which involved running each long and strange link (each a mess of numbers and letters with .onion at the end instead of .com) through a program to check its safety. The dark web was full of scammers. People would throw out fake links to well-known markets, collecting a person's data – Alek was using an advanced VPN as well as Tor – and then stealing from them.

Alek finally found an Amazon-like marketplace, which listed all kinds of drugs (legal and illegal), fake IDs, clean needles, and 'hacking services'. Alek scrolled through, ignoring the *ping* that told him Inquisitor had responded in the other browser.

WildNet, was set up so that the most-reviewed and most-liked items were at the top. Alek found a service for 'find location via IP address, can sometimes bypass VPN, message for more details!' It had thirty-seven five-star reviews, some of them with text.

Alek went back to the other window.

I'm even thinking of drawing up a business plan, Inquisitor had written. *There is so much potential, here.*

Alek went back to the dark web browser. As he made his purchase, he thought about explaining all this to Liuba. She liked to think she was sharp with tech, but all this would've boggled her mind. *I'm going to find him,* he would've told her, if she wouldn't overreact and try to get him sectioned. *And he's going to give me what I want.*

A business plan. Was he joking? Did he honestly think Alek would find that acceptable?

Alek was in charge. *Him*. Finally, he'd found something he was good at, something he could work towards, with true salvation at the end, true pride... Nobody was going to take that from him.

Chapter 13

Vicky

"This is good," Nat said, sitting at her computer with her legs crossed, her braid hanging over one shoulder. As Vicky sat on her bed, she felt like she and Nat were bonding in a way they hadn't in years.

Nat turned and smiled. "It's *really* good, Mum. People are taking your side. People are sticking up for you."

Vicky felt a weird twist in her chest, a mixture of... pride, almost. And something else. Something ugly. The glare of the camera, the moist hairy lips curving into a perverted smile as he gave some ugly instruction.

"You're helping people share their experiences with trauma."

"Really?" Vicky leaned forward.

Even better than the subtle warm glow inside Vicky was the clear pride on her daughter's face. Somehow, it made all of it – the blackmail, video one, the argument, the creep with the bones, video two – worth it. "Seriously." Nat frowned. "I won't ask why you really made it, though."

Nat looked lost and a little afraid for a second. But then she forced a smile. Vicky reached over and touched her hand. "Is something wrong?"

"I'm not an idiot, Mum," she said. "I know this wasn't about some *bet*."

Vicky tried not to let the shock show, but she knew she had failed from the way Nat pulled her hands away. But Nat didn't seem angry, exactly. "*Was* it because of the childhood stuff?" Nat asked, quietly. "I mean, maybe we used it as an excuse... but maybe it's an excuse *and* it's real? Did you have a mental—" She paused, took a breath. "Feel a bit poorly, Mummy?"

She winced when the *Mummy* slipped out. Vicky kept hold of her hands. Her baby was on the verge of crying. She didn't deserve to be lied to. Nat hated it. She hated secrets. She always had, ever since she was a little girl, demanding to know what Daddy and Mummy were whispering about, to the point of learning Father Christmas wasn't real... and then being *glad* she knew the truth, smiling proudly up at them.

"Mum?" Nat said again.

Vicky could've lied. It would've been simple. Nat would've believed her. But she just couldn't do it. "No," she said. "It's complicated. I wish I could tell you."

Vicky's voice cracked. She didn't mean to, but she started crying. Nat slid into her lap and they held each other; they cried together. Vicky thought Nat would ask some follow-up questions, but she didn't. Instead, she just nuzzled into Vicky. "I love you," she said.

"I love you too." Vicky held her tightly. "Is something else wrong?"

Nat stiffened for a moment, but then said, "No."

"Nat?"

"No, really. I just want to help you."

"You have. That video saved me."

"We have to be ready," she said. "He might make another one."

"We can't just keep—"

Nat sat up with that excited and engaged glint in her eyes again. "Mum, this is how it happens."

"How what happens?"

Vicky knew it was wrong, but it was just so sweet to see her daughter this excited. "Get famous. Make careers out of it. We could become millionaires."

"This isn't about that."

"I know, I know," Nat said quickly, but she was still smiling. She stood up, out of Vicky's lap, and dropped into her computer chair. "I'm just saying."

"Is that what you want to be, then?" Vicky asked. "No more dentist?"

"I wanted to be a dentist when I was like, twelve."

"Wrong – it wasn't even last summer."

"Yeah, well, I guess we'll see?"

She stared at the screen, hit refresh. Vicky felt another weird stab of guilt when she leaned forward, peering at the number. Mini fireworks went off in her head when she saw that it had gone up. More views. More likes. More comments. More shares. More endorphins.

"It's his move now," Nat said. "The longer he takes, the more *our* story becomes *the* story, right?"

"I think..." Vicky playfully tickled Nat in the side. "You should go into politics."

Nat giggled, slapping at her hand. For just a moment, Vicky forgot about all this nastiness.

Chapter 14

Alek

Alek decided to dress Modern-Faced as he got ready to leave.

He wore jeans, a jacket, a cap, a shirt, regular middle-class clothes. He left by the small, locked exterior gate, rather than the bigger ones used for cars.

Across the street, there was a tree and a bench, and a small park just beyond it. Alek spotted them straight away. Did she think he was stupid? It was Natasha, Vicky's daughter, the teenage girl sucking on a green, ugly vape pen and staring at his house. Another girl was with her, slighter, blonder, sort of mousey. Natasha blew a big cloud of vape and turned away.

Alek should've left it. She was just another stupid girl making stupid-girl decisions. But this was clearly not coincidence. Perhaps Vicky had sent her as some kind of spy. Or maybe it had something to do with Maksym.

"Natasha, right?" he said.

She yelled over. "I'm not doing anything wrong."

He laughed. "I didn't accuse you. But is it Natasha?"

"I didn't know you lived here."

He laughed again. The street was quiet. In the park, an elderly lady walked her insanely tiny dog. Alek couldn't make out the breed. It looked like a rodent on a lead. "I'm not accusing you of anything."

"What, then?" she said, as her mousey friend looked down, clearly terrified.

"I'm a fan of coincidences," he told her. "But you really shouldn't vape, you know."

"Yeah, yeah, whatever..."

Alek really should've left it, but her dismissive tone was cruel and unnecessary. "If I were you, I'd smoke that filth somewhere else," he told her. "We have a housing association and a neighbourhood watch around here."

"Ooh, scary," she said, and her little mousey friend giggled.

"Is something funny?" Alek called over.

The girl turned away and Natasha said, very loudly, "Just ignore him, Mia."

"What's so funny?" Alek persisted.

But then he heard somebody coming. He turned to find two men, mid-fifties, beer bellies, one in a polo shirt and one in a football T-shirt, both of them unfit, red-faced – drinkers, by the looks of it. "You know these girls, mate?" the football boy said.

Alek looked down at them. The difference in their height and size was unmistakeable. "One of them is the daughter of the woman who pissed on my grandfather's grave," he told them. "The other one is a little rat."

"Don't call her a rat!" Natasha suddenly exploded.

"Look, mate..."

The man started, but Alek couldn't be bothered. With the girl wailing and the man trying to puff himself up and act tough, Alek took a step forward, meaning to walk down the street. Then the red-faced polo boy tried to half get in his way, but he wasn't sure about it. Alek tilted his head at him. Really? The man took a step back.

He would've liked to have had a longer conversation with

them; he didn't like being laughed at. But as much as some people might like to pretend, Alek wasn't an insane person. He walked down the street, walked toward town. He was going to arrive in Cornwall by late evening. He'd have to overnight there, and return in the morning. But he'd get what he needed.

Nigel Laxton lived in a picturesque setting. His house-with-a-view had a Ukrainian flag in the front window, which instantly won him some points. But Alek was tired. It was dark and cold. He hadn't been able to sleep on the train because a baby was wailing continuously, with no attention from the mother, just another mindless moron zombie staring down at her phone. The only thing that stopped Alek from saying anything was that the trainline had recently implemented a new anti-harassment campaign for women; no doubt he would've been Kafka'd into the fucking dirt if he'd dared to speak.

Alek hammered on the door. His body felt sticky and stale. Less than a minute later, a light switched on and a silhouette appeared. He opened the door, his anger draining and turning into abject terror when he saw who it was. He was late thirties, going grey, but with a full head of hair. Fit, but somehow soft despite his lean build.

"Hello, Nigel," Alek said.

"Uh, uh."

Alek smiled. "Please relax and invite me inside."

"It's almost midnight."

"I know, and I'm very tired from all this travel. I'd like a cup of coffee. I came straight here from the train station."

Nigel's eyes were wide, his hand trembling slightly. Alek just kept staring at him. Nigel was making a choice – and then he made the wrong one. He tried to violently shut the door.

What a moronic, seriously deluded thing to think he could do; Alek simply stepped on the threshold, blocking the door with his knee, then used his body to bump the door open and wriggle inside.

Alek sighed, then grabbed a big fold of Nigel's shirt and shoved him up against the wall. "I wanted to do this in a civilised way," Alek said. "But this is fine. You know what I need. Email, password. And the password to the email you used to set up the new account. I really hope you haven't connected it to any mobile phone or verification software security yet."

Nigel was trembling all over. He shook his head. "It's a new email."

"Excellent. Then I will take my account…" And his views. "And be on my way. How does that sound? No broken teeth. No trouble. No drama. Just a nice simple honest thing."

Nigel nodded slowly; Alek applied just a little more pressure to his chest with the bunched-up material. "Because you obviously understand that the video was never yours, don't you?" he said. "You have to know that…"

But Nigel *didn't* know it. Alek saw the micro expression, the eyeblink of protest.

"What were you thinking, talking about making *plans* together? It's my footage. My brand. My career."

"I thought this was about the war, the history," Nigel said quietly.

Alek almost gave him a whack; it was such a weasel move, trying to twist what Alek had said into some kind of selfish and pro-war message. "In the greater context, of course. *We're* talking about me and you. Now, now, let's hurry up."

Putting his hand on the other man's shoulder, Alek followed him into the living room. He sat with Nigel as he read out all the usernames and passwords, and then Alek, on his mobile, changed them. He then added security steps, linking them to his other email accounts, and added extra verification from an app on his phone. Now *his* numbers were *the* numbers.

When he was done, he stood up, brushing his hands on his trousers. He wasn't sure why he did that; he had vague memories of Maksym doing it, so maybe it was that. But there was no dirt on his hands.

"Thank you, Nigel," he said. "I'd like to make something clear before I leave."

"I won't say anything," Nigel said in a small voice.

"No, no," Alek corrected, sitting next to him on the sofa and gently placing his hand on the smaller man's knee. "Let me make it clear. If you *did* decide to talk, or make a forum post, or do anything..." Alek leaned close, his voice becoming a tender whisper. "You'll never see me again. You just won't wake up one morning. That's all. Do you live alone?"

"Y-yes."

"Then you'll rot until eventually, somebody complains about the smell and rings the police."

Alek stood up and left the house.

At least he would be able to make his video now... In fact, he had even brought one of Maksym's diaries with him. He'd used the charger on the train, so his phone was fully loaded.

"There are no values anymore," Alek said, as he curled his hand around the knuckle-duster. He'd done his research into this particular weapon. The mistake people often made was trying to punch normally, but it was more like knocking on a door; that was how one prevented injury.

The man was in his mid-thirties, well-to-do-looking except for the blossom of piss staining his lilac shorts, his hipster hair floppy over his eyes as he winced up at Alek. He tried, in vain, with his neglected muscles, to bluster his way out of the bindings. The dirty rag in his mouth prevented speech, for which Alek was grateful to himself; he'd heard enough of this man's soul already.

"At any other time in human history, or in many other countries, your flagrant disregard for the wellbeing of your child and the mother of your child would be culturally disallowed." Alek sighed; always, he had to reduce his speech for these morons. "What I'm saying is – you wouldn't be able to sit in a barber's shop, bragging about, as you said, 'leaving that boring bitch and banging a right horny slut'." That was the thing with this man – he looked well-to-do, but he was filth. "Oh, you don't remember? You don't remember me sitting behind you? Listening? Everybody could hear you."

Alek knocked the door of the man's cheek and the man's face cracked as he slumped in his bindings, but the chair, bolted to the floor, prevented him from collapsing.

"You were bragging about abandoning the mother of your child, because she was, as you said, 'too bloody boring' for you. Don't you realise that you must be a seriously sick individual to do something like that?"

The man's eyes narrowed, and Alek could tell what he was thinking – he was the sick one, was he? So Alek knocked the door again, again, and then he sort of blacked out, and when he sort of woke up, Alek could taste the blood in his mouth from where he'd chewed the man's earlobe off. He spit the blood in the man's ruined face; the duster had cleaned him up nicely.

"Rat," Alek panted, spitting again. "Coward. Freak. What about your child? What about your responsibility?"

Chapter 15

Vicky

At work, Vicky couldn't stop thinking about what Nat had said last night when they'd watched the video together. *'Mum, things can go really, really badly if the internet turns on you. Properly turns on you. It can ruin your life. All this petty stuff, the comments and the newspapers, that's nothing compared to what it could be. Have you heard of Luna Polly-Anne?'*

Vicky had searched the name, afterwards. Luna was a woman who'd appeared on some dating TV show. Viewer comments and harassment had led to her suicide. And there were other cases, too; families having to move, children being harassed in school. Nat was even getting comments about it online now.

'You can't let him win,' Nat had said. *'If he keeps fighting, we have to keep fighting.'* But how could Vicky do that without Michelle?

The day went by in a tick-tock torturous way, with each minute feeling like an hour. It was as if all that time on the phone was making everything else go slower in comparison. She just did her best not to go on her phone, even on her lunch break, or think about the next video.

There didn't really *have* to be a next video, but Nat seemed determined. Still, Vicky was in charge. She could've easily told her daughter no; it would just mean Nat would probably go back to being cold and distant again. Was it selfish to let this happen to be closer to her daughter? Was it pathetic?

At home, she found Nat sitting in the living room with Max on the armchair, playing his Switch. Her friend Mia was on the chair, cross-legged, scrolling on her phone.

"Mummy." Max beamed, when she walked over.

She smiled, a burst of love pulsing through her. She'd never get tired of his happy voice when he said *Mummy*. Whatever else was true, she and Seb made a good parenting team. "Maxxie." She leaned down and hugged him, then turned to find Nat smiling at her.

"Hi, Mum."

"Hey." Vicky smiled. "Hello, Mia."

The girl looked up shyly, like she was scared to be anywhere except behind her fringe. Vicky was the same at her age. "Hello," she muttered.

Vicky got dinner started. Nat rushed into the kitchen, joining Vicky at the breakfast bar, where she was sitting as she waited for the water to boil.

"Mum, have you seen it?"

"It's bad," she said bleakly.

Vicky clicked play. This time, Alek was sitting in what looked like a library. He had another leather-bound diary in his hands, reading with passion. His words were painful. "With a gun to my head, they forced me to watch as they violated my wife…"

"That's genius," Nat muttered, when a tear slid down Alek's cheek.

"Maybe he really is crying."

"Be real, Mum."

"I'm sorry." Alek cleared his throat. "I share this with you, so you know… I understand what abuse is. I understand how evil people can be. But for Vicky to use abuse as an excuse to piggyback off *other* people's trauma… that's wrong. But I've been in the wrong, too."

"He's an actor, Mum," Nat said, mesmerised. "He knows what he's doing."

Vicky thought he seemed genuine, but she didn't say anything.

"I shouldn't have caused a scene at her house. I shouldn't have called her *Vile Vicky*. That was overly passionate of me. Now, I'd like to take a more grown-up approach. Vicky – let's talk. I'm sure there are any number of podcasts who'd love to host us. If you'd be willing to speak with me, one on one, then let me know. Send me an email. Make me a video. And I'm sorry, Vicky. For your trauma. For what happened to you. But it doesn't make what *you* did okay."

The video ends with a fade-out to a photo of his grandfather Maksym, standing next to his grandmother's headstone.

"Oh my God, *Mum*," Nat exclaimed. "You have to do this. I mean, it's playing the game on his terms. But it's too good to pass up."

"Don't be so callous."

"But that's what he *wants* you to think," Nat cut in. "Don't you get it, Mum? None of this is real; you can't take any of it to heart. We have to use what we can. Are you going to make a video or not?"

Vicky shook her head. "No. I'm done with it. I've got no reason to. I've got my side of the story out there already."

"Then *I'll* make one," Nat said.

Vicky thought about the comments, the hate, the stress of it all. "No, Nat. We're going back to normal."

"You can't stop me."

"I *can*, young lady." Vicky realised she had let this go far enough; they'd drifted too distantly from a regular mother–daughter relationship. "I'll take your phone, your laptop, your tablet, everything. You are *not* making a video."

"I'll find a way, Mum," Nat said. "I'll tell him that I'll go on the podcast with him."

Vicky pointed to the door. "Go to your room until dinner's ready."

Nat laughed as she rolled her eyes. "Okay, Mum. Fine. I guess Mia can come too, right?"

Vicky knew it would lead to a fight, probably a drawn out one. This day had felt long enough already. She refreshed the page; Alek's video already had twenty thousand likes. She tried not to think about how many a response video would get. Or the podcast. And what about after that?

But she didn't want to be famous. Who would?

Chapter 16

Alek

"You've weakened any possible case," Mr Hurney said down the phone. "By apologising for the video—"

"She's not going to pursue a case," Alek told him. "And even if she did, we're beyond one video now. You see, I thought my popularity depended upon that one video. But my last two videos have gained just as much attention." He paced the office. "It's *me*, Mr Hurney. *I'm* the hit."

Alek hung up, in awe of himself. He had secured the account; he had furthered his popularity. People were still donating to charity, making videos adjacent and connected to his in the digital space, showing their donations and citing Alek as the reason for them. His latest video had swayed the viewership once again.

He wasn't sure about the ultimate goal, except that he knew it *had* to lead back to Makysm. It had to. He couldn't understand how there would be any logical alternative.

Alek checked his private messages. There were so many. A few were criticising him, a few threatening, but most were expressing support. The latest ones all mentioned a news article. He clicked through and found it on a popular news website... well, popular as far as they were concerned. *Their Ammo is Viral Videos: The War for Ukraine and Public Favour, a TikTok Zeitgeist opinion piece...*

There were a couple more tabloid style ones, too. One from a smaller website had the headline, *TikTok Titans Clash in Viral Vendetta,* which Alek liked. He was a *titan* now.

Newspapers meant hardly anything, but Alek went to his TikTok bio and put an email address for business and press inquiries. He had also made accounts on all the other major social media platforms. He had posted his video on them too, to lesser success.

If Vicky agreed to the debate, perhaps, finally, Alek would be able to do something about the mayhem she had caused.

He kept scrolling his messages, then stopped when he saw *Nat_in_the_Hat_2007.* The year in the name suggested the user was seventeen. Nat matched with Natasha. Was it Vicky's daughter coming to bother him again, but through the digital realm this time?

You shouldn't be messaging me, he wrote.

She was online; she replied almost instantly. *Why not? I'm my own person.*

Why were you and your friend loitering there?

What game did this girl think she was playing? Perhaps she thought she could record or somehow target Alek. But he wouldn't slip up... Still, was there a way to use her to get to Vicky? Alek had something that could blow Vicky's life up – he knew about the affair – but if he dared to use that, Liuba would hate him. Things were difficult enough with her as it was. He could just hear her now. *I told you that in confidence; I knew you were getting ill again...'*

He didn't know who the affair had been with. He had no proof. Would publicly accusing a woman in this modern feminist era end well for him? Alek had to explore further options.

Through Nat, he could get to the mother. Through the mother, his grandfather. Then: oblivion.

He wrote, *Loiter again and see what happens. Maybe tomorrow afternoon.*

What's going to happen? she wrote, but Alek left it at that.

Surely she wasn't going to be foolish enough to show up? They were enemies. If it wasn't for his love for his sister, and the fact he had no proof, he would've blown this girl's mother's life up. But maybe she *would* come; maybe the silly girl would think she was confident and capable and far more impressive than she really was.

David watched her video, wishing it would bring him some joy. He tried to remember the man he'd been in the pub all those years ago: the intellectual whose words alone had been enough to bag Vicky, the mother who'd become a shameless nympho just because he'd said a few words. But it all felt hollow; the world felt hollow. His tongue stung from the packet of sweets he'd just eaten, but also, it was like he felt nothing. Clicking off the video, he went to his favourite porn site.

It was like the front page was trying to make him look at the real nasty shit. He didn't want to; he was aware, really, that *this* sort of stuff was a bit too far. *Brother Pisses on Sister While Step-mommy Begs for More.* Or there was, *Eighteen-Year-Old Slut Cries as She Takes Big Mean Dick.* David didn't want to watch those; he was pretty sure he had a porn addiction. These days, any man could develop it. It wasn't his fault. But what was he supposed to do? They were *throwing* it out there, all the weirdest, most interesting, most disgusting things. The thing of it was, getting hard over the vanilla stuff – such as *MILF takes a throat fucking* – was becoming more difficult.

With a sigh, he clicked on a video of an *Extreme Gangbang*.

As he stroked, he began to let go of the shame. He began to even forget about Vicky. He began to forget about everything. He just saw her, felt her even, imagined he was there, and he couldn't be embarrassed because he wasn't the only one. This video had over a million views; it had thousands of comments. How could this be wrong, then? How could anybody judge him?

Chapter 17

Nat

Mia took out her phone. "Your mum's video has started, like, a podcast war. I thought *you* were going to be the famous one."

"I am," Nat said. "I just need some time, and a big bombshell, a big event."

"Like a sex tape?"

"That's gross," Nat said.

Mia shrugged, staring into space. "Maybe it would be worth it."

"Really?" Nat asked.

"You'd just do it. Get on with it. It wouldn't be fun. But then you could make, like, anything you wanted, a perfume brand or anything, all for a few awkward minutes."

Nat shook her head. Mia kept scrolling on her phone. The house across the street, with its vine-covered gate and tall walls, was like something straight out of a horror film, as Nat had told Mia. Even though the day was sunny, it felt eerie. After almost an hour, Mia huffed. "Are we going to stay here all day?"

"He'll come out. He replied to my messages last night."

"I don't care what happens anyway," Mia said.

She seemed determined to be in a mood.

"You know, if something happens, like if we get a recording of him acting nuts or something, we'll *both* be involved. *You* can use this too."

They both froze when the gate started to open.

Within moments, Alek stood over them, hands in his pockets. He wore a T-shirt, jeans, trainers. His arms were massive. He wasn't gym fit, more like... just big, like a tree trunk.

"Are you secretly recording me, then?" he said with an unhinged smile.

"What? No."

Nat laughed, but she was scared at the same time. She needed to keep a brave face for Mia. But this wasn't smart, really, what they were doing. It was necessary, though. Nat knew what she was doing, or so she hoped.

"Look." Nat showed him her phone.

Mia did the same, then stared right up at him with that angry look that even made her teachers flinch. "See? Or do you need to strip search us too?"

"I can categorically state that is of no interest to me," Alek said. "Why don't you girls come for a walk with me."

It wasn't a question. He turned into the park. Nat looked at Mia. Mia shrugged, then took the vape from Nat and took a big inhale. They wandered after the big man. A note of danger stirred in Nat's belly. They shouldn't be doing this. But there was a thrill too. Mia felt it; she took Nat's hand, grinned.

Alek looked over his shoulder with a smile on his face. Mia whispered in Nat's ear, "He's actually pretty hot."

"Don't be disgusting," Nat said.

But as they walked through the park, she couldn't help but feel like they were on some kind of adventure.

Chapter 18

Vicky

Vicky was speaking with Brad on Zoom. He was a booking agent with a huge smile. The podcast was a drama-slash-news-slash-variety show, which had gained massive popularity for its viral moments.

"So I'd have to come to London?" Vicky said into her laptop camera.

"Paid for by us, of course," Brad said. "You'll get the VIP treatment. But we have to decide soon. Things don't stay hot forever."

The host was a well-known figure in British television. Marty Graham was a sometimes charming, sometimes offensive, sometimes both, comedian-turned-podcaster.

"How long do I have?" Vicky asked.

"I'd say no longer than twelve hours. If it's a financial issue... We can arrange reimbursement."

Vicky swallowed, hoping she had a good poker face. She needed a manager for stuff like this; she wished Nat was there. "Okay, yes, that's interesting. Thank you. I suppose you have to wait for his decision, too."

"Alek's, you mean?"

"Yes."

"Oh, he's already agreed," Brad said cheerily. "He didn't even ask to hear the terms."

"I'll email you soon."

As soon as the call ended, she started biting her nails. Max and his friend were in the garden, bouncing on the trampoline. Seb walked into the kitchen with a coffee mug, looking at the floor.

"How did it go?" he said, looking out at the garden now.

"He said he can offer money. And they'll arrange travel."

"They want you in person so it's more of a circus. I don't get it. Isn't it over?"

"This podcast will..." She paused, wondering how she could explain it.

"It will make even more drama. It will make stuff even more awkward for me at work."

"Maybe this is about *my* career, not yours."

"What *career*?" Seb snapped.

"Not career," she said. "Just... my situation. I didn't plan on this happening. Maybe this is a way I can finally deal with my past trauma."

Seb bit down, clearly finding fault with what she'd said, but he didn't make a comment. He ran his hand through his hair and then looked outside at Max.

"At least the kids are happy," he said, but his voice was shaking. For a moment, she thought he might cry. "Right?" He looked at her, and for a bleak, terrible moment, Vicky feared they weren't in love anymore. The thought passed. But it stung. "Aren't they?"

Max was happy, bouncing higher and higher. Vicky hoped that Nat was happy, too.

Chapter 19

Alek

As Alek walked down the street with the girls, towards the town centre, he kept a skip in his step. He didn't want Nat or the little flighty one, Mia, knowing that he felt on edge about being out with them in public. But people walked by them, seemingly unaware of who Alek was. This confused him for a second – his numbers were doing so well – until he remembered the internet was a different neighbourhood. There was little chance of...

He realised right away he'd made a mistake. He'd been thinking about this happening; he'd willed it into existence. As they walked down the street that led to the promenade and the beach, a car pulled up opposite, a horn honking. A hungry-looking wannabe wolf was in the driver's seat, music pumping, cigarette dangling out of his mouth.

"It *is* him," a lady yelled from the car. "From the videos!"

"Are you all right, Alek?" He blinked. What the fuck? He blinked again. The rodent-looking one, Mia with the sunken cheekbones, was staring right at him. Alek was standing in the park, near his house; no, they were walking, walking through the park. The car had gone. Nat walked beside Mia still, vaping.

"Alek?"

"I'm fine."

"Where are we going?" Natasha asked, with another suck of her vape pen.

"You should ditch that disgusting habit," he said.

"Yeah, it's gross," Mia agreed.

Natasha snapped, "*You* vape, Mia!"

"I don't. I never would, either."

Alek nodded again, kept walking. He was starting to think this whole thing was pointless and dangerous. What were the chances he could get Natasha to turn on her mum, really? Perhaps if he hurt her... but he wasn't willing to do that. "Perhaps we should get right to the point, Natasha," he said. "I was going to take you to a memorial they have in town, but what's the point?"

He stopped, sitting on a bench. A young mother was pushing her son in a buggy nearby. They looked so happy and oblivious to how violent the world could be.

The girls paused, but didn't sit down. Alek didn't like what had just happened, whatever it was. That was crazy-person shit. He wondered if it was alcohol and lack of sleep. The man, the car, the scent of his cigarette, all so vivid, and then gone in an instant.

"Are you going to try and get a recording?" he said. "Hmm? Is that it, Natasha? Or make me believe you're some naïve little girl? Maybe you're hoping I'm a pervert."

Natasha stared at him, and Alek laughed. Mia laughed too, which was strange. "Please – do you really think I believe you'd ever turn on your sweet momma?"

"He doesn't want us for *that*, Nat," Mia said, and Alek had no idea why she was even speaking, or why she was here, except that he was happy somebody was agreeing with him.

The young mother kept looking over. She had hippie red hair and lots of piercings and tattoos. After a pause, she left her child by the swing, to walk over to the park fence. Alek felt sick to his stomach; what sort of mother left such a distance between herself and her child? Now Alek would have to watch the babe to make sure nobody took it.

The woman paused at the fence. "Mind if I speak to the girls for a sec?"

Alek shrugged. "I don't care." He kept staring at the baby.

A minute later, the girls returned. Mia was smiling and looked drunk; Nat was watching her friend sideways.

"I told her you were our uncle," Mia said, as though she expected Alek to be proud.

"That's fine," Alek said, relieved when he saw the woman return to her child. "In the years to come, if you decide to start a family, never do that, girls," Alek said. "Never leave your baby unattended."

"I wouldn't, ever." Mia clasped her hands together.

Alek looked at Natasha. "So, let's get something clear. You're trying to use me. I was going to try and use you. But I don't want it; I don't need to. I've got the podcast with Vicky. We're going to blow up the internet. And I'll collect the remains, like a hundred little bones."

Mia giggled and Alek found himself thinking of Liuba, how much he'd loved to make her laugh when she was around the same age.

"I don't know what you're talking about," Natasha said.

"I saw you in that video... I think pretty soon you're going to get in the game. In that case, controversy is your friend." Alek smiled up at her. "If we play this right, we can make you famous, Natasha. Easily tens of thousands of followers within the first few days of making your account – if not a million. Imagine hitting one million followers in record time."

Natasha couldn't hide it. Her eyes were wide. She looked

like a cracked-out junkie listening to her dealer serenade her with the latest strains of her beloved injectables.

"You could," Alek went on. "But you might be too immature."

"That reverse psychology crap doesn't work on me."

"But it's not reverse psychology," he said. "It's a fact. This will involve choosing your own path, Natasha."

She folded her arms, considering it. "I wouldn't do anything to hurt Mum," she said, then looked at her friend and muttered quietly, "She's been through enough."

"Your mum isn't the angel you think she is," Alek said, and then he did a bad, bad thing. He didn't mean to. But this would make it all so much better, so much easier. "Can you be grown up, Natasha? If I tell you something, can you listen calmly?"

Natasha glared at him. "Just spit it out."

"Why do you think dear Mummy made those videos, hmm? Because – and seriously, it's absurd – she had a little dalliance with a fellow, and he created a certain video, and this video showed certain unseemly things, and..."

She was rolling her eyes. "Yeah, ha, ha."

"It's true. Your mother had an affair." Alek was being mean, but there was something offensive about Natasha, about some silly little child thinking she could outsmart him. And that head shiver too, whatever it was, the brain melt she was giving him. Maybe it was being close to her. Like her family's breath was poisoned or something.

"You're lying." Natasha's voice was shaking.

"Want proof?" Alek said, recklessly. "Ask my sister. Tell her you've had suspicions. Make up a reason, but *don't* tell her I told you. Liuba won't tell you, but you'll be able to tell from her reaction."

"You're a fucking liar," Natasha hissed, taking a trembling step forward.

"Nat!"

Natasha stared at her friend. "Are you *defending* him?"

It was hilarious and absurd, this little bird's sudden affinity to Alek.

"If you tell my sister it came from me," Alek went on reasonably, "it will seriously hinder my ability to help make you famous. I can see the future, Natasha, and it involves *this* moment sitting on the top shelf in a hardback book in hot pink in Tesco; it involves a music career and appearances on TV shows and a reality-TV empire and a make-up brand. It means *you* choosing *your* path, Natasha. Go, ask Liuba; keep it secret. Then come back to me. We've got work to do."

Natasha had tears in her eyes. Alek didn't look at her. It wasn't as if he was some bully who enjoyed making children cry. But he'd let this show go on for long enough. "Maybe I'll just tell her *you* told me."

Alek ground his teeth. It sounded so loud, the scraping of enamel. He said, "I would much prefer if you didn't do that."

"Mum wouldn't do that. Not Mum."

"You don't know your parents," Mia snapped. "Nobody does."

"Come on."

Natasha grabbed her friend's hand. Mia tugged her hand away, looked at Alek. "I'm staying here."

A wave of revulsion touched him. He had to stop himself, before he said something nasty. What did she think she was? She was nothing in this, a spare piece. "Go with your friend. Nobody has any use for you."

Mia gasped as though some strong emotional connection between them had been severed. It was a pathetic and desperate display of something Alek didn't want to think about.

When they didn't leave – Mia was looking at Alek, and Natasha was waiting for her friend – he stood and walked back towards his house. His head was hurting; he wanted to hurt something else. Those girls, or Natasha at least, were poison. But he could use her. Unless she told Liuba what he had said about the affair.

Then what? He had to keep going; Maksym would want him to. He had the podcast... unless Natasha confronted her mother, and Vicky backed out, and it all blew up. *Fuck.* Was it time for some good old-fashioned blackmail? But then Vicky would go to Liuba. Why did he have to care about his sister so much?

"Why did you do it?" Alek said, seething, as the fat, revolting, arrogant, pathetic bloated thing blinked at him from across the room. Alek hopped from foot to foot, loosened his arms. "Hmm? You and your four 'lads', all of you bloated and sickening, all of you with too-tight chinos and no socks, all of you slaves to whatever your friend happens to be doing, hmm? Why did you do it?"

The man was slowly realising where he was: trapped in a cage with a real fucking animal. Alek was preparing himself to let the beast out of him.

"Wuh-what?"

Alek roared. "Why did you do it?"

"Do what?" the rat squeaked, beginning to panic.

"A mother and her child were walking down the promenade. You ran up behind her and shouted right in her ear. You terrified the poor boy and caused the mother to let out a scream. And then all your friends laughed and laughed and laughed and... and why? What was funny about that? What if that woman had heart problems? What if you'd caused her to trip, fall, bang her head? What if she'd suffered from PTSD, and your sudden, pathetic, so-

called joke triggered an episode? Don't you care? Don't you think, ever?"

"What, mate?" he said, probably still hungover, like that was an excuse.

"Do you even remember doing it?"

"I was so pissed, mate. What is this? Where's Larry? Is this a joke? Larry!"

"Hands up." Alek got into an orthodox boxing stance. "Let's see how tough you are without your buddies."

"Wuh-what."

"Oh, for fuck's sake."

Alek advanced on him, but it was an absolute joke. This man, so confident in mindlessly harassing and possibly traumatising a five-foot-six woman, shrunk against the wall. But the fight had already begun; Alek had given him fair warning.

"Let me recite a poem I wrote recently," Alek said, as he landed an uppercut to the body that sneaked below the floating rib and caused the man to gasp as though Alek had sucked life from his lungs. "The beautiful accuracy of the biggest knuckle driving through his nose/ The would-be hard man striking an involuntary pose..."

"Argh!" the man yelled, then threw the wettest blanket of a punch Alek had ever witnessed.

Alek withdrew just out of range and then swatted him to the floor.

"Brain rattled and with a bloody gasp, now he knows," Alek went on, as the man stared up at him, so adrift without his mates. "The next time he blusters could be his last/A blunder regretted only in living past."

Chapter 20

Nat

"Are you crying?" Nat asked.

Mia touched her face. "No."

Nat wanted to be there for her friend, but Alek had just exploded her entire world. Nat's first instinct was to go and ask her mum about it, but she couldn't stop thinking about what Alek had said.

The fastest-followed TikTok account of all time... make-up deals, TV shows... a life, a path, like countless other girls her age who had made it massive and were now millionaires, simply because they hadn't let people hold them back.

They didn't talk until they got to another park. This was all they did, sometimes – walk here, walk there, meet a few people, walk someplace else. It all seemed so empty, now that Nat had these big plans in her head. But it wasn't like she was going to abandon Mia.

Mia slumped against a tree; her arms folded across her middle. "Did I look desperate?" she finally said.

"What – for *him*? Mia... he's old. He's weird. He's not a good person."

"I don't need him to be a good person," Mia said. "He's big, Nat. Didn't you see the size of him? He's like... like *two* dads."

Nat shuffled closer to her friend, touched her hand. But then it was like Mia had snapped out of some kind of spell.

"I can help," Nat said. She meant it.

She could have money, freedom, opportunities. She would never need to rely on her parents again, and nor would Mia.

Taking out her phone, she found Michelle's number. Alek had clearly been talking about his sister, though Nat only knew Liuba was her middle name through Facebook.

Chapter 21

Nat

Breathe, breathe, breathe...

Nat had to keep reminding herself as they drove into the studio car park. London was magical and huge and inspiring. Everything seemed grander and more epic.

She stared at her feed, swiped, watched a video of a girl dancing, got bored, swiped, watched a funny video about a pit bull making friends with a rooster, swiped, swiped, swiped, watched a video that made her jealous, this online couple; the girl didn't deserve him. Swiped again – and there was somebody else's reaction to Mum...

She kept swiping away. Videos like that were appearing on her feed a lot. A man in a suit was waiting for them, probably like twenty-five or thirty, or maybe a bit older. He walked over, a big smile on his face. Nat wondered if he was looking at her weird or if she was imagining it.

"Vicky!" he said brightly, like he was Mum's best friend. "Brad? We spoke on the phone?"

Mum smiled, looking tired. She'd been driving for several hours. Nat had asked her to take them up the day before, so they could spend the night and then be fresh. But Mum had looked all stubborn. *'I'm not giving them any more of my time than I have to.'* Mum was bullshitting, big time. She was acting like she didn't want this. Acting like she was Miss Perfect. But Nat had heard the hitch in Michelle's voice when she'd finally worked up the courage to ring her yesterday.

'Did Mum cheat on Dad?'

'Why are you asking me this?'

And then nothing. Brick wall. She might as well have just said *yes*.

Brad smiled at Nat, now. "And *you* must be Natasha."

It was really over the top and dramatic, but she remembered her manners, nodded and said hello. He walked them down a narrow corridor. She wasn't sure what she'd expected, but it hadn't been this: a dressing room with a shower. Brad smiled from the door, never stopped smiling, actually. "You can freshen up if you like."

"That's his way of telling us we stink," Mum said, trying to smile at Nat.

Nat loved her so, so much. It hurt how much she loved her. But also... She felt sick. "Yeah." She laughed awkwardly.

"You can wait in here." Mum touched her arm and Nat almost cried.

"I'm fine," she said, keeping her hard face on, the one that wouldn't give anything away. "I want to be here."

"You're so wonderful, Nat," Mum said. Nat hugged her quickly so she wouldn't see how shiny her eyes had got. She tried to remember what Alek had said about the future, and her fame... all this being a line in her biography. *'I didn't want to hurt my mother. But I had to think of my future. Both my parents had betrayed me. What other choice did I have?'*

People would eat that up, surely. They would pay in some form for it. Nat had to be smart, bury her emotions. Fuck Dad. Fuck Mum. Fuck the world. Fuck it all. Alek thought he was in charge. He thought *he* was using *her*. But if this fame crap was really a game, Nat was going to win, no matter what it took.

"I love you," Mum said.

"I love you too." Nat squeezed her tightly.

After the hug, Vicky walked over to the small mirror and picked up something off the table. "How cheesy is this?"

She held up a coaster with big bold letters on it reading *The Marty Graham Show*. There was a small, round photo of him in the corner, purposefully round as though to really highlight his bald round head. He had a big, somehow annoying grin on his face.

"Have you listened to this podcast?" Mum asked.

They'd driven almost the whole way in complete silence. Nat had just kept staring at her phone, trying not to think about everything. "It's a joke," she told Mum. "He's always pulling stunts."

"Stunts like what?"

"I don't know. Like one time, he brought out this reality star's old teacher, because on the show she'd talked about not being able to tell the time and feeling really embarrassed in class. They brought the teacher out and sort of made her walk off the show."

"What, the reality lady?"

Nat nodded. "Marty Graham had a T-shirt on under his hoodie with a big clock on it."

"Oh, God," Mum said quietly. "I hope he doesn't try anything like that."

Chapter 22

Alek

Alek stared into the abyss of his black coffee, wishing he'd had more sleep last night. The five-star hotel the podcast had provided for him was adequate, but a big man like him had specific mattress requirements; he much preferred his own. Still, this was it – his time, his chance. He was spreading a message. He was – was this even about Maksym anymore?

He took a sip of the rancid coffee, thinking of his grandfather, the voice which had guided him ever since he'd severed his connection to the absurdly persistent impositions of the pharmaceutical companies. Maksym's voice would be nice to hear, and their plan would be lovely too. But what if Alek could do some good here? And really, were they ever going to save them all? Could they?

Alek trembled, scalding coffee swilling over the rim of the mug and onto his hand. He felt nothing. He was numb. His skin and his heart were numb. His mind was twisting against him. He was doubting. *Doubting.* Doubting his *grandfather.*

"Alek," Brad said, all teeth, the smiling fucking donkey. "Are you all right?"

"Am I all right?" Alek repeated, staring at him.

Brad fidgeted like a coward, like a man who'd never felt a punch to the mouth. "Your hand..."

Alek looked down at his coffee-scorched hand. "I suppose I should wash up before business begins."

He went to the toilet. In the hallway, of course, as if the universe was playing games with him, Natasha was just walking out of the women's. She put her hands in her pockets and put her head down.

"See you soon, superstar," Alek told her.

She tried not to, but the corner of her lip twitched and she smiled.

One of the clauses of the contract read, *The GUEST or any representative of the GUEST shall not under any circumstances seek financial retribution against the HOST for any perceived harm, excepting that which falls within the legal code, in which case the GUEST is free to seek legal but not financial recourse.*

Alek's lawyer had told him something like that would most likely not hold up if pressed with enough resources; he was salivating for a case of some kind.

Alek walked into the studio, shaking hands with Marty Graham. His head was freshly shaved and so shiny under the bright studio lights, Alek was sure he could see a large, brooding man staring back at him from Marty's scalp. "Hello, hello," Marty said brightly. "I think you're a little late!"

The clock told him how late he was. "Fifteen seconds."

Marty laughed tightly. Everybody was treating Alek like he was some animal they'd all unexpectedly been caged with. Vicky was already sitting at the podcast table, headphones on, looking hollow-eyed and nervous. Behind her, just out of view of the camera, Nat sat staring down at her phone, her hair across her face.

"Should've got a bigger chair, eh?" Marty grinned as he nodded to the seat opposite Vicky.

Alek studied the chair, then looked at Marty. "Have you got a bigger one? It looks extremely flimsy." Before waiting for a reply, he turned to Vicky.

"Afternoon, Victoria."

Vicky looked at him, but said nothing.

"So it's like that, is it?" Alek said.

"We can talk on the podcast; I've got nothing to say to you until then."

"Very moral-high-ground of you, well done." When Alek turned back, Marty was still looking at him awkwardly. *Up* at him, since Alek towered over everybody in the room; he even towered above the security guard standing just outside. Alek wondered if they always hired one, or if they thought he was too dangerous to be around.

"I'm sorry," Marty said, gesturing to the seat.

"Then *I'm* sorry—"

Alek turned and walked away. He was too damn tired. Sleep was important to a brain like his. His head was splitting. But this was tactical, too. Who the fuck did Marty Graham think he was? Alek was the orchestrator here.

"Wait, wait," Marty said. "Of course we can get you a larger chair. I was only messing."

"Ha, ha," Alek said dryly.

The funny part was, it was the big, burly security guard, his neck covered in grotesque tribal tattoos, who had to awkwardly remove the smaller chair and bring in what was more like a miniature armchair from the waiting room.

"Thank you, friend."

Vicky stared at the whole thing with a *Can you believe this crap?* face. That was good; she needed to learn just how small she was.

"Okay, shall we get started?" Marty said, sitting off to the side between Vicky and Alek, as though he was a referee. "First of all, Alek, do you want to explain to the listeners about the chair situation?"

Alek grinned, forcing his Modern Face into suave existence. "You've got a real athlete here, Marty – a real specimen. I mean, look at me." Alek waved his arms, laughing, and Marty's eyes lit up with relief. When would people understand that Alek had been acting his entire life? "Even *this* chair is too small."

Marty grinned, then turned to Vicky. "Sorry about the chair, Vicky."

"It's fine," she said quietly, not star quality at all, far too introverted.

"I'm just glad you two can be in the same room," Marty said.

"Unless Vicky tries to kick me out," Alek quickly replied.

"Maybe don't get blackout drunk and hog the trampoline, then?" Vicky snapped, and Marty laughed again, which was annoying, him laughing at her lame little jokes.

"You a trampoline fan, Alek?"

"I'm far more graceful than you'd imagine," he answered honestly. "But as usual, Vicky is doing what she does best – distorting reality."

"Oh, so you didn't use the trampoline?"

"I did, before I started drinking, and only for a short while... and anyway, we're not here to talk about *trampolines*. We're here to talk about the suffering and death of millions of people – the seemingly inevitable march of agony sweeping across a beautiful and bountiful nation."

"Bit rehearsed," Marty muttered, almost like a reflex.

"I'm sorry?" Alek said, staring at Marty.

Marty looked genuinely scared. "I said it's a curse. It seems. On the nation."

Hmm. It was a good lie. "It seems to be, yes."

"Yes, exactly," Vicky snapped. "And *I* need to make it clear that I have nothing but love and support for the Ukrainian people."

"Ah, yes, which is why you made a video *using* them, pretending to *be* them." Nat glared at Alek from behind Vicky, because they both knew the truth; they both knew why Vicky had really done it.

"I explained that," Vicky said, sitting upright, with way too much poise and dignity for Alek's liking.

"Oh, right," Alek replied, shaking his head and sighing.

She became combative, almost yelling. "You don't believe me? I've spent my entire life, since that sick man took my innocence, trying to put myself back together. I am so, so sorry to anybody I hurt or offended, but I promise it never came from a place of malice."

"You're just another person spitting in the face of Ukraine. Okay, Vicky. Let's say you're telling the truth."

She glared at him convincingly. "I *am*." She was a very good liar. Or was there a nugget of truth there?

"Even *that* doesn't absolve you," Alek said, eloquently. "It just means that you're another privileged person using those beneath you in the socioeconomic ladder for your own perverted form of personal therapy. So you feel bad about a horrible, tragic, *horrific* incident, which happened in your youth..."

He made sure to put emphasis on that, as well as to raise his voice and talk authoritatively anytime he thought she might interrupt.

"No, wait a second," Vicky snapped. "You're being absolutely disgusting right now."

"Oh, really?"

"I *deleted* the video. I haven't made an entire career out of this. I clearly regretted it."

"Ah, I'm sure your regret will bring all the victims of the war back to life."

"Now, hang on," Marty said, as if he'd forgotten what they'd already talked about. Alek had *told* him that Nat was ready to turn on her mother; it would give him a viral moment. When he'd arrived they'd had words, and Marty had smiled and clapped him on the arm. It was their plan; was he going back on it?

It was as if Marty's free-speech sensibilities, for which he was well known and on which he relied, were stronger than his predatory hunger for virality. Which was bad for Alek.

"You can't really believe she's responsible for the *war*."

"I believe she's responsible for a lot," Alek snapped, thinking of Maksym.

"I'm guilty of being selfish, of letting my childhood trauma rule me, but I would not – and I have not – ever hurt anybody. I would *never*. I'm just..."

She stopped, fighting back tears. It was so skilfully done; it was almost expert. Visibly, she went from strong to almost completely devastated to strong again, and then sat up straighter. "I just want to go back to my normal life."

"That's easy—"

"No, it's not," Vicky cut in. "Because you won't let me, Alek. It was all dying down, until your video. But you had to chase *your* fifteen minutes of fame."

Alek shook his head. "No, Vicky. That's not how this is, at all." What a bitch. Alek should've got more sleep. But what a *bitch*. "I'm doing this for my true homeland. I'm doing this for my grandfather." Which she most likely knew all about, anyway.

"If you're doing this for Ukraine, then could you answer a couple of questions for me?"

"What questions?" He looked at Marty. Had he been making plans within plans?

Marty chuckled, all shiny-headed. "Don't look at *me*, big man."

"Just two questions," Vicky said.

Alek shrugged. "There's nothing you can ask me that I have any reason not to answer."

It wasn't as if she was going to know about his cellar and his box and the rattling of bones. "How many bedrooms do you have in your home?"

Ha, ha, ha. She thought this was *it*. She was trying to play it. "Five," he told her. "It was my family's home. I'm not ashamed to admit that."

"Okay, great..." And here came another bitchy little smile. "And how many refugees are you housing?"

Oh, *fuck*. How had he not seen that coming? He'd thought she was going to take an economic angle, trying to brand herself as the hardworking mother and him as the aristocratic layabout. His mind scrambled for possibilities; the only way out would be to blame his schizophrenia diagnosis, but something inside wouldn't let him. He hated that diagnosis. It was like a stamp on his forehead. Yet, he couldn't tell her, *It's so I can chop up homeless people and shear their bones.*

"Alek?" Marty said.

"Uh... none, right now." He barely forced the words out; this was thoroughly annoying. "But I have a personal reason for that."

"What reason?" Marty asked, still with a smile, but with a journalist's edge to his voice. "If it's anything to do with your..." He trailed off when Alek communicated wordlessly that he would slaughter him if he kept going.

"With what?" Alek asked.

"Well... any personal issues."

Did he know about the diagnosis? "I just…"

"Don't want them there with you?" Vicky hissed in an ugly, unfeminine manner. "I made a mistake, then I deleted my video. But you're uploading video after video pretending to be some champion for this cause. And yet you've made the choice not to save four people – to house *four* people?"

"What does this have to do with anything?"

Alek didn't mean to slam his hand on the table. He honestly didn't, but this was just absolutely absurd! The way she was twisting it, the way she was making it seem like she was the clever one. It was a tricky, sneaky, almost admirable thing she was doing… and it was working well. She must've known from Liuba that Alek didn't like talking about this nonsense.

Everybody paused, like in the aftermath of an explosion, like in that scene in *The Great Gatsby* when Gatsby goes nuts and everybody just stares at him as though his skin has fallen away and shown the ghoul beneath. The security guard entered the room, folded his hands.

Alek adjusted his mic. "E-everybody knows she's twisting it," he said, annoyed by the stutter. "Maybe you'll edit this, Marty—"

"Edit?" Marty chuckled. "This is live; we told you that, Alek."

Had they told him that? Suddenly, the webcam-style cameras were making him feel like there was something else going on. Vicky was staring at him. Nat looked doubtful, as though she'd finally seen him for the nothing he was.

"Didn't you know that?" Vicky had a supercilious, repulsive smirk.

"I know some things, Vicky," he told her flatly. "About you. About your marriage."

Vicky's eyes popped out of her head. She looked sick. "What the fuck are you talking about?"

Marty did that very annoying laugh, as if he was trying to weasel his way into both of them somehow liking him. But they had a *deal*. He'd told him; he'd head-fucked the stupid girl until she was ready to devour her own mother. Liuba was going to hate him, but he couldn't let this woman win this.

"Let's just say—"

He let his voice boom, found he was sitting up, glaring at her. Part of him hated that he was doing this; they were giving Marty everything he wanted. He was so, so sorry, Liuba.

But then Nat stood up, yelled. It was exactly what Alek had wanted – except, she didn't look like she was on his side.

Chapter 23

Nat

"Will you just shut up, you perverted freak? Before I tell *everyone* what you're really like?"

Nat was shouting. Her throat hurt. She could actually feel the veins in her throat pushing against her skin. She glared at Alek, telling herself not to be scared. What the hell was he doing? Mum and Dad were... they had problems. But the *whole world* didn't need to know.

"Excuse me?" he said.

Mum looked lost, panicked. Nat stared at Alek, even when she got really nervous because Marty grabbed the camera that was facing him and turned it to Nat. This was *it*; she couldn't betray Mum. Maybe she deserved it, but she just couldn't.

"You, Alek. In the park. With Mia. My friend." Crap. She shouldn't have said her name. It was so hard to stop her voice from trembling, way harder than she'd thought it would be. "She's *sixteen*, and you were flirting with her."

"I was doing no such thing."

"Wait a second," Mum snapped. "You were in the park with my daughter?"

"He said he was taking me and Mia somewhere." *Fuck*. The

name again. And this was live. "But then he got all weird. He started talking with... with my friend, like, I don't know, like he thought he was our age or something."

"Are you *joking*, girl?" Alek roared, making the security guard move away from the wall, getting ready. "I would never... I have never..."

"Where were you taking them, Alek?" Marty said.

"To – to volunteer," Alek said, touching his head. "To make a *change*."

"Maybe you should *change* your tastes to somebody your own age!"

Alek sprung to his feet. Nat forced herself to stay still. Her heart was beating so hard it almost hurt. Mum was on her feet too, her hands raised like there was anything she could possibly do if Alek decided to go crazy. Then the security guard walked towards him. He was as tall and big as Alek, but he looked softer somehow, even with the tough-guy tattoos.

"What's your job, then?" Alek said, turning to the man.

"Come on, mate." The man stood a couple of feet away.

"And that, ladies and gents," Marty said, "is the quickest podcast in... Woah, woah!"

He yelled because Alek suddenly lunged at him. His whole demeanour changed. Nat fell into her chair from the shock of seeing Alek like that, how violent he was about to get... but then he stopped himself with a forced laugh, leaned over, pretended he'd only been going for Marty's mic. "And that, ladies and gents, is how you *really* end a show. Ha!"

The security guard followed him like he was an animal about to attack. Marty was dabbing his head with his shirt and pulling stupid faces at the camera. One of his employees was following Alek and the bodyguard down the hallway. Nat put her hand on her chest, trying to calm herself down.

"It's okay." Mum's voice was soft and she gently took Nat's hands in hers. "Oh, Nat, it's okay."

"I'm sorry, Mum." Nat's voice broke.

"Sorry?" Mum pulled her closer. "Whatever for? You did nothing wrong. You stood up for me..." Now it was Mum's voice breaking. "You're the best daughter I ever could've asked for..."

Nat hugged her Mum tighter, trying not to think about the cameras, about what a moment this would make. Mum had made mistakes, fine, but seeing Alek threaten her... It just proved Nat needed her mum. She hated that a little bit, but it was true.

Chapter 24

Alek

Back in Weston-super-Mare, in his big house, Alek talked on the phone with the man who called himself a lawyer. But Mr Hurney had no answers; he just fumbled and muttered about contracts, and kept saying they could *pursue options*.

Eventually, Alek slammed his hand on the table. It was just like in the podcast interview. Reality was fraying and weeping and bleeding, and its blood was sick poison to Alek's future: his hopes, his dreams. "Enough," he snapped finally, sitting in his study, at his desk, but no longer fuelled by the sense of victory he'd felt before. "Are you saying you're going to charge me an exorbitant amount only for the podcast to stay online?"

"We're talking about the Marty Graham show here..."

Alek hung up. The live show had garnered 20,000 views. The uploaded video currently had one million views, and climbing. It had only gone up last night. Comments flooded in, many of them saying things like, *You can tell he's a perv just by looking at him.* There were others who were defending him, but not many, and he didn't like the tone of them, either.

This #metoo crap has gone on too long! When will men get a break?

Alek had no desire to become some sort of misogynist figurehead. Women needed the protection of men; they were weaker and softer... also sneakier, meaner, more capable of social manipulation because they could never rely upon their physical prowess, but still...

More comments – 3,122 so far.

So this silver-spoon prick won't even put his money where his mouth is!

Did you see the way he snapped? Dude definitely has problems.

Let's see how tough he is. If I was the one sitting face to face with him...

His phone rang, disturbing his thoughts. It was his landline ringing; he had turned his mobile phone off to fight the notifications from social media apps – and news apps too, since both local and national papers were picking this up. It was like there were two armies forming, and *that bitch's* was growing far quicker.

He picked up the phone. "Hello?"

"Is this the kiddie fiddler?" a low, cowardly little voice hissed.

"Is this a brave man anonymously phoning somebody to try and feel tough and significant?" He hung up.

So Alek would have to get his landline number changed, too. What was he supposed to do? How was he supposed to stop this stain from marking him? He would never, under any duress, for any reason, even if it meant saving several million lives, hurt anybody who didn't deserve it... He would certainly never involuntarily claim sexual use of somebody's body.

Alek would've laughed if his TikTok account wasn't currently being attacked by an endless series of wannabe world savers, each one more annoyingly righteous than the last. The phone rang again. Alek snatched it up. "Go fuck yourself."

"Why aren't you answering your mobile?" Michelle said at the same time, then, "Woah, expecting a call from a friend?"

"My number has gone public," he told her. "Which means I'll be disconnecting my landline once this is over. Luckily, I haven't reached the point at which vultures have started congregating outside my house."

What if that *did* happen, though? Could he hire security? He had money, fine, but not *unlimited* money.

"Whatever. I want nothing to do with any of it."

"It's so lovely, Liuba, feeling supported."

"Did you tell anyone what I told you about Vicky?"

"You'll have to be more specific," he said.

"No, I won't," she snapped. "You know exactly what I'm talking about. The reason she posted the videos to begin with..."

"The affair. No, of course not. I'd rather sacrifice my whole career than betray you."

After a pause, she sighed. "Okay, good. But it's not a *career*."

On that cheery note, his loving sister hung up the phone. Alek disconnected it, then the world went dark. When he awoke, he was staring at the obliterated mess of the landline phone on the floor.

Alek grabbed his mobile phone and propped it on his desk so he was in frame. It was time for him to fight back. He had an idea, which made him uncomfortable; it would involve sharing things he'd rather have kept hidden. But he couldn't tolerate this, anymore.

He looked too tired, so he went into the bathroom and washed his face. Then he changed his shirt, brushed his hair, and returned to the camera. A serious, emotionally moved man looked back at him from the screen.

Clicking *record*, he said, "By now, I'm sure most of you have seen the podcast. You'll have heard Natasha's unfounded and, frankly, disturbing accusation." He wouldn't make the mistake of repeating it. "It is, also, absolutely absurd – and a clear attempt on mother and daughter's part to slander me. But there's one problem, and I really never wanted to share this publicly..."

Alek took a breath, seeming dignified, seeming like a man who simply shouldn't have to deal with something like this. "I'm a virgin. I suppose you could call me asexual; sex has simply never interested me. And to think I would seek *that* from a *child*..."

He shook his head, resisting the urge to smirk when he saw how he looked on the phone screen.

"It is true that I saw Natasha and her friend in the park; and it is true I told them I was taking them someplace... but I was taking them to see a *memorial* and *volunteer*. I wanted to show these young people the value of hard work rather than standing around outside my house, waiting to catch me out, and vaping. But then I realised my mistake – realised how cynical people might perceive it – and so I left them. I don't even remember her friend's name. I definitely didn't want anything like *that* from her..."

This next part would be difficult; Alek wished he'd swallowed his pride and done this during the interview. He didn't *want* to do it, but what was the alternative? Let the world believe he was what she said he was? Let her win?

"As for Vicky's other dig," he went on, "it's time I was completely open. I have a..." He almost said *diagnosis*. "The reason I have not housed any refugees is because, although I have tried many times, I am schizophrenic and the authorities won't allow me to – despite the fact I am on medication and haven't had any kind of psychotic episode in a long, long time."

He had never tried to house any refugees, but the internet was a short game, he was learning. He needed to fix this *now*, not in a few hours when everybody had moved on.

"If given the chance," he lied, "I would do far, far more than I have already. To my loyal and loving followers, I want to say, thank you. Thank you for not believing her lies. Thank you for not throwing a man under the bus without any evidence. Thank you for being you. I will be posting another diary entry soon. In the meantime, again, thank you."

He took a moment to look introspective and emotional before ending the video. After editing and uploading it – he cut out the pauses and added some background music – he went to bed and curled into a ball, closing his eyes. He stared into the darkness of his eyelids, trying to see it: those dead fields, the swollen and broken people, the bodies, the skeletons, the emptiness of lifeless air, all through Maksym's eyes. But all he could see was Vicky looking at him, a glint of excitement in her eyes, as if she thought she'd won.

***

Hours later, Alek woke with a dry mouth to the sound of somebody hammering on the door. His head was hurting enough through dehydration, so a visit from Liuba was the last thing he needed; it had to be her, since she was knocking the main door, not using the buzzer from outside the gate; Liuba was the only one who had keys to the main gate.

If she was banging the door this hard, this probably meant Natasha had told her he'd informed her about the affair. Dammit. He got a quick drink of water and then went to the front door. The silhouette told him right away that it wasn't his sister. It was a large, wide-shouldered man.

Alek threw the door open, staring at the typically English-looking man: bald head, thick neck, fat but still fairly strong, a barrel sort of build, wearing a football shirt. His cheeks were alcoholic-red. Behind him, Alek noticed, near his *open gate,* stood Natasha's little bird-like friend. What was her name? Mia, Alek remembered. She wasn't wearing her school uniform, though Alek was fairly sure it was schooltime. Or was she too old for that? Was she in college? He was so unused to being around these small people.

"Can I help you?" Alek asked reasonably.

The man snorted as if Alek had just said something funny. The girl looked terrified as she leaned against the gate, her arms folded, looking over at them as though she expected a fight. It was honestly so grotesque to suggest that Alek would touch her for his own gratification. She was basically a small animal to him.

"You can help me, mate," the big man said, something in his tone telling Alek he was usually used to being the bigger man. But not with Alek; few people were. "By staying away from my bloody daughter."

"How did you open my gate?" Alek asked.

"Your bloody gate was already open, your highness!"

"Right," Alek replied. "Well... I've never done anything untoward with your daughter. I've only met her once, and that's because she was hanging around outside my house. Did *she* say I'd done anything?"

Alek must've left the gate unlocked, which he did sometimes... but people didn't usually just barge in expecting some sort of welcome, as though they had earned the right not to be slapped for such blatant disrespect.

"She's too scared of you," the man snapped. "So just stay away, all right?"

Alek shrugged. "Sure. But if you visit me again and presume to enter my gate, locked or unlocked, without permission, I won't be happy."

The man sneered, or tried to, but with Alek just looking at

him calmly, clearly unaffected by the hard-man exterior the worm was trying to project, it was unconvincing. "Or what?"

"I will remove you," Alek told him.

The man snorted again; he was a piggish thing. "Remove me, eh?"

"Remove you, yes. Physically."

"Pretty tough for a kiddie fiddler, aren't you?"

"I've never done anything even close to that, sir," Alek said. "And I don't appreciate you repeating slander. Time to leave."

For a third time, the piggy snorted. Alek's hand was twitching. He was a good person; he didn't deserve this darkness in his life. "Going to make me, are you?"

"Does that seem like an intelligent question for you to ask?" Though Mia's father reeked of booze and sweat and cigarettes, Alek moved closer, walking onto his front step, looking down at the man. "You – clearly unfit, clearly overweight, clearly a smoker, disgusting and incapable in too many ways to name – think you can stop me doing *any damn thing I want to you?*"

He didn't mean to shout the last part, but it was like everything caught up with him. When he shouted, it was like the piggy pit bull finally understood how outclassed he was. He backed off, hands raised, looking like he hated himself for the response. But he still did it.

"You want to hang around with the bitch so much? Be my fucking guest!"

He stormed out of the gate – right past his daughter – before Alek registered who he'd meant by *the bitch*. He was talking about his own daughter. Mia leaned against the gate, trembling all over, tears streaming down her cheeks.

Alek walked over to her as, in the street, there was a tyre-squealing noise. Clearly it was the pit bull abandoning his daughter.

Mia looked lost and devastated and hurt on such a fundamental level, Alek instinctively wanted to make her feel better. But he couldn't forget who she was and who her friends were.

"Your own father left you," Alek muttered. "With a man he apparently thinks abused you."

"Yeah," Mia said matter-of-factly, as if there was no mystery here at all.

"Does that seem right to you?"

"I'd rather be here with you," she told him.

"Don't start anything like that," he said sternly. "If this is all a plan – if your dad left you here so you can try and make Natasha's lies come true – then you need to leave."

"It's not..." The girl rushed forward, then dropped her hands, as if she'd intended to touch him. "I just... I've never seen Dad that scared before. He's going to be angry."

Alek shrugged. "Let him be angry."

"It's not that easy for me," she said quietly. "If I went home now..."

"What?" Alek asked.

She glared at the ground, as though it had offended her. "It wouldn't be good."

"No?" Alek knew part of him might regret this. But it also felt necessary, even urgent. "Then maybe you should come inside."

"Really?"

"Just for a little while," he said. "But remember, I'm a grown-up and I have no interest in you. You're a child. Do you understand?"

She stuck her lip out, looking petulant, disproving the point she immediately made. "I'm not a child."

"You're a little girl, Mia," he said.

She kept staring at the ground. Then, suddenly, she broke down into the most gut-wrenching sobs Alek had ever heard. He would have had to be completely inhumane to ignore her, so he put his hand on her shoulder and led her to the house.

"How about a mug of hot chocolate?" he asked as she wailed. "And then you can decide what side you're on."

Closing the front door behind her, he leaned down so he was eye-level with her. Her cheeks were red from crying. She had a few pale freckles scattered across her cheeks, which he hadn't noticed before.

"I can help you, Mia," he said. "With anything. Your dad can't hurt you if you're on my team. But you have to do something for me."

She took a breath, as if getting herself ready, then spoke in a detached voice. "Okay..."

What she did next sickened him; her hands reached towards a place they never should've even dreamed of reaching, and Alek backed away. "*Mia*," he almost shouted. "You're a child. Even if you weren't—"

"What, you're really asexual, are you? You're really a *virgin?*"

"Yes," Alek said with dignity.

"If you don't want *that*, what can I do?"

The poor thing. She asked the question as though the idea she could be useful in any other way was foreign to her.

"Way more than you think, Mia," he said.

Chapter 25

Vicky

Vicky sat in the kitchen with a mug of coffee as Max did his homework at the table. As usual, he'd left it until the end of the summer. But she couldn't blame him. She thought they got too much homework sometimes, though she knew that wasn't a popular opinion. Vicky tried to quieten her mind.

But last night, Nat had admitted that it was *Mia* who had been flirting with *Alek*, and that he'd been completely uninterested. Alek's latest video had swayed people a little bit, but not much. Accusations stuck even without evidence; this was helped by the fact far more people had watched *The Marty Graham Show* than Alek's video.

Still, it hurt Vicky, knowing it was all based on a lie. Her mood didn't get any better when her phone vibrated. It was a text from Seb, asking if he should get anything in for dinner.

She replied to Seb, then a few minutes later, the front door opened and Nat walked in. She looked tired, her hair tied up, lots of dark make-up around her eyes and a thick shield of foundation covering her cheeks.

"Hey," Max said cheerily as she walked in. Vicky was so, so happy to see him smile.

"Hey." Nat forced a smile at her little brother. "Mum, can we talk?"

Vicky followed her into the living room. Nat shut the door, then turned, a shockingly grown-up look on her face. Lowering her voice, she said, "Mum, I know about the affair."

The world dropped out from beneath her. Vicky had imagined this moment so many times, but now it was happening, she knew she never could've prepared for it. She was dangerously close to hyperventilating as she dropped onto the armchair. "Oh."

Nat sat beside her, took her hand. Vicky squeezed it so hard she must've hurt her daughter. But in all the times she'd imagined this moment, she'd never thought Nat would hold her like this.

"Mum, I want to say I forgive you, okay? I forgive you."

Vicky wiped a tear from her cheek. "Just like that."

"We haven't got time to fight. We have to be on the same team. We can't let him win. That's why I had to say what I said, Mum – he was going to make the affair public."

"*He* knows?" Vicky said.

"He's Michelle's brother, Mum," Nat said quietly. "That's how I found out – through him. He was trying to make me turn against you or something, I guess."

When Vicky looked at her daughter, she instantly knew: Nat had been planning to do just that. That was why she'd been so distant and awkward during the drive to London. But she'd chosen Vicky. That meant something.

"It was a huge mistake. I never should've—"

"Mum, don't you get it?" Nat interrupted. "This isn't about that. About right or wrong, or anything to do with the past. Or anything else other than that we have to win. We have to keep going." She lowered her voice. "If we play this right, we'll never have to worry about money again."

"You don't have to worry about money now," Vicky said. "Every family has its ups and downs, but you don't have to be concerned. We're doing quite well." Relatively speaking, at least.

"Maybe things won't always be as stable." Nat's grim tone made Vicky wonder if she'd noticed the distance between her mum and dad. "Maybe we need a plan B."

"For what?"

"For life," Nat said passionately. "I'm going to make a TikTok account soon. It's time I got in on the game."

"Nat, I don't think—"

"Or I tell Dad about the affair," she said flatly. "I'm sorry, Mum, but there's no time. How long do you think this will last? The only thing that separates a one-hit wonder and somebody who actually makes a career is that they never stop playing, Mum. *Now*'s the time to work hard so we can reap the benefits later."

For what felt like the millionth time, Vicky had to remind herself that this bright, engaged, *cutthroat* young lady had once been a tiny baby in her arms.

"It looks like I've got no choice," she said.

That made her feel better. At least she could tell herself this wasn't her doing.

Nat took Vicky's hand again. "This could get really ugly."

"More so than it already has?"

Nat looked at her as if to say, *Don't be naïve, Mum.*

Vicky felt resigned. And, weirdly, there was a light feeling in her chest, relief maybe. Nat knew, and she didn't hate her. That in itself was a miracle.

Chapter 26

Nat

Nat lay on her bed, *on*, not *in*, because there was no way she was sleeping tonight. Every second she spent sleeping was another second she wasted. College would be starting soon; she couldn't even imagine what it would be like walking down the hallways with this stain on her. Maybe her mates would support her, but maybe not. It all depended on which way it went. She thought about texting Mia again, but what was the point? She wouldn't reply.

Nat kept scrolling through the comments on the video podcast.

Her smile faltered when she came across a heavily upvoted reply. *Let's not rush to judgement, here. We don't know the full story. This is an accusation, nothing else.*

"Fuck you," she whispered, wiping her thumb and scrolling through more comments. Then she changed social platforms and started scrolling through memes. People were taking Alek storming out of the studio and putting him in different scenarios.

She clicked onto reels on Instagram. It was Alek, yelling, with the caption, *When they don't got mustard sauce.* A manager is pleading, 'Sir, sir, I'm sorry,' with Alek lunging towards him just as he'd lunged at Marty. The manager fell at just the right time, then the video ended.

A notification appeared on her screen. *New message: Mia. (Total unread messages: 78.)* She clicked her texts, ignoring the rest of the messages. She'd been ignoring them ever since this started. Some were from sort-of friends; others were from people she hardly ever spoke to. She had to do this on *her* terms.

What do you need, Natasha?

I'm just glad you're alive!

Maybe I should've texted.

Where were you?

Dad made me tell him where Alek lived. He drove over there and got in his face. It was so embarrassing, Nat. It really made me feel small and pathetic, and like I wasn't real.

The house creaked. From the bedroom next door, she heard a rustling. She wondered if Max was awake too. Maybe they all were, because they knew, soon, their lives would explode. Nat with college. Dad with work. Mum because of the lie Nat had told. And Max? Was he getting swept up in it all?

I'm so sorry.

I can't believe you said that on the podcast. I can't believe you put me in this position.

Mia, I'm so sorry. I tried ringing you.

How the fuck would ringing me make a difference? You already did it!

Nat felt like something terrible was about to happen. She tried to ring Mia, but she rejected the call right away.

I can't talk. It's too late.

I want to make this up to you.

Nat knew she shouldn't put anything too obvious in a text, but she also felt like she was losing Mia. She had to control some of the damage.

We can do this together.

Do what, frame an innocent man for something he didn't do?

Mia, he's not a good person.

Mia saw the message, but she didn't respond. Nat sent several follow-up texts, and Mia saw each one, but she was refusing to respond. Nat didn't know what to do. She felt like she was suddenly full of energy. She couldn't just lie there, doing nothing. Maybe she could walk to Mia's? But her dad would go mental.

Almost an hour later, as Nat was lying there sweating like crazy into the sheets, she got a text. Her belly dropped. It was a link to a TikTok video.

Nat clicked it. Mia appeared on the screen, looking small and scared, yet somehow brave at the same time. She was sitting in a garden, against the wall of a house. Nat wasn't sure if it was Mia's house or not.

"I feel like I have to do this," Mia said in a small voice. "Nat is my friend, but..." She paused, fighting off tears, and Nat knew they were genuine. She knew that, for Mia at least, this wasn't a game. "But I can't let her tell lies about me. She said Alek tried to... do something to me in the park, flirt with me, whatever, hurt me, I don't know. But it's not true. It never happened. I don't know why Nat would say that, but it's just not true."

The video ended, just like that. Simple and to the point. The view counter was already at 90,000. The video was uploaded only 30 minutes previously. It was exploding. It was going to erupt. By the next day, views would be in the millions.

Nat shot off a text.

> So you've picked your side, then.

> This doesn't have to be about sides.

> You're wrong. You just picked yours. That means anything goes now.

A small part of Nat knew how cruel this was. But Mia had just ruined her life!

> Anything I feel like using, I'll use.

> Nat?! What does that mean?!

Nat closed the text thread and muted Mia. She'd been the only one Nat *hadn't* muted, but there was no more special treatment. Nat would be cold, even against Mia. Going back to her text threads, she began to unmute people. She knew it was wrong; even as she did it, she knew, but what other choice was there? Let her family burn?

First, she texted Joel, a rugby player who was always trying it on with her.

> Mia is such a lying bitch!

She went through her contacts: friends from dance class, the shy girl from art, the helpful one from science. She responded to every single unread message except for Mia's... and in every single one, she made her reality, *the* reality.

Nat had to make herself believe it now too, or she'd never be able to keep going. Mia wasn't an innocent, loving, beautiful person who'd suffered unfairly too many times; she was a lying, conniving bitch. Nat flipped a switch; she could feel bad later. Now it was war. No time for feelings.

Nat sat up, practising her angry whispering until she got just the right tone.

Chapter 27

Alek

What an eventful night it had been... Mia's video had gone live yesterday and tonight, as a rebuttal, Natasha had revealed her true colours in a night-time tirade. Alek was almost impressed. Nat sold the lie well, staring with furious, tired eyes at the camera. "I can't believe Mia would do this. I don't know what's wrong with her; I don't know why she's covering for him. But I would *never* lie about this. Why would I? Mia is just trying to make me look bad. *Mia* is the liar – she's sick in the head!"

Just like that, the video ended. As Alek sipped his morning coffee, he couldn't help but smile. Natasha had clearly taken a cue from his video with its sharp ending.

The comments told him that this newest exchange had created another battle, almost evenly matched. Some questioned why Mia would lie about this. Others thought that Alek was creepy enough to pull something like this off. *Don't you know that's how groomers work?????*

Suddenly, the main doorbell went. Alek hadn't made the mistake of leaving the gate unlocked this time. Adjusting his shirt, he went outside in his slippers. He opened the side gate and looked out. Three people stood in a small cluster. One of them was holding a camera.

"Mr Bodar?" a youngish man said, approaching with a notebook in his hand. He had floppy blond hair. "My name is Raymond Simmens and I'm with the *Mercury*." It was the local paper. "We were wondering if you had a few minutes?"

Alek was actually genuinely delighted. "Sure. Would you like some coffee?"

The man flinched, seeming shocked. The camera man was taller, skinnier, younger. The third was a young woman, maybe around twenty, looking at Alek with the sort of wide, overly inquisitive eyes that made him wonder if she had an ulterior motive.

"This is my cameraman, Chuck," Raymond said. "And our intern, Izzy."

Alek nodded. "Shall we talk, then?"

He led them inside, hoping he didn't smirk too obviously when Raymond paused at the closed-off cellar door. "What's down there?"

"Oh, just my torture tools. And some dead bodies, of course. Ha!" Alek winked and Raymond laughed nervously. "I'm still designing my man cave," Alek went on. "It's closed off until then, for safety. Mould concerns."

Alek led them through the kitchen and into the overgrown back garden.

"Wow, it's like a jungle out here," Izzy the intern said inanely.

"Make yourselves comfortable," Alek said. "I'll make some coffee. How do you all like it?"

In the kitchen, making the drinks, he could hear them muttering through the window. They didn't think he could hear, but Alek was listening carefully.

"Seems like a nice enough bloke..."

"A bit eccentric..."

Izzy the intern then said, "I like him. Even *she* said he didn't do anything."

"At least he's friendly."

He carried the drinks through on a tray, then sat at the table, folding his hands. "So, what would you like to talk with me about?"

"Well... everything." Raymond chuckled. "Honestly, you're the most exciting thing that's happened to this town for a long time.

"Do you mind if I record? Sometimes it's easier than the old pen and pad."

Alek smirked. "Sure, but only if you promise to put me on the front page."

"This probably will be front page," Raymond said.

"At least *he* agreed to meet with us," Izzy muttered, drawing a sharp look from Raymond.

"Vicky wasn't amenable?"

"Shall we get started?"

Alek shrugged. "Sure."

"First of all, why don't you tell us a bit about yourself?"

Alek decided he'd need to be as honest as possible. He'd already disclosed his schizophrenia, so there was no use in concealing it now. "When I was a child, I spent a lot of my time alone. Reading. Imagining. Or going for long hikes and runs. Eventually, I read English Literature at Oxford, but then I became ill... mentally ill, you understand, and I had to drop out. This led to several years of psychotic bouts and drug addiction..."

Alek paused, remembering those foolish days. "I mistakenly believed that by using recreational drugs I could prevent the episodes and defeat the symptoms. But I was wrong. This cycle – which included some visits to the hospital – was interspersed with work for the family company, until it was sold, and volunteering."

Raymond just watched, seeming pleased, so Alek went on. Perhaps interviews were not usually this easy. Alek almost wished he hadn't shared the part about the drugs, but he had to go for the humanising angle.

"In the parks, mostly, and sometimes in the local charity shop, though I haven't done that for a couple years. I haven't had a very exciting or noteworthy life, it's true, but I try to be a good person."

"Which brings us to the latest scandal on the *Marty Graham Show*."

"Ah, yes, a vicious and unfounded accusation, which the so-called victim herself says never happened."

"Why do you think Nastasha would make such a claim?"

"Because she doesn't want the world to hate her mum. She thinks she has to slander me to save her mother. I'm sure she's a lovely girl and she's doing what she thinks is best."

Alek had to take this angle, even if he despised the little stirrer. If he revealed the truth about Vicky's affair, he would only look like a bitter, miserable man trying to tear down a woman. Natasha had almost done him a favour by going this route instead.

"But she's wrong," Alek went on. "I would never hurt anybody, least of all a child. Without meaning to get political or offend anybody, I would gladly see the death penalty for such crimes. To be accused of it is absolutely sickening to me. And if her lie takes hold and disrupts my life, believe me, I will be seeking recourse."

"Legally, you mean?" Raymond said.

"There are libel laws for a reason," Alek replied. "But I'd like to keep it out of the courts, honestly. The truth is, I'm a wealthy man. It wouldn't be fair. I'd much prefer for Natasha to come out and reveal the truth."

"It seems Natasha is claiming that you somehow forced Mia to make that video—"

Raymond was cut off by the sound of the main buzzer. Alek stood, wondering who the hell it could possibly be. Liuba hadn't visited him since this mayhem had begun.

"Excuse me for a moment," Alek said, wondering what they'd do if he told them he was leaving them to sit mere feet from a buried corpse.

Alek went to the main gate. A muscular man stood there. He had a skin-fade haircut with shaved lines through his eyebrows. Beside him, Mia stood awkwardly, staring at the ground with her hands clasped.

"We need to talk, mate," the man said.

Alek gritted his teeth. "Who are you?"

"Jack. Mia's brother."

Alek grabbed him by the front of the shirt and pulled him close. Baring his teeth, he glared. "Come back in an hour. I've got the fucking newspaper here, you idiot. How do you think that would look, Mia showing up here? Fucking hell."

Alek shoved him, hard, and the boy made a little weasel-like sound as he fell backwards.

Returning to the garden, Alek said, "I'm sorry. Where were we?"

"We were talking about Natasha's claim that you forced Mia to create the video."

"Pfft." Alek waved a hand. "That's absolutely absurd. I don't even know the girl."

Chapter 28

Mia

"The bloke's a freak," Jack said, walking just ahead of her in his angry way. Once, she told him he looked like Dad when he walked like that, but that just made him angrier. Mia couldn't believe it when Jack turned and walked away; only Dad could usually bully Jack like that.

"Maybe," Mia said. "But at least he actually cares about my feelings."

"What makes you think that? I mean, really?"

They were walking around the nearby park, at the far end, so that the reporters wouldn't see them when they left. They started wandering around the pond, past dog walkers and couples and old people and happy little kids who had no idea.

Mia rubbed her face when she felt the tears coming. She stared at the water. Jack didn't do anything, because Mia had told him not to. She didn't like crying. When Jack hugged her, it just made her cry more.

"Nat has turned everyone against me. Literally the whole college."

"Delete those apps, then."

"But I still have to go *back*."

"Maybe you could change college. Or do a gap year?"

She just sighed. Mia couldn't believe that Nat would do this. Her best friend.

Jack looked at her. "Tell me the truth. Did Alek try anything with you?"

"No," Mia told him. "You can ask me a million times. He *didn't*. Actually, *I* was flirting with *him*."

"Don't say stuff like that," Jack snapped. "You're a kid. He's an old man."

"He's not old. And I haven't been a kid for a long time."

Now Jack looked like he was the one who might cry. He stared at the water, his fists clenched, his body shaking. "I'll kill him, Mia," he said, and they both knew he wasn't talking about Alek. "I swear."

"No, you won't," Mia said.

They both watched the water for a long time. Then Jack started walking again. When it was time to go and see Alek, Mia actually had a smile on her face. She had it all worked out now. Before, she thought she had to be like *that*, but Alek wasn't like *that*.

Alek was the dad she was *supposed* to have. *Her* dad was a mix-up. The world had made a mistake. Alek was her protector. He'd never hurt her.

"Why are you even here?" Alek said when they arrived, greeting them at the gate and quickly waving them inside.

He was so much bigger than her dad, tall and wide and strong. He was wearing a colourful shirt. He shut the door behind them.

"I need to make sure you're not a kiddie fiddler, mate," Jack said, puffing himself up.

Alek just smirked. He'd got angry before, but that was only because the journalists were there. They couldn't blame him for that. "I'd rather die than do that, sir. I've got no interest in your sister."

That stung, but Mia didn't let it show.

"Anything else?" Alek grunted.

"Just that, if you have touched her, or ever do, it doesn't matter how big you are." Her big brother's voice trembled. "I'll mess you up."

"Okay, yes, yes, you'll mess me up. Now, are we done?"

Jack shrugged. "I guess we are, yeah."

As Alek tried to wave them back towards the door, a flutter of panic moved through Mia. She knew it was probably silly and childish, but she felt an attachment to Alek. She didn't have anybody else anymore.

She somehow managed to speak up. "No, we're not done."

Alek smirked at her. She tried not to lose her cool. "Nat has been texting everyone. Everyone thinks I made it up. They all hate me."

"What am I supposed to do about that?"

"Help me," Mia said, trying not to cry, hating how hard she had to try. "I want all that stuff you said you'd get for Nat."

"You want to be famous?"

She wasn't even sure. But she knew one thing. "I just don't want to go back to college as the person I am now. I want to be... different. Special. Better."

Alek's expression slowly shifted from disinterested to intrigued. "Hmm, maybe I *can* use you. But you have to promise, Mia, that you won't get squeamish. The lines are clearly drawn now. Me and you versus Natasha and Vicky. Can you deal with that?"

"Yes. I hate Nat. She stabbed me in the back. I wish she was *dead*."

Even Jack gasped. But Alek didn't look shocked. He smiled; he looked proud.

David hated the idiots at his job. As a compliance officer for an electricals insurance company, he was mostly able to hide behind his desk, so he didn't have to deal with the pricks. But there were days, like today, when huge deals were made out of nothing. Nobody knew that David was behind the Vicky thing; even if they had, they would all be too stupid to realise the significance anyway. Caroline was leaving for a new job, and apparently, because she wouldn't be here to celebrate her birthday next week, everybody was going to sing happy birthday. It was a joke. He didn't even know or like Caroline.

He spent the morning dealing with the necessary, boring bullshit he had to deal with. His job was mostly writing letters, or, really, slightly editing letters and emails. He had templates he could work from. It was mind-numbing. It was the system, the way things had been constructed, the rich funnelling the crappy jobs to people like him. And what choice did he have? Like it or lump it, that was his bloody lot.

Just after lunchtime, he heard something coming from the floor below. David was on the top floor; he'd worked his way up the greasy, pointless ladder. Directly beneath him was the cafeteria.

Voices rose, happy and annoying. *"Happy birthday to you..."*
"It's not even my birthday yet!"
"Oh, don't be so literal all the time, Caroline!"
Laughter, and then they kept singing, and for some reason David found himself leaning back in his chair, grinding his teeth from side to side. What the fuck was this? They'd just gone down there without him. He didn't care, but how rude were these people? That was the issue with the modern world. There were no manners anymore. Nobody understood even the

concept of respect. So this was what it was all about: making him feel small, making him feel like *he* was the loser.

It was the middle of the day. They had work to do.

"Happy birthdaaaaaaaaay to Carolinnnnnnne, happy biiiiirthday to youuuuuuuu!"

Everybody clapped obnoxiously loudly, drawing as much attention to the sad exchange as possible. He didn't care, obviously, that he didn't have to sing that inane song. Celebrating birthdays was a pathetic thing. As if people deserved recognition for surviving another year. But... well, it was rude – very, seriously, offensively rude – leaving him out like that.

About twenty minutes later, his co-worker Jackie returned to the desk opposite. She looked at him like he was a piece of dirt on her shoe, nose upturned. "Oh, hi, David."

'*Shut up, you whore,*' he wanted to say. But he could never bring himself to do it. He wasn't scared of the consequences; he didn't care that her husband was a big bloke. He wasn't afraid of human resources, or anything like that. He just didn't want the hassle.

"Hi," he mumbled, staring at his computer screen.

Chapter 29

Vicky

Nat threw the local newspaper down. The front page showed Alek standing in front of a wild-looking garden, the big letters spelling out a pull quote. *"I'm eccentric, but I'm not a bad man..."*

"They *never* do articles like this." Nat dropped into the seat opposite, angrily folding her arms. "You need to give me my stuff back."

Vicky had confiscated her phone, her tablet, her laptop and her Kindle when she had learned that Nat had turned half the college against Mia. She was finding it difficult to even look at her daughter.

"No, Nat," Vicky said, still feeling like the world had dropped out from beneath her.

"I *had* to do it," Nat hissed.

Vicky looked at her daughter, ignoring Alek's smiling face from the front of the newspaper. "It isn't *true*. Poor Mia."

Nat huffed, shaking her head. They were sitting in the kitchen, the sound of Max on the trampoline filtering through the open doors. "We have to fight back. We're winning, but—"

"Winning? Everybody is disgusted."

"Yeah, maybe some people are. But others think Mia is just confused. We need to keep going. We can't just sit this out."

There was a warm, ugly part of Vicky that thought Nat was right. But how many lines were they going to cross?

"This is about your future. If I let you go down this path, what sort of mother am I? This ends here."

"We don't get to decide that," Nat snapped. "Come on, Mum. I *know* you want this too. Me and you together, remember?"

Vicky almost faltered. But she felt sick because of how little Nat seemed to care about how wrong this was. She seemed perfectly comfortable turning against her best friend.

"You've been friends with her for years," Vicky said.

"I'm thinking about the future, not the past. That could've been *you* in the newspaper."

"They asked me; I told them no."

Nat deepened the fold in her arms, glaring. Vicky looked out at the garden, remembering the man with the bones, wondering if she'd dreamt it, wondering if she'd dreamt this whole awful thing.

"Why would you do that?"

All of this was ugly. It had started with something sickening and gross, an affair she deeply regretted. Even worse, it had led to Vicky contributing to her own daughter's decay. "I never imagined you'd do something like that. Especially to Mia. Everything's changed."

Nat looked at Vicky as though she was speaking in a different language.

"So, you'll just let him win?" When Vicky didn't reply, Nat went on, "Seriously, Mum, we're in too deep. If we back out now, our lives are completely ruined. There's no coming back from this. If he wins, wherever we go, we'll always be *losers*."

"We've already lost," Vicky said, letting the mother in her

speak. Not the confused, abused little girl; not the woman who just might've wanted some fame. Not the person desperate to be friends with her daughter instead of a parent. "It's over."

"Give me my stuff back, or I'll tell Dad about the affair," Nat said flatly, glaring. It was the same threat she'd used two nights previously.

A flutter of panic touched Vicky, but it was quickly followed by a depressed pang. This was what it had come to, then – her own daughter threatening her. "Do what you feel is best," Vicky said. "But this has to end here."

"It's too late for that."

"You're forgetting who's in charge, Natasha," Vicky told her. "In fact, go to your room."

"Are you serious? And do what?"

Vicky raised her voice. "Go to your *room*."

Nat huffed and stood up, dragging her feet as she left the kitchen and walked down the hallway. Vicky's breath was coming far too fast. She stayed where she was, trying to do a crossword, stubbornly ignoring her phone, which she'd placed screen-down on the table. She didn't need anything except this pen and paper. It didn't matter if, when she returned to work on Monday, she'd get more crap from her co-workers. So far, though her name was plastered all over the internet, nobody had showed up at her house. She wasn't *that* famous.

The front door opened and Max came running in with a big grin.

A moment later, Seb walked in, an awkward look on his face. "Max, why don't you play your game for a little while."

Max ran from the room.

Seb sat at the table with a sigh.

"What's wrong?" Vicky asked, the awkwardness between them still taut.

"I saw Martin at the garden centre."

Martin was Laura's dad, and Laura was a friend of Mia's.

"He thinks Mia's making it up," Seb said, the corner of his lip twitching, almost like he was relieved. "Apparently, quite a few of the parents do. At a party last year, Mia was being…"

"Being what?"

"Quite provocative."

"Imagine if somebody said that about Nat," Vicky said in disgust, thinking of the small, haunted girl.

"She likes to push the boundaries, make up stories, play games." Seb frowned. "Would you prefer if everybody thought our daughter was a liar?"

"I'd prefer…" She trailed off. *The truth*, she was going to say, but that would just be more hypocrisy.

"Nat was trying to defend you on that podcast," Seb said. "It's not *her* fault her friend is a liar."

"She's turned the whole college against her *best friend*. Doesn't that seem like a big deal to you? Am I the only fucking sane one?"

"Mummy?" Max said from the doorway, his games controller in his hand. "I need batteries."

His expression was one of heartbreak that he'd seen them arguing, a tiny bit of innocence chipped away. Vicky rushed over to him, and scooped him up into her arms. "Can Mummy play the game with you?"

"Haha, yeah," he said, making an effort, but she could tell he was shaken.

Chapter 30

Seb

The headache was vicious, but that was nothing new lately. It'd be easier for Seb to think of a time recently that his head hadn't been splitting right down the middle. Work was a nightmare; every update had more people gossiping, more people watching him. Thankfully, he had a big, private office and enough power that people generally didn't come right out and abuse him. But how long would that last for?

Nat made him jump when she opened the door. He'd been standing out there, lost in thought. Or maybe delaying. She frowned. "Hey, Dad."

"Did you and Mum have a fight?"

"She's being a total bitch."

Seb lowered his voice in a harsh whisper. "Don't talk about your mother like that."

"Oh, come *on.*" She had that sick grin on her face, like she thought she had all the power. Seb was being held prisoner by his mistakes. It was his fault; he should've left Mia alone. It had made things so complicated. "I need your help. I need my phone. Or let me borrow yours."

"You're grounded, Nat," Seb told her. "Your mother wants this to end now. No more drama."

"Dad, that would be the biggest waste ever. I don't think you get how big this could be. One day, all of this will just be a line in my biography, in my best-selling book."

Her voice was warm and excited, more like the Nat he remembered before the blackmailing, before the fame chasing.

"Are you going to make me say it, Dad? Get me my phone or I'm telling Mum."

Seb swallowed, feeling sick. A little voice whispered in his head that he should just do it, whatever she wanted, but this was one step too far. Seb and Vicky didn't have the perfect marriage, clearly, but they always did a decent job – Seb thought so, anyway– of raising their kids. Better than many, maybe most people did. Their childhood was far better than Seb's had been, anyway.

"Then you'll have to tell her."

Nat narrowed her eyes. It took Seb a moment to realise what looked slightly different about her; she was wearing eyeliner. He didn't like it. "I'm not joking."

"Neither am I. This has gone on long enough. I made a mistake. I... I made a series of mistakes."

"You know Mum's Team Mia, right? If she found out what you did with her... what you two did *together*..."

Shame gripped Seb, but he didn't let it show. He had to go back to being the man he was before. He had to try and be better. "Tell her, then. It will cause more problems for your parents' marriage. It'll make life even more difficult for your baby brother. Go on, Nat – tell her."

Seb turned away in disgust, walking down the stairs, sick with himself, sick with his daughter and sick with the world. He wished somebody owned the internet, so he could find him and kick the living daylights out of him. He'd crack his head open for making the thing that was tearing his family to pieces.

In the living room, Seb picked up the other controller and pressed start. Max grinned as Seb's character appeared on the screen.

Chapter 31

Alek

"It has like a thousand views," Mia said, laughing meanly as she showed Alek her phone.

She, Jack and Alek were sitting in his garden. It was the first time they'd met up since agreeing to work together. Alek had spent that time cleaning his house and tidying up the garden, purposefully ignoring the internet to let the stories percolate and spread. With no counterfire from Vicky or Natasha, it had given him chance to plan a truly impressive offensive.

Mia laughed again, showing the screen to Jack when Alek didn't respond.

"What is it?" Jack asked.

"Some girl from Weston. Apparently, Alek threatened her once because she didn't know what the Holodomor was. Imagine not knowing *that*." She gave Alek one of those strange, fond looks that made him uncomfortable.

"I remember her." Alek shrugged. "But she's nothing, nobody. We've got way bigger concerns. Jack, how old are you?"

"Twenty-four," he said, in that nervous way he had. He was probably used to being the biggest, scariest person in the room. Or the garden.

"So you're old enough to become Mia's legal guardian."

Jack shifted uncomfortably. "Uh, I don't know about that."

"Jack wants to move," Mia said bitterly.

"Move where?" Alek asked.

Jack kept shifting around in his seat, a mixture of guilt and indignation affecting him. "I'm old enough to have my own place. A couple of my mates are saving up too. We're going to get a flat together."

"And leave your sister behind," Alek said, thinking of Liuba. For all her faults and her insufficiencies, Alek would never have abandoned her, especially if she was suffering in the way Alek was almost certain Mia was. He waved a hand, leaning forward, resting his elbows on his knees. "How much money do you have left to save?"

Jack, of course, looked utterly confused by this reasonable question. "Not too much. Not sure, off the top of my head."

"I've got enough money to put you up in a two-bedroom flat someplace, with room for Mia."

The girl beamed again in that annoying way.

"Dad won't like that," Jack muttered.

"Are you really that scared of that man?" Alek laughed, then clapped his hands. Perhaps he did it in an abrupt manner, because Jack flinched and even Mia moved away, looking at him cautiously. "Here's the thing. None of this matters. It's time we really took control of this situation. But it's going to mean *everything* changes. This isn't about Ukraine anymore."

Both of them looked confused, as though they were thinking it had *never* been about Ukraine. But it had – for Alek, it really had. But where was Maksym? The game needed playing for its own sake, now. *'We just walked on and on, looking for something, some morsel, but... nothing.'* Alek pushed the voice away, because it was fake anyway. Maksym didn't give a damn, so why should Alek?

"But you'll never let go of your Ukrainian pride," Mia said like a trained cultist.

"Mia, you're not going to like where I take the conversation next," Alek said, ignoring her comment. "But it's necessary. We have the power to completely rock the internet. We have the power to destroy Natasha for daring to weaponise the mobile phone-obsessed culture of your sad little college hierarchy against you."

"Okay..."

"But we have to acknowledge what's happening here," he went on.

"I did some reading during the last couple of days. Your behaviour towards me heavily indicates some kind of abuse, and your father's attitude and demeanour makes it obvious it was him..." Alek waited as she almost started crying, but she managed to keep it together. "I'm sure he said lots of things to you, Mia, about what would happen if you ever told anyone. I'm sure there were threats. But this is bigger than him." He chuckled, mirthlessly. "And so am I."

Alek knelt beside Mia; he took her hand. It clearly meant a lot to her. She clawed on tightly, desperately. Alek told her, "The world is a vicious, ugly place. Every single second, the most evil thing you can imagine is happening somewhere. If you walked down any street with X-ray glasses, the things you'd see... but you have a chance, Mia. You can fight back. You don't have to live in fear. Don't let it own you. *You* own *it*."

Mia swallowed. "But how?"

Alek let go of her hand, standing up with a grin. "We upload the most explosive interview ever put to film."

Chapter 32

Vicky

Vicky sat in the supermarket car park. Her manager was never usually this understanding. Taking holiday, especially at such late notice, had never been this easy.

Seb was home right now; his workplace had basically told him to do most of his work remotely. When Vicky had asked how bad it was for him there, he'd just looked at her bleakly. They were becoming circus sideshows.

She almost logged in to her social media apps. But she'd been ignoring them ever since she learned what Nat did to Mia, ostracising her like that. Though Vicky had confiscated her devices, Nat wouldn't give up her passwords.

Vicky shoved her phone into the glovebox and took a moment to compose herself. None of it was real, at the end of the day. If she ignored her phone, the world was the same. She was just a regular woman going on a regular shopping trip. Leaving her phone behind felt liberating.

She took her time on every aisle, soaking in the normality, ticking off each item from her list with an intense sense of satisfaction. She was about to reach the line of the self-service trolley section when she spotted him. Dave. He was standing by the shampoo with that casual, lazy smile on his face. Maybe he felt her glaring, because he turned; the smile widened.

He strolled over way too casually. "Morning, superstar."

Vicky shocked herself; she spat right in his face. Luckily, they were the only ones in the aisle. Dave rubbed his face furiously with his sleeve. "What the fuck is the matter with you?" he hissed.

"Get away from me, or I'll do it again."

"Do you really want me to—"

Vicky grabbed his shirt and wrenched on it. She surprised herself by how hard she did it. She shocked herself with the rage bubbling out of her, especially in public. "Do what you want, you perverted *freak*. But just know something – I'll get you back. I'll find a way to ruin *your* life." As she said it, she knew it was true. She'd get her revenge, whatever it took.

With that, she pushed her trolley away. He laughed, but she could hear the uncertainty in his tone.

When she got home, Vicky was shocked to see that there were several cars parked outside their address. A small crowd was gathered on their front garden: teenagers, children and a few adults, all of them holding phones. Vicky sat at the end of the street, watching as Seb stood in the middle of a circle, moving his hands as he spoke. She felt like she was in a fever dream. Was she suddenly a politician's wife?

Vicky climbed from the car, grabbing the groceries. By the time she reached the crowd, Seb was already walking inside. They turned to her, cameras aimed, and immediately people started yelling. A gaggle of teenage girls started *screaming*, in fact, *swearing* at Vicky. One of the fully grown men shoved a camera at her and said, "Do you have anything to say to Mia Price, Vicky? Any words of support?"

"Do you support your daughter's behaviour, Vicky?" another person yelled.

None of them looked like journalists; it was more like a group of regular, bored people had converged on her front lawn. Even the adults asking questions seemed more like wannabe internet stars than reporters.

Vicky went inside. Seb was waiting at the door, quickly shutting it behind her, and putting the chain across.

"What the hell's going on?" She dropped the shopping on the counter.

"Mummy?" Max ran down the hallway.

She leaned down and scooped him into her arms. She didn't realise how badly she was shaking until she cradled him to her chest, feeling his small hands grip her desperately. Over the top of Max's head, she gave Seb a look. Seb shook his head slowly. His eyes were hollow.

Nat appeared at the top of the stairs. "She uploaded it *last night*, Mum. But I didn't even find out until those people turned up!"

Oh, God, another upload. There was always something else. From outside, the teenage girls began to chant. *"Vile Vicky, Vile Vicky!"* A few teenage boys joined them, but it didn't sound very enthusiastic... not yet, at least.

"Let's not talk here," Vicky said quickly, when the chanting changed to *"Nasty Natasha."*

"Don't worry," Nat said dryly. "They've already done that one. Dad, what did you say to them?"

"I politely asked them to get off our property."

"But you didn't say anything about me or Mia, or anything?"

"No."

Nat sighed. "Phew. I need to work out how to play this."

"There's no *playing* this," Vicky said in disgust, carrying Max through the house and into the garden. Normally, he would rush straight for the trampoline, but even that didn't interest him right now. He just stayed sitting in her lap.

A moment later, Seb appeared, with Nat following soon after. "Don't you even want to see the video?"

"No," Vicky replied. "I'm sick and tired of videos, honestly."

"Max, can you go inside?" Nat said.

"I want to stay here."

"I need to talk to Mummy about something. It's only for grown-ups."

"It's fine; I'll take him," Seb said, leaning down.

Vicky sighed, but let her son and husband go. She would have much preferred to just sit there, holding him. "Do you want to see it?" Nat asked. "It's almost forty minutes long, though."

"I don't need to see it," Vicky said numbly.

"It basically starts with Mia talking to her brother. She's saying she wants to get an interview with Alek. Apparently, Mia's some aspiring journalist now. Anyway, during the interview, Alek turns it around on her... Mia breaks down. She starts talking about her dad. Her abuse."

"Oh, Jesus," Vicky said. "Oh my God."

"She says I knew about her abuse when I started cyberbullying her. That's what she called it. *Cyberbullying*. Because of those texts I sent to our college buddies. Can you believe that?"

Vicky massaged her forehead, hating her gut reaction to her daughter's tone. Her mind flashed with the thought, *What an ignorant, stupid girl*. And she hated herself for it.

"I need my phone, Mum," Nat said. "Those girls outside – they're from another college. And one of them is the boyfriend of a girl in my year. I bet people are talking about me. I have to get ahead of this."

"You're still talking like it's a game," Vicky told her. "But I've told you – it's over. You crossed a line."

"Mum, my *life* is over if I don't get this under control."

"Under control? How?" Vicky was almost shouting. "You've pushed your so-called best friend into a public breakdown! You've made half the fucking town hate us! You've ruined our lives!"

Vicky didn't mean to jump to her feet; she didn't mean to wave her hand in Nat's face. Nat flinched, which just made Vicky even angrier. It was like she was trying to pretend that Vicky was going to hurt her. When Nat burst into tears and ran into the house, Vicky didn't follow her. Instead, she took out her phone. It wasn't difficult to find the video; all she had to do was unmute her notifications and read one of the many messages she'd received containing a link to it.

Whether or not it was staged, Vicky wasn't sure, but the video started with someone Vicky assumed was Mia's brother interviewing her from off-screen. "Why do you want to talk to him, Mia?" "Because I think he'll understand." "But why? I don't get it." "He's a good person. He has a good heart." "But you barely know him." "At least let me try..." The video then cut; Mia was approaching his large house. When Alek appeared, he told her in an understanding, caring way that she shouldn't be wasting her time with petty internet drama.

But then Mia broke down; she began to sob and beg. If it was an act, the girl deserved an Oscar. Finally, Alek agreed and the video cut again to Jack, Alek, and Mia sitting in what looked like an office. The camera angle and the audio quality were good.

Vicky sat, paralysed, as Mia brutally and with devastating honesty recounted incidences of abuse from her father. Jack sometimes cut in when Mia glanced at him, but not often. And the whole time, Alek sat there looking so empathetic, so understanding, so kind and good-hearted.

"That's – that's why I acted like that before, I think," Mia said at one point, between gut-wrenching sobs. "I don't know what – what else – love is."

Vicky wiped a tear from her eye. Nobody could watch this and think it was just another part of the game. Nobody could watch this and doubt how real the emotion was.

"Nat knew about it," Mia went on. "But she didn't care. She wanted to spread rumours anyway. She wanted to cyberbully me anyway. I have to go back to college and she's turned *everyone* against me."

"And she knew what you were going through at home?" Alek said quietly, with a sombre undertone of disgust.

Vicky looked up to find Seb watching her from the kitchen window. For a moment, Vicky could imagine it was weeks ago, before the blackmail. Just another lazy, sunny summer's day. He gestured with a mug now, silently asking her if she'd like a coffee.

Vicky gave him a thumbs up, even though the gesture felt wildly inappropriate. There was nothing good or thumbs up-worthy about any of this. From one side of the garden, their neighbour – an elderly lady called Margeret – cleared her throat.

"Good morning, Margeret," Vicky said. They weren't exactly close, but they had always got on.

"They're being awfully loud out there," Margeret replied. "Awfully crude, too."

"I'm sorry," Vicky said reflexively, though what was she supposed to do about it?

"I hope nobody rings the police," Margeret said. "They

could, you know. Noise complaints. Feeling threatened in one's home. I really hope nobody does that."

The elderly lady might as well have come right out and made the threat. With a tut, she turned away, leaving the wall which separated their gardens. Vicky knew that most of the street probably felt the same way. But the question returned to her: what could she do? Go out there and scream at them to leave, with all those phone cameras aimed at her? She sighed, went inside, and decided to call the police herself.

Chapter 33

Nat

Nat had asked Dad what they should do. It was the first time since she'd learned about him and Mia that she'd gone to him for advice. But the truth was, this was getting scary.

Dad's shoulders were slumped. He'd looked defeated, and also guilty about being so defeated. He must have known the truth was bound to come out soon too. But all he'd said was, "They can't stay out there all day."

That was the only answer he had and it was just crap. *Why* couldn't they? Nat glared at the group of girls when they started chanting again. There were ten of them now. Nat knew at least four of them by sight alone. They were probably livestreaming to like, ten people.

If Nat had *her* phone, she could've done something.

Leaving the window, she went to her vanity unit, opened the top drawer and took out her emergency bottle of vodka. Jack had bought it for her a few months ago. Nat had kept it there in case of a party or something. But in recent weeks, it had been becoming a lifeline. She unscrewed the cap, tossed her head back, gulped. It stung her throat; she gulped some more.

She quickly put it back. Her head was already getting woozy.

Was there any way she could come out of this with what she wanted, now?

She dropped onto her bed and closed her eyes, the room spinning quickly around her, like the mattress was trying to throw her off it. Dad had let her watch the video on his phone, snatching it away quickly so she wouldn't read the comments. But she'd seen the top one with thousands of likes.

I don't care how old she is, Natasha is clearly a sociopath.

How was that fair? Nat went back to the drawer, to the vodka, took another big sip. For the rest of her life, Mia's story would be *the* story. Nat would be the cyberbullying bitch, *Nasty Natasha*, who tried to use her friend's abuse against her. Is that what she had done? No, they were twisting it. They were getting it all wrong.

She had to find her phone. She had to save herself. Spinning around on her vanity unit stool, the room seeming to dance and blur, she thought about the corner drawer in the kitchen. Mom had kept her electronics there before. Or there was the storage unit in the footstool in the living room. Nat would bide her time, then check there, then... then what? Make a video saying, '*Sorry, everyone. I did know Mia was being abused by her dad, but I tried to turn the whole college against her anyway.*'

She buried her face in her pillow and screamed.

Chapter 34

Alek

"You think you can turn my own family against me?" Mia's dad, whose name was Nigel, apparently, was roaring down Jack's mobile phone. He was clearly drunk, slurring, his voice crackly. "Is that it? You fucking... mental... *fuck?*"

"As eloquent as your insults are," Alek told him, as Jack and Mia watched anxiously from across the table, "they seem counterproductive."

"Do you have any idea who you're talking to?"

"If you have a problem with your son and daughter associating with me, I suggest you take legal action. But please know, sir, that if you go down that road, I'll be forced to use every resource I have to take any legal course of action I see fit."

"Tell her to change the video!" he roared down the phone. "Delete the video!"

Alek hung up the phone, then slid it across the table to Jack. "He wanted to talk to me. We talked." Alek shook his head. "He's clearly a selfish pig of a man."

"Mum's in pieces," Jack muttered. "Everybody's going mental. All our mates. All his mates. All her mates. Everybody's asking if it's true and that. It's getting really out of hand."

Alek gestured to his kitchen, which was tidy, clean, a scent of lemon in the air. "Everything seems quite peaceful to me, Jack."

"But what about when we have to go home?" Mia's voice sounded like it might break at any moment. She'd been like this ever since they recorded the video. There was something detached in the girl's eyes, like part of her had disconnected from everything.

"You don't," Alek told her. "You and your brother can stay here."

"Really?" Mia's eyebrows shot up. "Won't that look bad?"

"I don't care how it looks," Alek snapped. "We've put things in motion now. Your parents won't go to the police... in fact, the police might decide to visit them. Unless you're lying?"

"I'm not lying!" Mia squeaked in disgust.

"Look at it like this. Jack is my friend; there's nothing wrong with him staying here. You're his brother; there's nothing wrong with you staying with him. In the meantime, it gives us time to plan."

"Plan what?" Mia asked, a note of dread in her voice. That was annoying, honestly, because she'd seemed so certain in the beginning.

"The next step. Mia, you created a YouTube channel with *zero* subscribers and views. Your first video is currently at..." Alek checked his phone, then blew out a whistle between his teeth. "Almost one million views in less than twenty-four hours. Don't you think you should capitalise on that?"

Chapter 35

Mia

Mia wanted to make him happy, wanted to make him understand that she was on the right team. But it was like she was living in a constant state of fight-or-flight. Ever since she'd agreed to the video, it was like something had sort of jolted her out of her body. She'd always thought she did a good job at hiding that ugly, unshareable part of her life. And now almost a million people knew about it. She wondered where this was going to go. What next? More videos? More talking about it? She'd made herself into even more of a freak.

"Are you okay?" Jack asked, touching her hand.

She forced a smile. She could tell he wasn't sure about this either. But Alek was big and persuasive, and this was what Mia had *said* she wanted. Fame. Her name out there. A chance to be different.

"How do we make it about other stuff?" Mia asked Alek.

"I don't follow."

"How do we make it about... you know, not Dad and all that stuff?" She really hated how much her voice trembled.

"Don't get sentimental," Alek said. "This was about my grandfather's tragic experience in the Holodomor, once. What those people suffered pales in comparison to whatever you went through."

Mia's eyes stung. This man was supposed to be saving her, but she had a dirty, used feeling: a familiar twist in her belly. "Fine, okay," she said. "I get that. But I'm just asking."

"We have to use what we can." Alek's eyes had a dreamy look, as though he was looking directly at all his future fame, envisioning his name in lights. "I know it might not be comfortable for you, Mia, but clearly, it has to be preferable to the alternative. Or would you rather go home?"

"No," she said quickly. "I want to stay here."

That was something she was completely certain about. This big house was so much better than their house, with the chipped wallpaper and the creaking floorboards and the bad stuff that happened at night.

"Good," Alek said.

The only bad part was that Jack had started to steal from Alek. She'd first seen it earlier when they walked in. In the living room, he'd casually slipped a small silver ornament into his pocket. If Mia knew Jack, that wasn't the first thing, either. She wanted him to stop, but she was scared of making him angry. If he left, would Mia still be allowed to stay here?

"Your next video shouldn't feature me," Alek said. "We don't want it to look like I'm pulling your strings, do we?"

"No, that would be a real shame," Jack said, with a whole lot of unhelpful sarcasm.

Alek ignored the sarcasm, then clapped his hands together. "I'm making another coffee. Want anything? No? Okay."

He walked into the kitchen, leaving them in the dining area. Jack immediately started looking around, not even trying to be sneaky about it. He was clearly looking for something to steal.

"Stop it," she hissed. "Don't steal from him. He's helping us."

"When we stop being useful, there's no way he's letting us stay here. So, you enjoy it while it lasts. Me? I'm getting some insurance."

Mia wanted to argue, but then Alek returned with a big grin on his face. When he looked at Mia like that, all her doubts went away. There was pride in his eyes. He looked prouder of her than anybody had ever been. "Mia, your video has reached a million views!"

A million people knew about the most shameful and horrible things that had ever happened to her; she felt sick. She smiled. "Wow, that's amazing."

"It's just the start," he said, winking, with an almost boyish look.

When he left them again, Jack stood and went to the display cabinet, fiddling with the drawers.

"Stop it," Mia hissed.

He turned to her with that vicious look on his face, the Dad-like look. "When this is over, we'll be left with nothing. This isn't going to last forever. You'll thank me for this. Trust me. I'm making sure we've got a future."

"You just want to move into that flat with your mate."

"No. It's too late for that. I can't leave you with him now."

"Nothing's changed."

"What sort of brother would that make me?"

She knew he meant – what sort of brother would he *look* like.

Chapter 36

Nat

Nat stayed in her room all day, falling in and out of sleep. She sobered up a bit and decided that she'd wait until night-time to find her phone. Eventually, the people gathered outside had left. They weren't being paid to do this, so maybe the novelty had worn off. For a while, anyway.

At around eight, Dad brought her a plate of chicken nuggets and potato wedges. "I'm not hungry," she told him.

He stood at the door, holding the plate, a grimace on his face. "You have to eat."

She folded her arms, sat up; maybe she was still drunk. "You're forgetting who's in charge."

He looked at her like she was insane; perhaps that *was* an insane thing to say to her dad. She had never spoken to him like that before. She hadn't even dreamed of it, even when she was blackmailing him successfully.

"Just eat some dinner."

"I'm *not* hungry," she snapped.

"Fine. Suit yourself."

He left her there, which was lucky. If he'd come into the room, he might've smelled the vodka on her breath. She waited until she heard him go downstairs, and then went quietly into the bathroom to brush her teeth and swill mouthwash around her mouth. Then she quickly went back to bed, waiting, waiting. She heard Dad put Max to bed, then a while later, Mum and Dad started to settle down for the evening. Nat ignored the gurgling in her belly.

Just when she thought it was a good time to start looking, she heard the floorboard creak outside her bedroom. A moment later, Dad's voice: "What're you doing?"

Then Mum: "What if she's hungry?"

Something about this almost made Nat cry. She closed her eyes and rolled over just in case they checked on her. There was something so... *regular* about it. It made her almost wish life could go back to normal... but it was too late for that. She had to be strong. The door creaked as it opened. Mum walked into the room. Nat stayed very still. Even when Mum leaned down and gently kissed her on the cheek – and Nat felt a strong urge to turn to her, grab her, hold her – she stayed still and kept on pretending.

"She's asleep," Mum said, outside her bedroom door. "I just wish..."

What, Mum? But then she walked out of earshot. Nat was left to wonder – and then harden her resolve again. She couldn't waste time worrying if Mum cared about her. If the day came when she was a millionaire, she'd look back on this as just something she'd had to do. Still, she'd do her best to bring Mum with her somehow. Whenever she found a way out of this. First, she had to assess the damage. She needed her phone.

She crept down the stairs, stopping every time they creaked. The vodka was still doing its work on her, but she managed to get down the stairs quietly. She went to the drawers in the corner of the kitchen, made to open them... then smiled when her fingers grazed across a small metal padlock. Mum knew *she* knew about this drawer, so, instead of moving Nat's stuff, she'd decided to make a point. She was playing games.

Nat almost swore. She *needed* her phone. It was like she could feel it pulsing through the drawer, like it was talking to her, lighting certain parts of her up. There were who-knew-how-many people out there, all with something vicious to say about her. Not knowing exactly what they were saying somehow made it more painful.

Not only had Mum cheated on Dad, she was also ignoring the fact that Nat had saved her ass. And instead of being rewarded, treated like a grown-up and included in plans, Nat was being punished.

She tugged on the lock. The drawer rattled slightly. Nat was sure that Mum had installed the lock herself, when she saw an inch-long gap open up. She hadn't properly installed it. Nat saw the edge of something shiny and black; it was her phone, and suddenly she was flooded with purpose, with intention. She felt beautifully awake.

Pushing her finger through the gap, she clawed at the edge of the phone, using her nail to drag the edge of the case until it was at the entrance to the drawer. Then she angled her finger so that she could pull it upward. But the angle was wrong. The phone was wedged. She gritted her teeth, pushed the phone back, rearranged it. How long did it take? She didn't care. She was so focused. If only her history teacher could see her now.

Finally, through trial and error, she was able to get her phone. She almost cheered as she went to the kitchen table and turned it on. As she waited for the screen to blink to life, she paced up and down, opening and closing her hands as tension moved through her.

Her phone turned on, connected, then...

It was mayhem. She'd never seen a notification screen like this. The screen kept flickering as more messages arrived, both texts and notifications from social media apps. Then the screen went blank, as the phone died. Nat turned it back on. Her heart was pounding so hard, feeling like it was climbing up her throat.

Finally, it turned back on. This time, it survived the notifications. Nat's hand trembled as she picked up the phone. She had over a hundred texts, two hundred Facebook messages to her private account, and literally thousands of TikTok and Instagram messages.

In the group chat with her friends, she was shocked to find them talking about her like she wasn't there, just because she hadn't responded for a couple of days. These were her friends who didn't know Mia, but even *they* were talking as if Nat was guilty, disgusting.

Is that true about Mia?

Nat???

Where is she???

That's so not on if it is. If Nat used that against her.

Calm down. We don't know anything.

Nat has always been mean.

Hey!

It's true. We all know it.

Tears pricked Nat's eyes. But anger gripped her chest harder, with more purpose. They were already reframing all the jokes and pranks; Nat could see them on some podcast or TV show, making innocent jokes seem mean, twisting her behaviour. She clicked off the chat. There were *dozens* of variations of *go to hell/I hate you/burn, bitch.* One DM came from a boy she'd gone out with for a bit last year. *What the fuck is the matter with you? You're evil, Nat. Sincerely, everyone at the fucking college.*

Nat was crying now. Tears made hot tracks down her cheeks. How could everything change so fast? She'd expected *some* backlash, but this was far beyond what she'd imagined. She went to her other apps. So many of her 'friends' had messaged her, basically cutting ties before things got even worse.

I don't know what's going on with you, but let's just cool if for a while, yeah?

That was the tone of so many of the messages. Her world was crumbling.

She went to the podcast page. It was now at 1.2 million views and rising, and there was a link in the comments to a YouTube channel: *Mia_th3_Minx_001*. She was always using *minx* for stuff, and everybody thought it was lame, but not anymore. All the comments were calling her brave, courageous, heroic... and any comment that mentioned Nat was negative. *Her family's the problem! Just look at her mum...*

Nat kept reading. So many people were speculating about her state of mind, her mental health, her capacity for evil. People joked that she must torture animals; others speculated that she must be experiencing even worse abuse than Mia to 'act out' in such a way.

Nat ground her teeth from side to side as she read the replies. She had never, not in a million years, expected Mia to use *this* as her defence. Nat knew on a hazy level what Mia went through with her dad, but her friend never came right out and said it.

Then the realisation hit her. It must've been him. Alek. The interview was framed as if Mia had chased *him*, but she bet it was the opposite. But did it matter? Would it change anything? Her world was falling to pieces either way.

The tears kept coming because the comments did. She tried to tell herself these people didn't know her, but it didn't seem to matter. They wanted her dead; they argued about the best ways to kill her, using code words like *unalive* so that the comment algorithm wouldn't automatically remove their hilarious death poem.

Eventually, she slammed the phone down on the table and went to the counter, grabbing a bunch of kitchen towel so she could wipe her face. But she couldn't stop crying. It was like the comments were whispering in her head. *'Unalive... Evil... Must have serious psychological problems... I'm sorry, but we can't be friends anymore... I didn't know you were this sort of person...'*

"Nat?" Max said from the doorway.

She looked up through blurry eyes to find her little brother standing there with a scared look on his face. He frowned at her, almost like he was judging her too. But then he rushed over and threw his arms around her, pushing his face against her hips.

"Please don't cry," he said.

She leaned down and tightly wrapped her arms around him, savouring his warmth and the support... the support he might not even have offered if he fully understood the truth.

"It's okay," he went on when she kept crying. "Is it online stuff?"

He made it seem so small and easily managed with that phrasing. *Online stuff.* Thousands, tens of thousands, hundreds of thousands, millions of people. All screaming for her blood. And why? Because Alek had won the battle. That was it, the source of all her problems. If Mia had remained onside...

Nat went to her phone.

"Should you be on that?" Max said nervously.

She sent Mia a text, details of a meeting. "I'm putting it back. It's okay."

Max frowned again, but he didn't say anything as she slid

the phone into the drawer. She hugged him. "Whatever happens, I'm always going to take care of you, okay?"

"Mummy and Daddy take care of me."

But they might not always be able to. Nat had to make a choice – be hated for the rest of her life by everybody, everywhere she went, or go back to plan A: ruthlessly pursue fame. Switch off her feelings. Even if it meant doing something she'd never be able to take back.

Chapter 37

Vicky

The next morning, Seb made Max breakfast and then started remote-working at the kitchen table. Nat was still asleep, and they both agreed – without really discussing it – that they'd let her stay that way. The sad fact was that it was easier to let her sleep than to deal with her: deal with the huge ugliness of what she'd done.

"I'm going to see Michelle," she told Seb.

She walked over to the table, leaned down, and kissed her husband like she meant it. He made a muffled noise of surprise, then grabbed her and kissed her with the same passion.

"Where did that come from?" he asked.

"I love you," she told him, then kissed him again. "Let's try to get through this as a team, yeah?"

He smiled. "That sounds good to me."

With a little note of brightness in her chest, Vicky left the house. Luckily, there were no losers hanging around outside. They hadn't been actual paparazzi – Vicky didn't think Weston even *had* paparazzi – just a bunch of local kids and sad grown-ups trying to make a fuss and get some attention. Vicky drove through the town, actually enjoying sitting at a red light and watching an elderly lady walk her dog. It was a nice reminder that the world was actually ticking along just fine, even if *her* world had imploded.

Vicky was hoping to catch Michelle before work. Her friend hadn't been texting her as much as usual; Vicky hadn't been texting, either, sensing the shortness of the replies. Vicky could now guarantee awkwardness with the parents of all Nat's friends, and maybe some of Max's too, plus she still had the challenge of working out what to do with Nat. She didn't want her friendship with Michelle to turn to crap on top of that.

Parking up across the street, Vicky went over to the flat and pressed the buzzer. A second later, a busy-sounding Michelle said, "Hello?"

"It's me," Vicky replied, which normally meant Michelle would let her in.

"Oh..."

Vicky tried to laugh, but she felt stung. "Not got time for a cuppa?"

"I was just about to leave..."

"Are you walking to work today?" Vicky asked, knowing Michelle often did; the sun was shining. "I could join you."

"Uh, yeah. Sure. Okay. Sure."

Vicky began pacing in front of the flat. She wondered how long her friend was going to leave her out here for. Michelle had been with her through so much; she had held her hair as she'd vomited, shared secrets, had sworn to always be at her side. But Vicky could feel all of it fading away. She hoped she was wrong, but she didn't think so.

When Michelle finally joined her, Vicky felt unexpectedly jealous. She hadn't anticipated that. But it struck her hard, like a slap across the face. Michelle looked well. She was wearing her work clothes. Vicky had been told to stay far, far away from her own place of work.

"Hey," Michelle said, unwilling to look Vicky in the eye.

"Hey, you."

Vicky moved in for a hug, which Michelle let her do. Then she moved away as if she didn't want to be seen in public hugging a leper. Or was that just Vicky's mind playing tricks on her?

"Shall we?" Michelle said, nodding towards the footpath.

"Sure."

Vicky started walking, but Michelle made a noise. Then she said, "I walk this way now."

She nodded to another path, which led alongside the train tracks.

"Through that field?" Vicky asked, mapping the route in her mind. It made no sense. It would mean adding at least fifteen minutes to her journey.

"You're right," Michelle said, blushing.

Vicky let it slide, though it was clear what had just happened. Michelle didn't want to be seen with her. God. When had that happened?

"Are you okay?" Vicky asked as they walked the regular way.

Michelle plastered a fake customer-service smile on her face. "Yeah, sure. Same old, same old. I'm rewatching *How to Get Away with Murder* again."

"That's only the, what, tenth time?"

Michelle laughed hollowly. "Around that, I bet, yeah." More fake laughter.

The footpath took them through a park. A few young children and their parents were inside, making Vicky long for the early, early days before her children were even a little bit complicated. She remembered how simple and beautiful it had been to walk this tiny, pink miracle of a thing through the park, hear her squeal and sing and just live.

"Michelle, hi!" A woman called over. She was what Seb would call a *designer mummy* – fake lips, fake chest, branded clothing. She was aggressively chewing gum and as they walked over, the tempo of the chewing increased.

"Morning," Michelle said. "Vicky, this is Chantelle. Chantelle, this is…"

Michelle stopped talking. Clearly, Chantelle didn't need to be told who Vicky was. Her demeanour changed instantly. She narrowed her heavily made-up eyes and then pushed a fake smile onto her face, just like Michelle's. Maybe this would be Vicky's world forever: fake smiles all round.

"Anyway," Michelle muttered awkwardly. "We should get going."

Chantelle beamed. "See ya soon, hon."

They turned and walked away. Michelle's shoulders were slumped. Vicky couldn't take it anymore. When they had left the park and were walking down the busy footpath, people walking and cycling to work, Vicky said, "It's all right. You can walk the rest of the way alone."

Michelle flinched; they moved off to the side, under the trees which bordered the path, as people walked by them, most of them wearing headphones. "What are you saying?" Michelle snapped, way too aggressively.

"It's fine," Vicky said, trying to keep her voice calm. "We don't have to dance around it. It doesn't have to be a big deal."

"What doesn't?"

"You don't want to be seen with me!" Vicky yelled with way too much aggression, then quickly lowered her voice. "It's obvious. But it's fine. I understand. Maybe if the positions were reversed, I'd be the same."

"It's not that," Michelle said in a weak, small voice.

"Come on," Vicky said. "I saw how you were just now – with Chantelle, was it?"

"She's just somebody I say hello to sometimes."

"You don't have to defend yourself. I'm not trying to make you feel uncomfortable."

"Then why show up?" Michelle said. "We both know there's pretty much nowhere you can go right now and not be the centre of the attention. Everywhere you go, people are going to whisper, point, maybe even go further than that. I don't want that. I'm sorry. I just... I can't."

She turned and walked away. Vicky didn't follow her. Instead, she went back the way they'd come. As she walked past the park, she saw Chantelle and two other women clearly watching her. They were all wearing bright, stylish tracksuits. Vicky felt frumpy and, from the way they were staring, dirty somehow. Guilty. Without letting herself think about it too much, Vicky walked over to the park fence.

"Chantelle, was it?"

The woman aggressively chewed her gum. "Hmm-mm. Vicky, yeah?"

"Is there..." Vicky almost bottled it as the other two women glared at her as though she had a death wish for daring to challenge their queen. "Is there something you want to say to me?"

Chantelle sneered, then made a *you don't want to know* face. "I don't know you, love."

Vicky wasn't sure if she was relieved or annoyed. When she turned away, Chantelle made a scoffing noise, then said not-really-under-her-breath, "And I don't *want* to know you, bitch."

Her friends laughed like they were back in school. Vicky pretended she hadn't heard and kept walking. It stung, but she *had* asked for it. She was almost tempted to ring her manager and ask if she could go back to work. She didn't relish the idea of being home all day, with nothing to do but think, obsess, scroll...

When she got home, Seb was waiting for her, his briefcase already packed and his formal work clothes already on. "Is your phone off?" he asked.

"Yes," she told him. "Sorry."

How could it *not* be off? Any time it was switched on, she was just more tempted to scroll and read and hate.

"You're okay to watch the kids?" he said, already rushing out of the door.

"Yeah, sure. Why do they need you in all of a sudden?"

"Client meeting," he replied. "We thought he was in London for another day, but apparently not. I shouldn't be gone too long."

It made Vicky sad, how clearly nervous he was about being in the office. She took one of his hands, looked at him with intent. "We're not bad parents, Seb. Nat just made a mistake. With enough time away from her phone, she'll realise that."

"I know. She's a good girl. But what about everybody else?"

He gave her hand a squeeze and then left.

Vicky checked in on Max. He was in the living room, playing his game. They were letting him stare at that screen far too often, but, honestly, she was just happy he wasn't on social media. She'd much rather have him slaughtering wave upon wave of digital enemies than reading all the horrible things people were saying about his mum and his sister online.

She picked up a book and tried to read, but it was like the digital world was tugging at her, screaming at her. Every time she tried to read a page, it was as though her ability to maintain a reasonable level of attention just turned to dust. She did her best to try and focus on the page, the story, but the events seemed so meaningless. She was glad when Nat walked into the room, even when she dropped onto the other sofa with a huff, her arms folded.

"Is this about your phone, or have you found a new problem?"

"Oh, ha, ha." Nat stubbornly stared off into space. The back of Max's head trembled, like the stress of the constant arguing was getting to him. It was another tick in the bad mother column, something Vicky seemed determined to contribute to.

"You'll see one day. This is for the best."

"Am I allowed out, at least?"

"Are you forgetting what being grounded is?"

Nat huffed again, then said, "I need to catch up on my homework. At least let me go to Terri's to study."

Terri was an old friend. Vicky almost asked, *She still likes you?* She'd done her best to hide how awful it was from her daughter, but she wouldn't be able to keep it buried forever. That was the main reason she was hesitating. Terri would surely let Nat see her phone.

"Can't she come here?" Vicky said. "And wait a sec..."

"She got her dad to ask Dad, God," Nat snapped. "I'm not lying to you *all* the time."

Just most of the time. "What homework is it?"

"Law. Psychology. I mean, everything, Mum?" Nat said, like it was obvious. "Please?"

"You're aware I know her mother?"

"Yes, I'm *aware*."

"Let me ring her, then."

Nat shrugged and Vicky took out her phone, hating the wave of nerves which moved through her. She had been friendly with Janine, Terri's mum, for years. She'd never had any reason to be nervous or on edge around the woman. But now, clearly, she *always* had a reason. That was the most sickening part of this new reality; she no longer had the luxury of not being self-conscious.

She took a breath. After pressing *call*, she experienced the most pathetic tightening in her belly, a fist of nerves as though she herself was a teenager again.

"Hello?" Janine said.

"Hi, Janine. It's Vicky, Natasha's mum."

She wasn't sure why she added that last part. Janine had seen who was calling when she looked at her phone... and they'd spoken so many times.

"Oh, hi," Janine said. Did her tone slightly change? "How can I help?" Was that overly official?

"Nat mentioned she and Terri discussed doing some studying together?"

"Ah, yes, later this afternoon, right?" Janine said, *seeming* the same, at least as far as Vicky could tell. Maybe she was misreading the whole thing. "I'm happy to pick her up and drop her off if you'd like?"

"Uh, sure," Vicky said, caught off guard. And, as pathetic as it was, she was grateful for how normal this felt. "That sounds lovely."

"Is four okay?"

"Sounds great."

"Okay, bye!"

After hanging up, she found Natasha looking at her with a small smile.

"This is to *study*," Vicky said. "I'll be speaking to Janine after. If I hear you spent half the time on Terri's phone, no more study breaks. Am I clear?"

"Yes, Mum," Nat said. "Thank you."

David rolled another cigarette, lighting it and blowing the smoke out of his kitchen window. Sometimes, he thought about just sitting here and smoking until his lungs gave out, until his whole body gave out, until there was nothing left. He'd just woken from a nightmare, which was thankfully becoming hazy now, but not hazy enough. He'd been strapped to a chair, and he was pretty sure the past version of himself had been giving him a speech: the skinny, handsome version who had stolen Vicky from her husband and fucked her silly.

"What's the matter with you? Have you given up? Don't you have any self-respect?"

He finished the cigarette and began rolling another. He was developing a yellowish stain on his fingers from holding the cigarettes, but smoking was often the only thing that distracted him from everything else. Even if the taste was sickening, and even if he often thought about quitting, nothing else made the thoughts stop.

He could be better. He could do better. But it was so unfair, the way things were stacked against him. After lighting the second cigarette, he took out his phone and went to one of his online accounts. He had several under various names. Going to Vicky's latest video, he wrote, *I'd love to skull fuck this slut.* And then he logged out and went to another account, and commented, *Does anybody else believe anything she says? I know a lying bitch when I see one.* Another account: *I'd love to piss all over her face.*

He felt sick; he was smiling. It was pathetic how easily triggered people were. He knew that, when he logged back in, he'd be flooded with replies, outraged and righteous, people who pathetically thought they were making the world better by replying to a comment on a website. It was a fucking joke. They were, all of them, the so-called do-gooders. Especially the women. They were the sorts to go on their precious marches about global warming while wearing jackets made by little Chinese kiddies who were basically slaves. Everybody was a hypocrite.

On his third cigarette, David did something which, on some level, he knew was too far. But it was also too *easy*, and therefore tempting. He went to the memorial page of a teenage boy who'd recently jumped in front of a train and traumatised a train driver.

Using a fake Facebook account, he wrote, *Your son should be ashamed of himself.*

Then he refreshed the page, waited, refreshed it again. Here they came, the notifications, the appearance of red, like blood, leaking from the notification bell symbol.

What is wrong with you?

Nothing. It was *them* who had the problem. They were trying to celebrate this little shit as though he meant something. But that was just the thing these days, the truth nobody wanted to accept. Nothing meant a damn thing anymore.

Chapter 38

Alek

Jack had looked shell-shocked and physically sick when he'd appeared at Alek's gate. Mia hadn't been with him. It was strange seeing Jack alone. And the absence of Mia made Alek wonder if there was some scheming going on; she *still* hadn't posted another video, something to grow her social media presence without attaching herself too much to Alek.

But that wasn't the point. Apparently, Mia's dad, Nigel the abuser, was dead.

"He rang my mum before he did it. Told Mum to tell Mia he was sorry and he couldn't live with himself. He's gone."

And then Jack had turned and walked away, his posture tight.

Alek was currently waiting for a call with Mr Hurney, his lawyer, to connect. As the phone rang, he listened for Maksym's voice, for any sign, for a whisper, something to hint at the world within the world. But there was nothing. As shameful as it was, whenever Alek thought about their mission nowadays, it all felt faintly... unrealistic? Otherworldly? Somehow, all of *this*, the real world, was becoming more important.

When Mr Hurney answered and the annoying pleasantries

were out of the way, Alek got right down to business. After informing him of Nigel's suicide, he said, "The police have confirmed it with the family. He's definitely dead. Could I be found in any way liable for this, Mr Hurney? At least this more or less confirms his guilt. *Public* opinion will be on my side, but what about the law?"

"What are the chances his family might seek legal recourse?"

"Low, as far as I understand it," Alek said. "I get the sense he was a sadistic, abusive bully and that's about it."

"Good, good," Mr Hurney replied. "Mr Bodar, while I have you on the phone, please let me talk with you about the entertainment management side of the business. I was loath not to mention it before..."

Alek listened as he talked about his friend's fame management company, or something like that. Alek was thinking about Mia, her public response to this. She had to spin it right; she had to play it for everything it was worth. Cutting Mr Hurney off, he ended the call and then rang Jack. He had taken the boy's number specifically in case he needed to get hold of Mia. So far, that hadn't been necessary.

"Yeah?" Jack said, answering.

"We need to talk. Me, you, Mia."

"Why?" Jack said in that infuriatingly passive tone.

Alek resisted the urge to snap. Perhaps it was fair to give Jack some time and space to process what had happened. But then, wasn't it also fair to wonder how in the name of all that was holy this was supposed to be a *sad* event? An abusive piece of filth was dead.

"We need to..." What if the little snake was recording? "Can you come by or not?"

"Let me ask Mia. She's in a real state."

A real state. He didn't even understand how this could be

the case considering who they were speaking about. They were talking about a real *animal,* the sort of beast angry men would have taken turns beating in the good ol' days.

"Huh-hello?"

The girl sounded as though she'd been crying. Alek would have to play this right. Sooner or later, the news would become public. He tried to imagine what this girl wanted, and it was clear: a father. He made his voice softer. Or tried to. "How are you feeling, Mia?"

"He's gone," she said, and Alek almost screamed. The *way* she said it was grotesque. It was like she was speaking about a saint. Not a *rat* like Nigel the abuser.

"I know. Oh, Mia." Even Alek wasn't sure what he meant by that. "I know it can't be easy. I hope you're not alone."

"I'm with Mum and Jack," the girl said, fighting back tears. "And later..."

"Later?" Alek said when she cut off. He was really getting sick of the way her voice shuddered and danced every time she spoke. He understood that grief was powerful; he'd felt very upset when his own, non-abusive father had died. But this was just so *much.*

"Nothing." She sniffled.

"What're you doing later?" Alek said again, wondering if she was hiding something.

"*Nothing.*"

For the first time since Alek had met the girl, she sounded as if she had grown a backbone. He wanted to tell her, *This is the best possible outcome we could've hoped for. The abusive pervert is dead and we've got the fuel for twenty more videos.* But she was too busy grieving the man who had violated her innocence to be receptive to such reasonable words.

"Okay, Mia," Alek said instead. "Will I be seeing you soon?"

"Uh, I don't know."

"I want to see you, Mia," Alek went on. "I want to make sure you're okay. Why don't you ask Jack to come by with you later?"

"Mum doesn't think it's a good idea. She says, now Dad's... Well, I don't have to, now."

Alek's teeth were beginning to hurt with how often he was grinding them.

"Mum's being really nice," Mia went on, no idea she sounded like the most naïve and moronic person who had ever lived, no idea she sounded like a complete fool, in fact.

"Your mother was happy to let you stay here when your paedophile father was alive because she knew what would happen to you," Alek finally snapped. He couldn't help it. This was just absurd. "She was too afraid to make him stop." Alek hardened his tone when he heard Mia sniffling on the other end of the line; as long as she didn't hang up, he knew he was making progress. "*I'm* trying to help you, Mia. I'm the only one. And you won't even agree to meet with me."

In the background, Alek heard Jack. "Mia?"

Alek grunted. "Mia. You need to tell Jack to bring you here later, understand? I'll make us all some dinner."

"We'll see if we have time," Mia said after a pause, and then she hung up.

Alek went to his computer room and began to set up the camera, but it wouldn't work if it just came from him. He needed Mia at his side. Or, better yet, he needed Mia to respond in such a way that it made Alek seem like a supportive, harmless older man. Perhaps Mia might do a short video announcing her father's death, then say something like, *"I think I need to do this as a podcast. With Alek. It was so much easier with him last time."* Or whatever, and then, oh, they'd do the podcast, and Alek would set *just* the right tone. By the time it was over, the audience would feel like avenging angels, like their attention on the first podcast had led directly and gorgeously to Nigel the abuser's death. But first, he needed Mia to co-operate.

"You sentenced a child predator to just two years in prison," Alek said, his voice cold, his demeanour cold, everything cold. There was no use getting emotional with somebody this deranged.

"I–I–I..."

He was an upper-class man with a posh accent, who had never experienced even the most cursory brush with violence; Alek knew that without even having to ask. Yet, he'd had the temerity to allow a molester to be free, to do it again. How was that acceptable? That boy's life would never be the same. Every interaction, every relationship, would be marred. Even if he was of unusually stoic character, there would be aftershocks until his very last breath. And this was happening every single day, all over the country.

"Have you ever had a penis in your mouth which you did not request?" Alek asked. It seemed, to him, a very simple question.

But the man's eyes became bulbous, and the ugly purple veins on his alcoholic's neck writhed like Medusa's snake protesting at the lack of eyes to claim, and he began to blubber as though there was some pity owed to him.

"Hmm?" Alek snapped. "Have you?"

With no answer forthcoming, Alek pushed the button on the knife, revealing the sharp blade, then reached down and grabbed the naked man's shrivelled old cock.

"You're about to," he told him.

Chapter 39

Seb

Walking into the office, Seb felt every eye in the place turn to him. It had been like this, on some level, ever since Vicky had first started uploading her stupid videos. He'd hated it from the start, the added attention, feeling like he was being mentally picked apart in a thousand different ways. Even when he nodded to people, it was like there was a delay. How many of them had seen Mia's podcast? People were probably thinking, *What sort of father is he?* But Vicky was right. Teenagers made mistakes. Nat would learn. This would pass.

Seb went into his office to get ready for the meeting. The work, at least, was rewarding. They were currently working on the copy for a lung cancer charity. This included major advertising campaigns and all the paraphernalia; there was even talk about Seb writing a piece for their blog, since his dad had died from lung cancer.

Checking his email, he was surprised that Lucas hadn't attached any notes to his email about the meeting. Usually, there would be an agenda; all Seb had was his email.

Can you come into office? Airway Angels
wants a meeting.

'Airway Angels' was Lucas' nickname for the charity, since they came across as very religious and zealous. But as long as they were paying the bills, nobody really cared. Seb had known immediately he would have to leave his office to go and speak with Lucas. They were around the same age and had started within a year of each other, but Lucas was one rung ahead. Even so, they were still friendly. Usually. But this was the first time Seb had been in the office since everything got so irretrievably messy.

Seb left his office and ventured into no man's land.

He knocked on Lucas' door. "Yep?" Lucas called.

"It's me," Seb replied.

"Ah – come in."

Lucas was leaning back in his large ergonomic desk chair. Seb's office was classic, with a dark carpet and an oak desk; Lucas has a modern, metal desk and he'd had hardwood floors installed. Lucas stood, tossing a stress ball from hand to hand.

"Seb, mate," he said.

Seb really didn't like his tone, but he put on his best face. "Lucas, mate."

Lucas rolled his eyes. "I know. I'm acting like somebody's died, or something. But let's be honest – you know everyone's talking about you."

"Yeah, I felt it the second I walked in. What're they saying?"

Lucas frowned. "What do you think they're saying?"

"Probably that I'm a terrible dad. Speculating about my marriage. Finding any reason they can to hate me, because that's what the internet is telling them to do."

"Yep, pretty much. I'm sorry." Lucas sounded genuinely

apologetic. "You need to get this under control, Seb. It's beginning to affect your reputation in the workplace."

Seb knew right away. "There's no meeting, then."

"I thought it would be better if that's what the email stated," Lucas said. "The big boss has been on my case, Seb. A potential client mentioned you to him directly – and not in a good way. Something about some online scandal. In *our* business... It's costing us business."

Vicky brought in decent money with her part-time hours, but their family relied on Seb's work. More than that, he was proud of it. He got a deep satisfaction from supporting his family with a profession he had spent time and effort getting good at.

"Do you understand what I'm saying, Seb?"

"Fix the drama. Or I'm getting fired."

"I'm sorry. Shit. Really. Just think of it like this... See this office? I've got word I might be making a move soon. You know I'd put in a word for you."

This was one of the reasons Seb could never resent Lucas; Lucas genuinely did look out for him. But the few times Seb had tried to take their friendship outside of work, Lucas had seemed awkward, making Seb feel like the unpopular kid pushing his luck.

"It'd be a big bump in pay," Lucas said. "A *very* nice bump. All you need to do is make all this go away."

"How am I supposed to do that?" Seb said, his tone getting sharp. "What am I supposed to do? Snap my fingers and make that podcast disappear? I told Vicky when we got Nat her phone, I said, it's not good for kids. It messes with their heads. And look – Nat's obsessed. Scrolling twenty-four-seven. And there was Vicky with her stupid little videos, but at least she got over that, and..."

Seb broke off, breathing heavily. "Sorry, mate."

"It's all right. Maybe you need to vent."

"I'm sick of it," he went on. "If I had my way, *none* of us would have phones."

"Find a way to make it stop," Lucas said. "Can't you get your daughter to release an apology video or something? Or can't she make up with her friend? Maybe that'll fix it – then keep them off the internet."

"It's easier said than done," Seb said, thinking of all the times he'd let Nat blackmail him these past few months, all the times he'd failed as a dad. It had made her feel too powerful; it had most likely led to this, at least to Nat's part in it.

"Losing this job would be criminal," Lucas said. "Especially if I get the promotion."

"I'll try," Seb replied, but he wasn't sure what he could do. Far too often, he felt powerless when it came to social media. He sometimes posted photos of his running machine readout to his Instagram, where maybe four people liked it on a good day, and that was it. Even with this job, he handled copy; the act of getting the copy out there was beyond him.

"Have you seen the podcast?" Lucas asked a moment later.

"Yeah," Seb replied, remembering when he'd watched it with Nat. "It's moving."

"Devastating," Lucas said, nodding. "That poor girl."

Seb hated thinking about Mia, but he nodded in agreement. "That poor girl. The world's a bad, bad place."

"Hmm, yeah," Lucas said, suddenly seeming distracted. "Look, Seb..." He leaned forward, lowering his voice. "Do you remember before, when my mate was out of town? I was wondering if we could do the same thing? I know it's not a good time, but—"

"My bloke's moved," Seb cut in quickly, the excuse he'd decided on if this ever happened again. He'd hoped Lucas would never address it: the one time Seb had bought cocaine for him. He'd felt dirty the whole time. "Sorry."

"Ah." Lucas leaned back. "That's a shame. Anyway, remember what I said."

Seb nodded. How could he forget?

"Do you need me in the office for anything else?"

"Nah, probably better to pull the old remote-working card, mate."

Returning to his office, he spent some time working on his laptop. He didn't want everybody to see him leaving so quickly after getting there. It was all about appearances, after all.

Chapter 40

Mia

Terri was the go-between, with no particular loyalty to any one social group. Some of the other kids hated her for that, but Mia had never judged her. She understood that, sometimes, a person just needed to be a certain way. They had to make themselves whatever shape the world required of them. Like Dad had done with Mia, shaped her. And now she missed him; it hurt how badly she missed him, or the idea of him, or the Dad-shaped hole, or something. Even the idea of replacing him with Alek now seemed stupid.

Mia tried to focus on her phone. Terri's text read:

> Mum said Nat's mum has said she can come.
> Are we still on?

Wiping her face, Mia ignored the noise coming from the living room. Jack and one of her cousins were playing cards and Mum was crying loudly. A gameshow was playing in the background. The tones of everything clashed too hard.

> Yes

Mia replied. Terri had no idea about Mia's dad; nobody did. Well, they knew about her *dad*, about the stuff that went on in secret, the stuff Alek had come out and acknowledged like it was easy, seeing right into her heart, her soul.

Nat had sent Mia a message last night.

> Mum's keeping my phone from me. Arrange a meeting at Terri's. Get one of her parents to contact mine. Say it's a study session. Tomorrow. Please, Mia.

Mia liked the sound of that *please*. The news about her dad had just made her want to do it even more. When her mum walked into the room with that sad look on her face, Mia wanted to slap her, spit at her, hug her. Instead, she scrolled on her phone as her Mum started boiling the kettle.

"I'm going to Terri's in a bit," she said.

"Terri who?"

"My friend. Terri," Mia said in blatant disgust.

Mum just bit down in that scared little way and turned back to the kettle. Mia felt like she might cry all over again, which just made her so angry. She shouldn't have been able to be so mean to Mum and get away with it. Mum was just so weak, so snively, so pathetic... exactly like Mia was being. She needed to get a grip.

"I'm sorry," Mum said quietly, still staring down at the kettle, her back to Mia. She started trembling all over, like she was going to boil up, then her voice got all melodramatic and crackly and she said, "Sorry, oh, Mia. I'm so sorry. Mia."

Then she actually collapsed into a ball on the floor. Mia remembered in English class once when some funny boy had said, '*Miss but how can you collapse into a ball? This isn't Pokemon!*' And they'd all laughed. But her mum did it, right then: she sunk down, inwardly, like she was shrinking in on herself. She started making snorting sounds. Mia retreated into her head. She didn't have to listen to this. Now it was *Mum's* turn to be sad and have a big pity party about how sad she was.

"What's going on?" Jack said.

"Mum's crying and saying sorry." Mia stared down at her phone; a glamorous influencer was handing out hot dogs on a busy, grimy, obviously American street.

Jack rushed over and knelt down next to their mum. "Mum?"

"I'm sorry. Oh God. What sort of mother am I?"

"Jack, I need you to take me to Terri's," Mia said. "It's important."

She left the room before she said something she'd probably regret. Mum was always making everything about herself. It wasn't like she and Dad had even been together, really. She was always breaking up with him because he was a bully and everything else that he was, then letting him back in. What was *wrong* with her? Mia went upstairs and started putting on make-up. She didn't want Terri or Nat to know she'd been crying.

It was time for Mia to stop letting everybody else decide everything for her, do things *to* her. It was time for *Mia* to choose. That was why she wanted to meet with Nat – especially before she saw Alek. Alek was... confusing. She felt like, sometimes, he wanted the best for her. But other times, like on the phone earlier, he sounded mean.

"She's a wreck, Mia," Jack said when she came back downstairs, ready for Terri's. They were in the hallway; the cousin and the cry-baby were in the living room.

"Really, Jack?" Mia walked right up to her older brother. Since seeing how small and scared he was around Alek, he didn't seem so big anymore. "Really? *Really?*" Suddenly, she was screaming in his face, almost crying, which would ruin the mascara and eyeliner she'd spent so long applying.

Jack didn't get angry, which was surprising. He just hugged her.

"Can we go?" Mia said into the warmth of his chest.

"Yeah, all right," he replied.

———

Terri's mum was being way, way nicer than usual. The second Jack dropped her off, Terri's mum rushed out, down the path. "Hey, Mia. How are you?"

"Fine, thank you..."

"Janine," she quickly filled in.

"Janine, thank you," Mia said, nodding as she followed her into the house. "Thanks for doing this."

Janine frowned. "I'm just letting you girls get some homework done."

Was that really what Janine thought was going to happen upstairs? No – in fact, they were going to reshape their entire world. Mia hadn't wanted any part of this. She didn't choose this. But what other choice did she have?

"Do you want a drink? Something to eat?" Janine seemed desperate for Mia to say yes.

"Are they upstairs?"

"Yes – Natasha got here a few minutes ago."

"Is it okay if I just go up?"

"Sure, sure, sure!"

Mia didn't like the way Janine was looking at her. It was how she had never wanted to be looked at: like a victim. That was probably why, even if Alek was a user like the rest, she preferred him. At least he treated her like her own person... within limits. God, life was confusing. She went to Terri's room, putting her ear against the door. They weren't talking. She pushed the door open.

Terri was reclined on her bed, a magazine open in her lap. Nat was in the desk chair. She leapt up as soon as Mia walked in. How could Mia hate Alek, when he had made this possible? If Nat had had her way, *Mia* would be the one with bloodshot eyes and ratty hair, fear covering every part of her.

"Uh, all right?" Nat said.

"Hey, Terri," Mia made a point of saying, then walked over and hugged her. *This* part was something Mia liked on some level; every girl in her year was suddenly being far, far nicer to her.

Terri gave her a real hug. "Hey, Mia. You okay?"

"Yeah, thanks." Finally, Mia turned to Nat. "Hey, *you.*"

For a split second, Nat's real reaction flashed through her features. It was nasty and superior, the way she always was, the supreme leader of school, now college, and life. But then she remembered what role she was supposed to be playing. She tried looking all sad, as she walked forwards with her hands extended, like they were about to be best friends again.

"Don't touch me," Mia said coldly.

Nat stopped.

"Because of you, I had to tell the whole world..." Mia didn't even want to say it. All through the podcast, she'd felt like she wasn't even the one really speaking. She'd felt like Alek was dragging the words out of her. Except, she *was* the one speaking; she was *willingly* saying all this stuff. Nobody was forcing her to. "I had to tell *everyone*, Nat!"

"I'm sorry," Nat said, but Mia didn't believe it.

"You're sorry because *I* won," Mia hissed. "You would've been happy if everybody hated me. If everybody was calling me a liar and a bitch, saying I was mental or whatever. You would've *loved* that."

"No." When Nat swallowed in that melodramatic way, it was like she was doing an impression of Mia's mum. It was annoying. "I wouldn't, Mia. I just did what I thought I had to do."

"Have you looked online?" Mia said. "At the comments? Have you read them?" A warm feeling moved through Mia when dread visibly gripped Nat. "Everybody *hates* you. And guess what? You deserve it."

Nat huffed and went back to her chair. Mia sat on the bed, next to Terri, who immediately started rubbing Mia's back. It was the sort of thing Mia could never have imagined her doing before. None of them said anything for a long time. Then Nat made another annoying huffing sound and said, "I want to make this right."

"You want me to help you, you mean," Mia snapped.

Finally, the real Nat came out. She hissed, "Is that so fucking bad? You asked if I saw the comments. You should see my *texts*. People are sending me death threats."

"Well, people have a lot of sympathy for..." Mia hated this so much. She also hated that little soft piece inside of her that felt sorry for Nat. Not too long ago, she would've been the first one defending her friend.

"But I didn't know," Nat said, red-eyed, staring.

"You knew." Mia looked out of the window at the clouds. "You asked. But this isn't about that. It's not about *that*." Suddenly, she was on her feet. She was almost crying again, as if she was the one who was doing a Mum impression, all rattly-throated, scared and pathetic. "Not everything in the whole world has to be about *that*."

"Mia, Mia," Nat said like she had so many times before, in that supportive way, as she reached over and took her shoulders. "It's okay."

Nat had always been the best at calming Mia down from panic attacks. Mia hugged her now, even though it pissed her off. She needed the comfort, even from this... this person. This traitor. She hugged her so tightly. Nat was sobbing. "I'm sorry. I'm so sorry." Mia was sobbing too, but she didn't let herself say any words. If she did, she might talk about Dad, or she might say she forgave Nat.

"Can't we fix it?" Nat said between sobs. "Me and you?"

Mia gently but firmly disentangled herself. One of the reasons Terri was so good in her role was that she could basically become a piece of furniture, pretending she hadn't seen anything about what had just happened. She wouldn't gossip, either; everybody knew that.

"No, Nat," Mia said, trying to make herself hardened again. "*I* can fix it *for* you. *We* can't fix anything. But I can't trust you."

"You can!"

"No, I can't," Mia snapped. "But I've got an idea. I've got a way to make sure you never, ever betray me again, Nat. You're not going to like it, though."

"What is it?"

Mia felt sick to her stomach, but she *had* to be sick if she was going to do anything at all in this world. *It* was sick. *Everybody* was sick. If life had taught her anything, it was that everybody, at some point, would do some horrible, ugly thing. Mia said, "I want you to strip. Then I'm going to record you dancing around."

"You're a fucking freak," Nat snapped.

"Oh, yeah," Mia said sarcastically. "I want it like *that*. No – it's because I'll always know then, Nat, that you're sorry. And that you'll never be able to betray me again, because you won't be able to. I'll have... collateral."

Terri stared from the sidelines, looking openly interested.

"I'll give you five seconds," Mia said. "If you say no, then, it's all fair game from now on. I'm going to eat you alive, Nat. Me and Alek, we're going to ruin you *and* your mum."

"Alek," Nat said, shaking her head. "If I do this, we have to find a way to get rid of him. It has to go back to just being us."

"I don't know how I feel about him," Mia said.

"If I do *this*, Mia, it means I'm all in, right? It means I've proved I'll do anything."

"Will you, though?" Mia walked right up to her ex-friend, stared into her eyes, enjoying the closeness, enjoying this feeling. Like *she* was in charge for once. "Anything?"

"I've got an idea that'll fix everything for us," Nat said. "But it'll ruin my family. And it will make Alek hate us."

Mia took a step back, waving her hand. "Nope. We're not talking about *any* plans until you pay the price."

"Are you serious?"

"Five..."

"Mia—"

"Four..."

"Please—"

"Three, two..."

"Okay, okay."

"I'll watch the door," Terri said, as Mia took out her phone.

Chapter 41

Alek

Alek refreshed several national and local news websites. Many of them mentioned Mia's podcast. The articles mentioned trial by public opinion and giving trauma victims a chance to heal as counterpoints. Alek kept scrolling; this fame was good, a spark, but it wouldn't mean a damn thing unless he harnessed it properly.

Finally, his phone rang. It was Jack. "We're on our way."

"Good," Alek said. "Text me when you're here."

He hung up; Jack knew to text him when he was outside from last time anyway, but Alek had to make absolutely sure about everything. There were several avenues of attack for he and Mia; rather, for him *through* Mia. But first, he had to get into her head and make her understand.

Soon, they had arrived, and Alek went out front. Mia looked like a girl trying to be a woman, her face plastered in ugly make-up. Jack stood with his arm around her, which looked unusual.

"Come in, come in," Alek said, trying to be cheery.

But the sombre pair were having none of it. They moped their way into his house, down the hallway and into the computer room, sitting side by side on the short couch. Alek began to pace, then realised that probably wasn't the best way to begin a calm discussion, so he sat, but his foot wouldn't stop tapping.

Standing again, he said, "I'm sorry for your loss."

Jack stared at the floor. Mia made a *"huh"* sound.

"I'm sorry, Mia?"

"You're not, though," Mia said. "Sorry, are you?"

She glared at him, and Alek did something terrible in his mind. He would never seriously hurt a woman or a child, but in his mind, he did it. In a brutally and efficiently violent manner. "It's a difficult time," he said inanely.

"Do you *think* I should miss him? Cry for him?"

He wished Maksym were here to say some choice words. There was too much softness in this new, unbrave world; that would be his line of reasoning. It's too emotionally confused. Of course she shouldn't cry for him. But she seemed utterly broken by the matter.

"I think people grieve in different ways," he said like a politician. "But I'm here for you, Mia. For both of you."

He waited for Mia to give him what he wanted, some approval-seeking look, but she seemed harder with the harsh make-up. She seemed more stubborn somehow. Determined. But to do what? Oh, to be able to crack open a skull, read the thoughts. What was she going to do?

"I guess you want to talk about doing another podcast."

He *wished* he was talking with somebody who could, in a logical and unemotional way, assess the situation and produce a tactical social media plan, but that was clearly far too much to ask. "We're not here to talk about that."

"But you want to," she said. "I just want to mourn my dad, but I know you, Alek. I bet you've already got a million ideas. Just like last time. You made me do that first podcast. And look what it made Dad do!"

"It made him do the right thing!" Alek erupted, leaping from his chair, not meaning to. But... what else was he supposed to do? He'd suffered far more than one man could reasonably be expected to. He'd lost his grandfather; he'd lost his purpose. Now, he was trying to make the best of it, picking a new path, and *this* was his reward?

"Jesus Christ, Mia, he did you a favour. How many more times would he have raped you? How many?"

"Shut up!" Mia screamed when she heard the r-word. "Shut up! Shut up! Shut up!"

She leapt to her feet too, then ran from the room, down the hallway to the bathroom. Jack went after her, then stopped in the doorway, turning, glaring at Alek. When Jack looked like he was going to get tough, Alek snapped, "Go and steal some more, you pathetic little urchin." Jack's eyes went wide, and Alek said, "I know my house. I know my belongings. Mia would never steal from me. But you, Jack, *you* think you're big and important."

"I didn't do nothing," Jack said.

"I don't care. Take your little ornaments. Just never go in the cellar."

"Just building stuff down there, you said."

"Oh, yeah, that's what I said. But aren't you curious, Jack, a big house like this and so far, you haven't found a safe, have you?"

Alek wondered what he'd do if Jack somehow stumbled into the cellar. Could he do it – hurt somebody like Jack? Somebody who annoyed him, but wasn't *guilty* like the dirty abuser hobos? Would Jack's bones be worth anything?

Mia came back, black streaks down her face, pouting like her life depended on it. "Let's just talk," she said. "I know you've got ideas. No Dad stuff. No arguing. No drama. Just a mature conversation, okay?"

Alek nodded, glad she was finally seeing sense. She returned to her chair. Jack sat at her side, but he was even shiftier than usual.

"So, what do you think we should do?" Mia asked.

"The main thing to think about is what sort of audience you want to cultivate based on the reception to this traumatic event," Alek said as though he was reading from a textbook. He was relieved to finally be talking about something that mattered. He'd been strategising all day. "The best sort of following is a loyal one, so I think you need to reward the audience."

"Reward them?" Mia asked.

Mia's tone was infuriatingly innocent. She was talking as though she didn't have the vaguest idea of what he could possibly mean. And she was the one who'd said she wanted to have a grown-up discussion; it was a complete joke. "The audience – especially the commentors who, by their very nature, have the potential to become long-term fans – resonated with your raw emotion. When you spoke about the first time—"

"Stop," she said abruptly, perhaps sensing where he was about to go.

"Mia, it's almost at two million views. Have you read your emails? You're being offered sponsorship opportunities. Someone wants to represent you. A talent agent. You could be huge!"

"I don't care. Just don't talk about it."

He almost laughed. Even Jack was looking at his little sister as though she had just wandered into insanity territory. The details about her abuse were out there for anybody to listen to; she'd cried extremely public tears over her father. He really, really wished Maksym was here right now.

"Okay. Well, they resonated with you," he went on. "By extension, they hated your father." Which *she* should have done, but the little girl was moronically determined to feel conflicted. "If you were to come out and suddenly paint him as a sympathetic and complex character, it would call into question the verisimilitude of the first podcast, which could be damaging."

"The *what*?"

"He's saying it'll seem like you were lying," Jack put in.

Alek chuckled. "Clever lad."

Jack flinched, a nasty, common sort of angry look on his apish face.

"So, if I say I'm sorry my dad's dead, it's a bad thing for my social media career?"

"Do you really need me to spell it out? Your father's death doesn't have anything to do with you. Ultimately, it's a vehicle for your audience to express their righteous rage. Just look at that recent memoir. What was it called? *I'm Not Sorry My Uncle's Dead*?" He couldn't remember exactly. "It doesn't matter. She openly talks about some family member being dead, and that she was pleased they were dead, because they were a bad person. People loved it. Loved her. Loved the book."

"But what if it's not how I really feel?"

"How do you really feel, then?" Alek said, hoping he did a passable job of hiding his impatience. There was just something so grotesque about this whole situation. He didn't know how clearly the head-fucked little thing needed him to say it; her father was a C-H-I-L-D R-A-P-I-S-T. Did she need him to sing it for her?

"I don't know," she said, picking at his sofa in an annoying manner. "I'm not even sure I want to do any more podcasts. I might even delete the first one. I don't want Dad's death to become a circus, you know?"

Alek kept his Modern Face on, but he was on the edge of completely losing it. Alek was a clever man; once he fixated on a topic, he felt confident he had the ability to navigate it. Maksym had left, or Vicky had taken him, or something. But *this* was his new purpose. Fame. And then... then he'd start a charity to help Ukrainians, or something. He wouldn't forget them.

"I don't know, actually," Alek said. "It seems to me that would be a very foolish thing to do, in fact. All over the country, all over the world, scared little girls are being abused. Those sick men are telling the terrified children: '*It's your fault. I'm doing this because of you*'." Alek had scanned several internet forums, accumulating hundreds of comments in the space of an hour, all first-hand testimony. He felt confident in what he was saying. "If you run away with your tail between your legs, what does that tell them? Think about *them*. You're free now, Mia. They're not."

"I want to help them," she said, raising her voice, putting a nicely judged sob into it so that she seemed fragile. "But maybe I don't want to do it your way. Maybe I want to help them in *my* way."

"But your way will mean throwing this chance in the bin," Alek snapped.

"You just don't want me to do anything without you."

"Obviously, things are going to work better with me included. Just look at the podcast, at the audio and video quality. Do you have any idea how much those cameras and microphones cost? Do you have any idea how impressive it is, me being able to rig them up so quickly, to produce a podcast so quickly, with crisp, clean audio and video? You're taking lots for granted, Mia."

"But I don't want—"

"Fuck what you want!" he exploded, not meaning to, but the little bitch really wasn't seeing the point. He stood over her, making Jack bristle a bit, but he didn't stand up himself, just glared at Alek. "You need to think, Mia. Think about the chance you've got here. You need to play this right. If you delete the first podcast and don't record another one, your dad's death will be just a blip in the news. You have to *choose* to be famous."

"What if she doesn't want to be?" Jack said. "She needs help. Counselling. Space and time to recover."

"She'll have all the space and time she needs when she's a millionaire," Alek snapped. "When you get famous, *then* you decide what you want to do with your life, not the other way around." Alek felt like he was explaining the most basic, obvious things, but they were determined to make it difficult.

"What if I buy my own camera and my own microphones, and do my own podcast?"

"That wouldn't be a good idea, Mia," Alek said, clenching his fists, wondering if he had it in him to hit a child. It was a sick thought; he felt wrong just thinking it. But could he, if he had to? Could he do it? No – he didn't think so. Especially not a girl. Just the thought of it made him feel like a monster.

"There's nothing stopping me."

"*I'm* stopping you," Alek said.

"How?"

"I'll find a way," he snapped. "I don't know details yet, but if you do this without me, you'll regret it. I can fucking promise you that."

"So basically, you want to use my a-abuse..." She couldn't even say it without her voice getting all shaky. "And my dad's death, so you can become some kind of internet agony aunt, or whatever?"

"I'm trying to help you."

"But you will have other guests on the podcast after me, right?"

"It's on your channel," he pointed out.

"Yeah, but, you'll make another channel. You'll use these podcasts to make a name for yourself."

"You're stating the obvious."

"So you're using me, then? Just like everybody else."

"Oh, not *just* like everybody else," Alek said, returning to his chair. "Though, it seems pretty obvious to me, that's how you want to be used."

He knew he had to stop talking. He was supposed to be taking on the loving father role, using kindness to win her over. But she was behaving like a spoiled, ignorant brat and he just couldn't bring himself to treat her with anything other than complete contempt, which was what she deserved.

"What?" She sat up, having the gall to look outraged.

"You're dressed in an overly mature and promiscuous manner," he told her. "You're going to attract the attention of boys and sadly, men, who only want one thing for you. Maybe if you didn't dress like such a—"

He stopped himself, took a breath. He was going too far. But the world was getting too harsh, too bright.

"Like a what?" Mia said. "Go on – say it!"

"I shouldn't have snapped. Mia, I went too far."

"What were you going to say?"

"Does anybody want any coffee? Tea?"

Alek left the room quickly, ignoring their replies. He couldn't be near them. It was almost as though Mia was purposefully antagonising him. It wasn't as if he'd said – or almost said – anything unfair, either. She *was* dressed in an unwise way.

While the kettle boiled, Alek went to the kitchen drawer where he'd taken to keeping Maksym's journals. They, at least, would bring him some solace. He was still trying to choose one for his next video. He opened the drawer – and it was empty. No journals. He knew for a fact he'd left them right there. Just last night, or perhaps two nights ago, he'd read one of his most beloved entries.

Would Jack have taken them? Perhaps he was planning to

use them in a future video? What would happen if Jack and Mia outed his grandfather as a cannibal? Would the audience understand that it had been a gruesome and evil time, and gruesome and evil things had been necessary, or would they judge him? Alek checked all the other drawers, but there was nothing. No journals.

When he returned to the computer room with his coffee, he watched the boy... the young man, really, even if he tried to appear more like a teenager with those stupid shaved cuts through his eyebrows. Mia had her arms folded, pouting at the floor. How interesting.

"So, when should we record the podcast?" Alek said.

Mia laughed in a disbelieving way. Alek needed them on his side. If they turned against him while having the journals... but did they have them? He'd have to turn his house over.

"We're not, Alek," Mia said, saying his name like it was difficult. "I need time to think."

"Time to think about your dead paedophile father," Alek said. "Look at you – you almost start crying just from me saying that. But that's what he was. It's pathetic that you won't accept it."

Mia stood up, looking at her brother. "Can we go now?"

"Yeah." He stood too.

"We need to record the podcast soon," Alek said, watching Jack. "This evening, or tomorrow at the latest. I'm heading out of town for a week after that."

"What, where?" Mia asked, unable to hide her interest, the poor, deluded thing.

"London to see a friend," he said. "Reach out to me *soon*. I'll be leaving late tomorrow night. Midnight."

"That's weird," Mia muttered.

"It's what I like to do. I take an overnight Uber."

"That must be expensive," Jack commented.

Alek almost grinned; the little thieving fool. Maybe he would take the bait. If so, Alek would find out where his journals were. Taking them was like breaking into a museum and defacing a piece of the past. "It is," he told him. "But I can afford it. As you of all people know."

"What?" Mia said.

Alek chuckled. "Your brother has been stealing from me. Didn't you know that? But it's okay; I forgive him. As long as he doesn't take anything I'll miss."

Alek gave him a serious look. In his mind, he was shouting, '*Bring me those journals back!*' He often wondered when somebody would clearly receive one of these messages. Jack gave no sign of having heard him. As Alek walked them out of the house, he knew he had to try something drastic. Before opening the gate, he took Mia's small, clammy hand.

"Mia, I'm sorry," he said. "I shouldn't have been so cruel. Please remember how much I care about you."

She didn't say anything. She looked so lost, so unlike who she was pretending to be.

Alek shut the door behind them, locked it, then rushed inside, getting ready to turn his house upside down and inside out. The only places he didn't need to check were the cellar and the garden, because he knew for a *fact* he hadn't stored them there, and... and there was something about the cellar. The door. It made him feel bad, panicked almost.

Chapter 42

Nat

Nat waited for the knock on her door. She knew it would come eventually. She had actually started reading a book; it was written in a flashy stylish way, about a princess who was ready to do whatever it took to become queen. She was ruthless, backstabbing, focused. Nat couldn't relate to her completely; there was still too much softness in her. But she was actually relieved that the weird, depressing video Mia had recorded was hanging over her head.

Nat had gone along with it, as Terri watched with sick, curious eyes. Mia looked sick too. But now, whenever Nat started to feel guilty, she just thought about the video. She told herself, *I'm being blackmailed.* How was she supposed to hate herself for that, exactly? She had no choice.

Dad knocked on the door. "Terri's on the phone," he said.

"Okay. I'll come down."

They *still* weren't letting her have access to her mobile. Nat thought about sneaking downstairs at night, but what was the point? She knew what was waiting for her. She left her room and went into the kitchen. Max was on the trampoline with two of his friends, his world completely unaffected, so that was something, at least. But what about after the next recording they were planning? *She didn't have a choice.*

"Hello?" Nat said, picking up the landline.

"Mia messaged me. It's done. She wants to do the study session on Thursday."

That was in two days' time. "Why not just get it over with?" Nat asked.

"She seems really, really low, Nat," Terri said. She had a note of accusation in her voice, and Terri was normally the best at having no opinion at all. "I think she just needs some time."

But they didn't *have* time. Each day that went by was another day of people hating Nat, writing more nasty comments, sending her more messages. But as long as they sorted this soon, it would be okay... wouldn't it?

"Okay, Thursday then."

"She also wanted me to tell you about her dad, but you have to keep it a secret."

"What about him? I thought he left town?"

"He took his own life in a bedsit," Terri said. "Mia's mum says the police are going to release his name soon. She says that will make it all even bigger."

"Did she say anything else?" Nat asked, unsure of what she was hoping for. Maybe some sign that they could go back to being friends, not just partners-in-crime.

"No," Terri replied. "See you Thursday. I'll get Mum to talk with your parents about it."

Nat hung up, then forced a smile when Dad walked into the room and over to the kettle. "Another study session?"

"Yeah, Thursday. Is that okay?"

"I think it should be fine." As the kettle boiled, Dad walked over to the small table the landline was on. He took Nat's hand. She could see how much of an effort it was for him; it was like his instincts were trying to warn him away. "I know things have been tough for us, Nat. But I think something good could come from all this. Once this blows over—"

"Blows over?" Nat cut in. "Dad, the world hates me."

"You'll see," Dad said in that confident, annoying parent way.

Guilt twisted in Nat's gut. She almost broke down, started crying like an idiot. But she had... no, she didn't have to be strong; she didn't have to turn off her feelings. *She had no choice.* She kept repeating it in her head, *no choice no choice no choice,* until it stopped sounding like words anymore. It was just a cold fact. Mia was in charge now.

She watched Max jumping up and down, a big grin on her face. She'd take care of him. Whatever happened, he'd always have a trampoline and friends, and the latest video games.

Mum walked in a second later. It was weird having them both in the house all the time during the summer holidays.

"*This* one wants to know if she can do another study session on Thursday," Dad said, talking like everything was normal, like it was last year and none of this had happened, like they were just a regular family.

"Sure," Mum said, giving her a loving look, just like the old days. Nat almost burst into tears. She wanted the old Mum-Dad-Nat connection back, the family days out and all that. But it was too late. The world already despised her. If Mia released the video, it would be so, so much worse.

"Thanks," Nat said, then she got up and went into the bathroom. Sitting on the cold toilet seat, she buried her face in her hands and screamed. She tried to remember what Alek had said in the park: her name in lights, a memoir, all of it.

She tried to see herself standing on a red carpet one day. Her dark hair would be beautiful and shiny as it flowed down her back, and she'd wear a dress, maybe a corset-top, red, stylish and sexy; maybe she'd even pose with one hand on her hip, the other on her head, so confident the cameramen would climb over each other, reaching and twisting to get the best angle, their lights flashing, blinding her, making her forget all the things she'd had to do to get there.

Going to the sink, she splashed her face, stared, tried to tell herself she was confident. She *could* do this.

"I have no choice," she said, to make it real. "I have no choice. I have no choice."

She was crying again.

Chapter 43

Alek

"Well, I think it's a very nice thing you did," Liuba said the day after his meeting with Mia; Alek still hadn't received any word from her or Jack. To make matters worse, there was also no sign of the journals, despite Alek searching every single room. He'd even stood outside the cellar door, trying to make himself do it, but it was like the connection to the old way of things would sever this new, sharp concentration he'd discovered since he'd begun pursuing fame.

Liuba sipped her coffee. "That podcast clearly helped her work through a lot of emotions."

"Didn't you see it?" Alek asked. "She basically chased me down."

"But who bought all the equipment? Who helped her upload it?"

His sister really was a great person sometimes. She hadn't even needed Alek to point this out to her. Mia had needed him to shout it in her stupid face and even then, she didn't understand.

"I just wanted to help her," Alek said. "This weird situation threw us all together."

"Are you going to keep making videos?"

"I'm not sure. Maybe not. It seems this is all becoming about much more than Ukraine. Mia was different; helping her meant something. But I'm not sure videos for the sake of them are a good idea."

As usual, Alek was doing a good job at telling Liuba what she clearly wanted to hear. If Mia finally came through, he'd be able to justify another podcast easily... and he'd be careful to craft his persona to fit any and all future endeavours. *If* Mia came through. What if she didn't? What if, worse than simply not ringing him, she stabbed him in the back?

"What are your plans for the day?" Liuba asked. It was lunchtime; she'd swung by from work.

"I need to do some cleaning," he said.

Really, he would most likely spend the day pacing and waiting for his phone to ring. And when midnight came, he had an Uber to catch; he'd already booked it, just in case. *That* was the only thing that brought him any kind of positive emotion. The rest of his life was bleak. Not only was Maksym gone; now, his words were, too.

"You?" Alek asked.

"Oh, the same. A bottle of wine. Netflix. It's all I've been doing."

"Sounds fun."

"It helps me escape."

Liuba gave him a look. Alek ignored it. If she wanted to get into an argument, or some kind of provocative situation, that was one thing. But expecting him to pursue her, beg her to tell him what was wrong, that was just absurd. He was content to let her drink her coffee in steely silence.

"I spent some time with Vicky the other day," Liuba said after a pause.

"Oh, right."

"I couldn't stand being around her," Liuba went on, and Alek almost smiled. "My own best friend. *And* I know the real reason she started this all to begin with – so do you, Alek. And I *still* couldn't stand it. The attention, or just wondering if we'd get attention."

"You're saying this like it's *my* fault. I didn't blackmail her."

"But when does it stop?"

When I have tens of millions of followers and the ability to be anybody I want to be. But if Alek told his baby sister about this very logical endpoint, she would most likely overreact in some way, as per usual.

"What do you mean?"

"The videos? The attention? Surely it has to stop, soon?"

"How much attention are you getting, really?" Alek asked. "Obviously, anybody who bothers you is a problem... but how much is it?"

"It's just the looks," she said, staring down into her coffee. "At work. All the time. I know people are wondering what's going on with me. Vicky has basically been told to stay away from the office. I'm your sister."

"But what do people say? How do they behave towards you?"

"They're polite."

"Maybe they're not actually thinking about you all the time," he told her. "Maybe they seem polite because they're just being normal, and a lot of this is in your head."

"Oh, I'm imagining stuff, am I?" she said, giving him a pointed look.

He aimed a big, fake grin at her, causing her to deflate a little. She knew she'd gone too far. But when she tried to apologise, he just magnanimously waved a hand at her. He didn't need her apologies.

"Anyway, love ya," she said, when it was time to go.

Alek gave her a sincere hug, feeling how badly she needed it. "I love you," he said. "Please try not to stress. And make up with Vicky; she's usually your rock."

Alek despised the bitch, but his love for his sister outweighed that, outweighed so much. It always had. He would give this all up for her, only her.

"It's just awkward..."

"It doesn't have to be. Tell her you hate me. Tell her you're never speaking to me again."

"Don't be silly. You're the only family I've got."

"Right back at you."

She laughed, and it was a wonderful sound. Once she was gone, Alek did a search for the journals again. He even went underneath the floorboards this time, but there was nothing. Why would Jack take those?

Finally, Alek rang Jack; he was tired of waiting around.

"What?" Jack said.

"Are we doing this or not? I've only got a few hours before I have to leave."

"Mia said you should leave her alone."

"Listen, it's..." He checked the time. "Five o'clock. That gives us a few hours. If you get here for nine, even, we can record something. Ten. Just get here, then I can edit and upload whatever we do, while I'm in London. Maybe you can record an intro and send it ahead."

"No, Alek," Jack said. "This thing, you, it was weird all along, mate. But now, after Dad... We just need space, all right? Have fun in London. Maybe we'll talk when you get back. When is that again?"

Alek's hand was tight on his phone. He wanted to break it. The little shit thought he was slick. "I leave at midnight," he said. "I'll be back in a week. Ring me when you change your mind."

But no phone call came. Alek refreshed news websites, putting in Nigel the abuser's full name, but there was nothing. Still no leak. Nothing on Natasha or Mia's social media accounts. During his searching, Alek found some empty notebooks in the style of Maksym's journals; at least, they would *look* similar in a black-and-white photo. Alek took them into the garden, arranged them, made sure the light was right. He wrote the caption. *May the darkness of the past capture the light of the future. Wishing you all a wonderful day. x*

It was generic and cheesy and, within an hour, it was amassing more likes than he ever could've imagined before. That was something, at least, but time kept ticking on. Alek drank coffee and even smoked some cigarettes. His nerves felt raw. He hadn't been sleeping. He'd started reading Russian literature, using a dictionary laboriously – not learning the language, just bluntly decoding the words.

Soon, it was midnight, time for his Uber. He made some arrangements before he left, and then he carried two empty suitcases out onto the street. He smiled to the driver and declined an offer of help, put them in the boot, then got into the car. The driver was a middle-aged man with glasses. From the way he glanced in the rear-view, Alek knew he recognised him from the internet.

"Evening," Alek said.

"Hello," the man replied. "Short drive."

"That's why I left a big tip," Alek said.

The man laughed nervously as he pulled away, driving to the end of the street, turning left, doing a wide circuit, then coming back to park by the kerb on the opposite side of the park across from Alek's house.

"Thank you," he said, climbing from the car then getting the empty suitcases. The man looked at him strangely and then drove away.

Alek carried the suitcases into the park and left them under a tree. It was dark, which was good, and empty. Even so, he crept along the edge and kept in full shadow. Finally he was able to creep up to the fence and lean down so he was partially covered by some bushes; he was able to see the front of his house from here. He struggled to think how somebody would climb the wall at the back, but the gate was doable, especially for an athletic man like Jack.

Alek wondered if he was wasting his time. But then his phone started to vibrate in his pocket. He took it out. It was Jack.

"Hello?" Jack answered.

Alek kept his voice low. What if Jack was nearby, in the park, watching the house too? "What?"

"Charming, mate," Jack said, laughing strangely; Alek suspected he was intoxicated. "We're ready for the podcast, all right? We've done some talking."

Alek almost bit, but then he heard a gruff voice in the background. "Tell him Mia's ready to come round now."

"Mia's ready right now," Jack said a second later. "She can't sleep."

"I told you. I'm away," Alek said.

"You've already left, have you?"

"My Uber just arrived. For God's sake, Jack. It's too late."

"Ah, fuck. Can you come back?"

"No. I promised my friend."

"But you can't be that far yet."

"The Uber arrived unexpectedly early," Alek said, feeling safe in the lie since he could also hear music in the background of Jack's call; he couldn't hear any music near him. "I'm at least eighty miles from Weston; I've got no intention of coming back."

"Even if she does the podcast without you?"

"Don't worry. I've got something for *her*, too. See you in a week."

He hung up. Obviously, if he *had* been going to see a friend and Jack called with a genuine podcast offer, Alek would've turned around. But Alek was not a stupid man. He wasn't going to be fooled by something so transparent. But what about the friend?

Alek didn't let himself think about that. Instead, he settled into his dark little corner and waited. At one point, an elderly lady walked by with a small dog. It must've been half past twelve by then at least, and she just tottered along as her old, fat dog waddled at her side. The dog paused, staring right at Alek in his dark spot, and then they kept going.

This was, he realised, exactly the sort of behaviour that could get him sectioned again. He was starting to get cramp lying like this.

But then a car pulled up onto the dark, dead street. Alek watched as two men climbed out, both of them clearly drunk. One was Jack; his shape was enough to tell Alek that. The other was taller, leaner, and seemed older somehow from the way he walked. They exchanged a look before walking across the street.

Alek had purposefully disabled both his security lights and his alarm as part of his preparation. Jack was clearly a person lacking in perceptive skills, so he wouldn't question it. And, luckily, they were both drunk. Though, there being *two* of them might be a problem.

They approached the gate, then after a short talk, Jack leaned down so the other man could climb onto his back. Alek began to slither from his spot like a reptile getting ready to consume his prey. The other man must've unlocked the gate, thinking the simple pull mechanism was all Alek used. He let Jack in, and then Alek slithered out from under the fence and began to approach his house.

What was he going to do now? He had been planning on scaring Jack to the point where the little rat might make something happen for him; maybe he could use Jack to get Mia to see sense. But with two of them, he wasn't sure. How would he get the other man out of the way first? Doing so would surely require hurting him.

He decided his best choices all involved knowing what they were doing in the house, so he stalked across the street. Even though this endeavour had offered up an unexpected obstacle, Alek couldn't help but smile as he walked back towards his house. He'd set the trap... and it had worked. It proved he was in control. Even if Vicky or someone or something had taken Maksym from him, *Alek* was in charge; he could still change the world.

Alek slipped through the narrow entrance and crept along the fence to the wheelie bins. It was eerily dark, atmospherically enhancing the situation. Alek found that his smile grew so wide, he had to be conscious of keeping his mouth closed, lest the whites of his teeth should show and give him away.

He could hear Jack and his oafish friend walking around to the side of the house.

"What'll we do?" Jack said, and the boy sounded sick to his stomach.

"Smash the bloody window."

"Won't anyone hear?"

"Nah."

Jack went, "Wait, wait!" but it was too late. A crash, shattering glass, and the other man was laughing, a real bullyish and look-at-me and aren't-I-impressive sort of laugh. Alek stayed pressed against the fence where it was darkest; Maksym would've likened this to avoiding the activists and their food-sniffing firearms. Alek got into the perfect position, watching as the other man cleared the glass away with a brick, then took off his jacket and laid it over the window.

He gestured to Jack. "Ladies first." When Jack hesitated, he snapped, "The fuck's wrong with you?"

"I don't know. It's just... he said the Uber just arrived. It *just* arrived. And then he said it arrived early."

Ah, that was true. Alek hadn't noticed that. That was thoroughly annoying.

"Well, he clearly ain't here. Jesus Christ."

The man climbed over his own jacket and into Alek's study. Jack looked up and down, then turned, and Alek could've sworn he stared right at him. There was maybe eight feet between them, and the fence was making the already dark night darker, but Jack didn't see; he just stared then turned.

Alek got a sick feeling as he watched Jack climb into the house, following his partner-in-crime. Something strange seemed to be happening here, something that would twist up the fabric of reality and might well spit Alek out. A voice whispered – not Maksym, but a real voice that meant something. "Turn back, Alek. You idiot. You stupid, pathetic idiot."

He pushed the feeling away, moving closer to the window when he heard them stomping towards the hallway. Alek slipped inside with far more fluidity than the drunken men had. He went and stood behind the open door, listening as they claimed the place with obnoxious footsteps.

"Where's his safe?"

"I don't know. I've never seen it."

"You said it was in the cellar, didn't you?"

"No, I mean – why would he tell the truth about that? I bet he's set a trap down there or something."

"You're so fucking paranoid tonight. Lay off the gear, all right? You can't handle it."

"I'm fine."

The gear. Jack was a young man and, like Alek had once upon a time, he was experimenting with allowing chemicals to hijack his consciousness in the vain attempt to leave behind this painful world. Alek almost felt sorry for him.

"We should check," the man said.

Alek felt borderline invisible and ethereal as he soundlessly stalked back into deeper darkness as their footsteps approached. The cellar entrance was directly opposite the room Alek was currently in. Alek thought about the last time he was in there; it had been with the hobo, and things had got very messy. But he'd done a decent job at cleaning; it was never perfect, though, and if the men went down there, they'd see large petals of blood.

Again, that sick feeling. It was like there was something trying to filter into his skull. It was an emotion he had felt in the past, and he didn't like to think about it; it mostly meant that something ugly and impossible was going to happen. Loud wood-on-wood noises as Jack's friend began to remove the board.

"I bet there's nothing down there," Jack said.

"Look at this door, though."

"What about it?"

"See the scuff marks around the lock? He clearly uses it a lot."

"Or it's an old lock with scuff marks, Sherlock."

"Fuck it."

Bang, as the friend booted open the door. Alek winced, gritted his teeth and clenched his fists in the darkness, wondering if it was time for him to do something. Perhaps he could scare them by loudly announcing himself, forcing them to run from the house. Or he could leave via the window, walk around to the front door and pretend he was returning home. But something kept him in place. His head was swirling.

"*Coward*," something whispered, and he shook his head as though to rid himself of it. "*Pathetic coward.*"

Footsteps echoed from further away, but one of them, presumably Jack, had remained at the top of the stairs. Minutes passed and then the other man returned.

"Dusty as shit down there," he said, coughing. "I had a poke around with my light. You were right. It's gutted."

Alek thought of his workshop and his cell and the custom-built kitchen and the toilet and the big blossoms of blood and the flesh-carving and the bone-collecting and all the purposeful and intended bloodshed he had performed. Suddenly he was on his feet, sprinting to the door.

"What the fuck?"

Both men spun to face him. Alek leapt forward, grabbed the lean man and shoved him against the wall so hard the entire house shook. The man became limp and pathetic, but you're the pathetic one, Alek, and you always have been. You've never had the courage of your convictions. And then Jack was yelling, "*Stop, stop!*" and Alek's eyes were blurry, and he realised he had hit the bastard several times. He was on the floor on all fours, gasping, wheezing, panting like a dog.

"What is this?" Alek roared. but you know what it is, you know who you are, who you've always been, nothing, nobody, a joke and a mess of a man, wishing you were special, but you're not; you never will be. "Explain." And he kicked the man in the stomach.

Jack turned and ran. That was a mistake. Oh what a big man, and Alek chased him and kicked him in the small of the back, like a coward – no, he had to – and as Jack fell the front of his face crunched against the door.

"Shut up!" Alek yelled and he turned and went to the cellar door, flicked the light switch. But no light came on. There had never been any light. It smelled musky and cold.

"Where's your torch?" Alek asked the lean rat weasel.

"Fu-phone," he wheezed. Both of them were incapacitated, oh how impressive you are, Alek.

He grabbed the man's phone and went to the cellar door and turned on the torch and light washed across the jungle of cobwebs and exposed floorboards and walls covered in peeling paper and a spot of damp and... and no workshop. Just what did you think you were doing? Who did you think you were? What did you think you were going to change? Silly man in his silly shirt saying silly things silently severing his sentience with each solipsistic sigh of make-believe.

Go on, Alek, get them; grab them. Ignore the way they moan and whine. Ignore the way they beg you to stop. That's it; kick that bastard down the stairs into the cobwebs, the dust and the fakery. Jack is whining, but who cares? Get him; grab him. He's telling you he's sorry, but it doesn't matter. It *never* mattered.

Because you know they did this. He stared *right at you* outside. It was dark, yes, okay, any reasonable man could admit that, but it wasn't *total* darkness. Which means he knew you were setting him up; in hindsight, it was very obvious.

"Please, Alek, God please don't leave us down here please for the love of God, mate, please, Alek, he gave me pills I didn't want it but there were so many people there shut up no you shut the fuck up shut up but it's not fair leave him and not me please Mia needs me she needs me more than anyone please don't—"

He knew you wanted him to come here. They planned it. Jack is lying. He looked right at you. Jack must've gutted the cellar at some point when you let him into your home; is that it, Alek? Maybe you are the big bad wolf. No, don't do that. Jesus.

"Please, please, please!"

Oh, more gasping, more crying? And this time it's coming from you? And there goes your coffee machine. You're making quite the mess, blubbering as you trash your own kitchen, what a productive thing to do. And now we're back to the hold-knife-do-nothing routine, fantastic, with *more* tears, what a treat.

So, are you going to do it? Are you, Alek? Are you? Do it. Go on. I dare you. I double dare you. Ha, ha, ha. You won't. But you should. It's what they deserve.

Chapter 44

Nat

It was 1am. Nat tossed and turned as the pit in her stomach grew. She kept trying to tell herself it wasn't her fault – that she'd had no choice – but it felt like a hollow lie. And there was something else, something she'd never admit... She was excited. She knew this was going to be huge. And, hopefully, all the hate would also stop. Whatever it meant for her family.

The next time she checked her phone, there would be love, understanding, empathy, hope. It didn't matter if, in the real world, she'd only ever have the opposite.

Nat turned onto her front and pushed her face into the pillow. "No choice, no choice, no choice," she said, over and over.

The world would be different tomorrow; nothing would ever be the same. Dad used to joke she was being a melodramatic teenager when she said stuff like that. That was before all the internet stuff, when her problems, even when they involved other people, had seemed so private.

She began to cry, unable to keep up her mantra. She cried into her pillow. Tomorrow, she promised herself, she'd be strong.

Chapter 45

Alek

Alek opened his eyes. He was staring at the ceiling, an ache pulsing up and down his back. He wasn't sure how long he had been lying on the floor. He could hear the voices, just the usual, and he turned them down inside his head. He climbed to his feet and stumbled to the sink, lapping up the water from the faucet, drinking as much as he could get down him.

He found he was able to move; he was able to coldly go upstairs and take a quick shower. He'd had a shit and pissed in his underwear. He put it all in a plastic bag, ready for disposal, and scrubbed himself until it hurt. There were no sirens; that was good. Having a detached house had probably saved him.

Nothing can save you.

Alek found himself standing outside the cellar door with a hammer in his hand. He needn't have bothered. Alek hadn't closed the door. He switched on his heavy torch, something which could also serve as a weapon if needed, and found the cellar to be almost bare.

He had tied Jack and his friend together around a middle pillar, using a series of zip-ties to seal them back to back.

Alek focused, dissected the scene before him. Both men were awake, with big red angry eyes. Alek had stuffed socks in their mouths and bound them with duct tape. He didn't remember doing any of this.

Laying down the torch, he noticed something glinting in the light. This was good; he'd also apparently put their mobile phones into a tin case, first removing the batteries and the SIM cards. They were all in the glinting tin.

Alek walked over to the men, being careful to take a wide path just in case one of them swung their legs at him. As he approached Jack, he held the hammer out, ready at all times.

"Don't make any noise," he warned him.

Jack nodded. Alek quickly tore the duct tape free and then stepped back. Jack made noises of disgust, as he pushed the sock out with his tongue.

"Please," he said, his voice weak.

"No, no." Alek gestured with the hammer. "How did you do it?"

"What?"

"You stared right at me," Alek told him. "Outside."

"What?"

"You stared *right* into my *eyes*." Alek waved the hammer again and Jack flinched, though they were several feet apart. "You saw me, but you didn't say anything. You wanted me to see this. What you did."

"Alek, please, I don't understand."

"You came down here and you got rid of everything!" Alek snapped. "You filled it with cobwebs."

Alek spun and struck the wall with the hammer; cheap plasterboard caved in. He remembered the brick that had been there before, the layers of soundproofing. He could see it as though it was superimposed over his vision.

But you have no vision and never have had—

"Shut the fuck up," Alek snapped. "Just – shut up."

Jack stared, wide-eyed. He began to protest when Alek grabbed more duct tape from his back pocket, but he stopped when he saw the look in Alek's eyes. Alek taped Jack's mouth up and then went back upstairs, careful to close and lock the cellar door behind him this time.

He was hurting. He stared at the tin he'd brought upstairs with him, then decided to smash their phones and the SIMs into tiny pieces with his hammer, sweep them all into a dustpan, and pour them down a drain outside his house. He thought about doing it further afoot, but what if somebody saw him? Or a camera picked him up? The pieces he poured down the drain were tiny; he would just have to hope he had killed any means of tracking.

Back in the house, he got his plastic carrier bag of clothes. Could he burn them? But what if people saw the fire? Realistically, did he need to hide them? What was the purpose? It wasn't as though he had murdered anyone.

Alek put them in the washing machine with a healthy dose of white spirit and detergent, then set the temperature to ninety degrees. Afterwards, he boarded up his broken window, knowing he'd need to get it fixed as soon as possible.

The kitchen was a complete mess, absolutely trashed, and again, Alek was grateful nobody would have heard. Alek's hands still throbbed from where he'd punched the coffee machine (and the men). The gleaming silver unit had a giant dent in the side. The cuts and the swelling on Alek's knuckles weren't terrible, but they weren't ideal.

The most pressing question was: what was he going to do with Jack and his friend?

No, baby steps. Grab a mug. Get instant coffee. Open seal.

Ignore harsh smell. Spoon three, four, five heaps of coffee into the mug, boil kettle, pour water, use handle to stir because the coffee is so dense it is not mixing properly, sip, stir more. Sip boiling hot coffee, enjoy the way it scalds the tongue.

Would he have to kill them both?

Chapter 46

Seb

Seb woke to a text from his manager.

> You've fucked it, mate.

Lucas had attached a link to the message; Seb clicked it while Vicky snored softly beside him. He'd always loved the way she snored, the cute little breaths she took. He'd once joked she sounded like a magical creature, a fairy, and they'd both laughed like it was the funniest thing ever, high on love.

The link took him to a YouTube video. The channel name was *Not Fake Mia*. It wasn't the same channel she'd uploaded her podcast with Alek to, but when the video started, Seb saw it was clearly her. She was sitting on a bed, a cheap-looking microphone in her hand; the video quality was nothing like it had been before.

The video already had 70,000 views after just four hours. Seb started sweating, trying to focus. Nat was sitting next to Mia on the bed. He looked at his daughter, her face plastered in far more make-up than she'd had on when she'd left for study group.

Seb reached over and nudged Vicky, though he almost didn't want to wake her. He didn't want her to have to experience this too. She groaned and rolled over, then sat up sharply when she saw the phone screen.

"What?" she said, still half asleep. "*What?*"

"I know," Seb whispered.

"Seventy thousand views."

"I know."

He felt numb as Mia introduced the episode. "I know this quality is crap, guys, but we're done letting people tell us what to do, forcing us to lie, forcing us to be what *they* want us to be. Before I go on, I'm going to play something for you. So you know who Alek really is. He's not a good person; he tried to use me to become famous."

She brought out a phone, pressed play, held it to the mic. Crackly audio played. Weirdly, the low-tech graininess of it made the video seem more authentic. Seb's work brain was ticking away; people would love this. Nat sat there with an unreadable expression.

"*I just want to mourn my dad, but I know you, Alek. I bet you've already got a million ideas. Just like last time. You made me do that first podcast. And look what it made Dad do!*"

Then Alek roared, "*You need to think, Mia. Think about the chance you've got here. You need to play this right. If you delete the first podcast and don't record another one, your dad's death will be just a blip in the news. You have to choose to be famous.*"

Mia clicked off the recording. "There's more, but that's just to give you an idea of who he really is. After my last video, my dad... he unalived himself. I was confused and I reached out to Alek, thinking he could help me in some way. But he wants to be famous, that's all. He's obsessed with it. He doesn't care about Ukraine, or anything else apart from himself."

A pause, then Mia looked at Nat. Nat swallowed; she

looked scared underneath all that make-up. Vicky was shuddering beside Seb.

"My parents are exactly the same," Nat said, and Seb knew that his life as he knew it was over. There would be before this video, and after. He swallowed a big ball of phlegm and bile. "My mum took my phone so I couldn't get evidence, but I swear, she wants to be famous even more than Alek does. She was the one pushing me to get involved. She wants me to be her little Kim K. It's always the same – adults just demanding stuff from us. Taking stuff. But what about what *we* want?"

Seb almost smiled when he heard her righteous tone. She sat up, seeming capable, impressive.

"What about your dad?" Mia said.

"Mia..." Nat bit down, unsure, then sighed.

Mia glared at her. "I thought we were done with secrets? Everybody knows what *my* dad did to me – but what about your dad? What did *he* do?"

"Seb?" Vicky whispered.

"I'm so sorry." Seb had always been a good lad; that's what people said about him. Not exciting, necessarily, not the sort of person who lit the world on fire. He'd never been an addict or let a night out sprawl into a crazy weekend. He was a down-the-middle sort of bloke. And now he had tears in his eyes.

"He had no one else to go to, Mia."

"Just say it."

Nat sighed, looked at the camera, looked right at Seb. She seemed almost *sorry*. "A few months ago, my dad's manager wanted some coke. His usual dealer was out of town. So my dad – feeling like he had no other choice – asked Mia to get him some. Mia's brother has friends who are into that sort of thing."

"But *I* don't do that filth," Mia added. "And actually, those people I went to, they weren't really his friends. It was scary.

But your dad got so serious and intense when I said I didn't want to do it. He basically assaulted me, Nat."

"He shoved you against the wall. He threatened you."

"You did *what?*" Vicky whispered.

"It's not how she's making it sound – she was going to yell, bring the whole house down. I asked her to stop and, and I touched her arm, like you do in a conversation."

"You shouldn't have been touching her at all."

Seb swallowed, remembering how Lucas had grinned when he'd slipped him the bag.

"So, this is why we're making this episode. We don't want *them* telling us what to do anymore." When Mia looked at the camera with such conviction, Seb could easily imagine her becoming an icon for oppressed teenage girls everywhere. "We're taking back our lives. I know Nat made some mistakes, but you can't keep hating on her with all these comments and stuff. It's not her fault. If *your* mum came to you and begged you to make *her* famous, you'd do the same thing. The important part is, we're on the same team now."

Mia reached out, offering Nat her hand. Nat took it, then smiled at the camera. Seb knew that smile; he'd seen it on countless Christmas mornings, at the water park, after she'd scored a strike while bowling on her birthday. It was genuine.

"For the rest of the video," Nat said, "we want to talk about the pressure social media puts on us. All of us. We all know the feeling, don't we, posting a photo and staring at the likes, obsessing? We want to help *you*."

"As a team," Mia said, her smile growing, and Seb almost felt proud again.

"Vicky," He paused the video, turning to her. "I'm so—"

"I had an affair," she cut in, and an invisible fist struck Seb right in the gut. Before he could say anything else, Vicky sprung to her feet and ran from the bedroom, screaming like

Seb had never heard her before. "*Natasha! You are in big trouble!*"

Seb dragged himself to the bathroom and puked up yellow bile. His belly cramped as he dry heaved. He turned at the sound of footsteps. Max stood there with a teddy bear in his hand. He didn't normally carry it around anymore, but he sometimes slept with it. He had tears in his eyes. In the background, Seb could hear Vicky screaming; she never let herself go like this in front of the kids.

"*You can't fucking run from us!*"

"Daddy?" Max said, blubbering. "Daddy!"

Seb turned, just in time for Max to run into his arms. He held his son tightly. A moment later, Vicky was at the door, her face bright red. She looked wild as she waved a piece of paper. "She snuck out in the night – she's taken her phone, too. Broken the drawer. She doesn't give a *shit*."

"Vicky!"

Max shoved his face into Seb's chest, scared of his mother.

"I'm going to Mia's. She threatens us in the note. *Stay away, or it will get worse.* Our little Nat."

"Was that true, what you said?" Seb asked, even as Max kept crying.

"Yes," Vicky replied, seeming distracted.

"When?" Seb almost heaved again thinking of his wife with another man.

"Over a decade ago."

She turned away, walked into the bedroom and began getting dressed.

"Daddy," Max moaned. "Daddy. Daddy?"

All Seb could do was hold him. It wasn't as though he could say, '*Everything will be okay.*' How could he know that?

"You better stay here with Max," Vicky called from the bedroom, then stomped down the hallway.

Seb picked Max up and carried him into the bedroom, grabbing his phone as he went. He was halfway down the stairs when it began to ring. It was Lucas.

"I liked you, Seb," he said. "Really, mate, I did."

"Lucas—"

"You've breached your contract, buddy. *Lots* of negative press. Which means we're free to shitcan your arse without any notice. Why in the name of God would you use a *child*? Wait – no, I don't..." Lucas paused, apparently realising he might've just implicated himself. "It's all bullshit."

"I'm not recording, Lucas."

"For what it's worth, you were really good at your job, Seb. Really good."

Were. Lucas hung up, carrying Max into the kitchen and sitting him down.

"Want some breakfast, champ?"

Max looked up at him, tears running down his face, then bravely nodded. "Uh, yeah, Daddy."

Seb began to mechanically go through the motions, periodically refreshing the podcast. He couldn't help himself; it was a compulsion. By the time he was asking Max if he wanted jam or butter, it had reached 90,000 views.

Chapter 47

Vicky

Vicky's head was rushing as she drove wildly through the town, almost cutting a red light before coming to an abrupt stop that had a mother pushing a pram look at her like she was mental. And maybe she was, but she couldn't stop long enough to think about that. She just kept driving, the video replaying in her head. Her own *daughter* – all the love, all the memories, holding her and not believing it could be possible to love like this. She'd cried and smelled her daughter, breathing in that newborn scent, loving her so deeply, so *instantly*.

She parked up across the street. She was shaking as she walked towards the house. Mia lived on the end of a row of terraces. There was a motorbike out front, with no wheels, sitting on bricks. Vicky wondered if it had belonged to Mia's father. She knocked on the door, expecting to have to wait, but it snapped open right away.

Mia's mother stood as though she'd expected Vicky. She looked ready for a fight, hair scraped back into a tight ponytail, hands on her hips.

"Where's Nat?"

"I'm sorry, but she doesn't want to see you."

"Are you fucking *joking*?" Vicky screamed, really screamed, so that she could feel her veins pushing against her neck.

Charlotte had the gall to look affronted. When Vicky stepped forward, though, she quickly snapped out of it and dived at the door, managing to almost close it until Vicky wedged her foot and her shoulder in the way.

"Nat!" she yelled. "Natasha!"

"Please," Charlotte moaned. "This is stupid. Don't make me call the police."

"Call the police? You've kidnapped my fucking daughter. *Natasha!*"

"Mum, stop."

Nat appeared at the hallway door, standing near the shoe rack, her eyes red from crying, black make-up streaked down her face.

"It's okay," Vicky said, staring into her daughter's eyes, seeing her little Nat, the girl she loved and who still loved her. She saw her in there, even as Nat tried to hide. "Whatever made you do this, *whoever* made you do this, I understand. I accept it. I forgive you. Just come home."

Nat shuddered, shaking her head. "Muh-Mum."

"It's okay, baby. We can talk about it at home."

Nat stared at the floor. Mia's mother stood there, still half-heartedly holding the door, clearly not sure what to do. Vicky didn't want to move. She could tell Nat was on the verge of bolting back into the house.

"Just look at me, sweetheart."

Nat stared with wide, red eyes. She seemed to be on the tipping point, like any moment she would break and run into her mum's arms. But then she spoke to the floor instead. Her voice was heavy, thick with grief. "You know what you did, Mum."

Vicky shoved the door, then Mia appeared beside Nat. The

girl looked almost feral. Her hair was a mess. She looked like she'd been crying. She stared at Vicky with pure hatred, as though she was ready to physically hurt her.

"Are you seriously doing this? Are you *seriously* here right now?"

"Mia," Nat muttered.

"Get *out*," Mia screamed.

It was all happening too fast to process. A voice came from behind Vicky. "Love – that's enough."

She turned to find a small group assembled on the lawn next to the motorbike. There were four teenage boys, perhaps as old as eighteen, and a gaggle of girls. Vicky peered closer; she was almost certain she recognised them from before, when a small gang had formed outside her house.

"Why won't you leave me the *fuck* alone, you sad cunts?"

Jesus. What the hell had she just said? The moment the word was out of her mouth, she realised her mistake. But it was too late. Several of the girls were aiming their phones, sick smiles on their faces, like spirits possessed by their devices. The lead man stepped forward, a dusty dirty beard smeared across his jaw and neck. "We're just looking out for Mia. She's been through enough. She's always been a breath of fresh air around here and you're intruding. Time to leave."

A switch flicked in her brain. Vicky no longer cared what anybody thought of her. She just wanted Nat back, safe and sound. "Not without my daughter. She's taken my daughter!"

As Vicky yelled, a distant part of her noted that she sounded like a raving madwoman. Behind her, the door slammed shut. Vicky felt as though she'd blacked out. Then she jolted back to reality, realising she was hammering on the door with her fist. Even the feel of the wood against her hand felt distant as the reverberation moved up her arm.

"Natasha!" she screamed. "Nat! Please! Nat!"

Somebody touched her hand; she spun, slapped him... no, *almost* did. Thankfully, he ducked out of the way. Time seemed to slow as he slid out of range. Now, he regrouped and puffed himself up. "Go on, then. Do that again! I dare ya!"

Vicky knew she was defeated. She began hyperventilating as she walked towards her car, the mobile phones following her, seeming like *they* were the sentient ones and the girls were the appendages, trailing behind their devices.

Then something happened, which she'd thought was *long* past. When she'd finally made it to her car, a panic attack hit; she began to think of *him*, when she was a girl – the camera, the promises. *'You could be a model, sweetheart...'* Her throat was tightening and her vision blurred. She tried to start the car, messed up. The girls were laughing; she could hear them through the window.

Finally, Vicky sat back and shuddered, tears pouring down her cheeks. She looked out of the window, back at the house, and saw Nat, her baby, standing in the upstairs bedroom. Could she see her mother crying from up there? If she could see, did she care?

Not sure what else to do, Vicky started the car and pulled away from the small mob.

Chapter 48

Alek

Alek had the lawyer on loudspeaker as he dug. He was finding it difficult to remember the lawyer's name, dig, and not think about the video or the two men he had tied up in the cellar, both of them most likely with piss in their pants by now; it had been ten hours since he'd left them down there. He kept digging, grunting, as the lawyer spoke. Mr Gurney. Hurney. Something.

"We will of course have to proceed with legal action," the lawyer said.

Alek was standing shin-high in the hole, his forearms tight and swollen with exertion. His knuckles throbbed from the mayhem last night. But at least everything sounded somewhat quiet. It was *mostly* quiet.

He kept digging. Where was the body? He needed to find it. Alek hadn't taken *all* of the bones. He never did that. He remembered the sound of them rattling around in the box, remembered the voices contained within, their purpose... but the more he dug, the more dirt he found. Nothing but dirt.

"Mr Bodar?" the lawyer said.

"But..." Alek stopped digging, thinking hard. His brain was so sluggish, but he was aware of the fine machinery contained within his skull, even if it was functioning at a slower rate than usual. "When the situation was reversed. When I recorded Victoria, you said—"

"I laid out arguments we could use to combat any legality, yes."

"So won't they just do the same?" Alek roared, not meaning to raise his voice. But it was absurd. Was this man a moron?

"They might be able to try, sir, but they will of course not have our legal pedigree, or our resources."

"My money, you mean."

He needed time to think; he needed sleep. But any time he closed his eyes, time would pass, and that meant more hate, more comments. Alek had watched the video this morning, his heart hurting, realising that he had to think fast, think of something clever, something that would turn this around.

But from the way Mia played it, there was nothing he could do... or was there? *Think.*

You can't think. Just dig. Big dumb oaf. Just dig and find no bones because you were never special and you're never going to be special.

Alek climbed from the small hole, staring down at the dirt, shuddering. What was the point? Suddenly disgusted, he tossed the shovel down and went into the house, into the computer room, not caring about the dirt he dragged everywhere. It didn't matter. He sat at the desk, opened the video. It was currently sitting at almost 200,000 views. All of Alek's social media inboxes were flooded with messages, but Alek couldn't bring himself to read them. Even the message previews were sounding as loud as the voices.

Kill yourself, scum...

You're a piece of...

I'm coming for you...

Alek blinked, rubbed his eyes. The message which had just

read *I'm coming for you* had gone. That was weird; had the computer been hacked? He leaned closer to the screen. Several of the comments had disappeared. Where the fuck were they? This didn't make any sense. He had good anti-virus, but anybody who frequented the internet knew there was *never* anti-virus software capable enough to stop the most determined attackers.

He quickly shut the computer down and booted it up in safe mode, then selected his anti-virus and set it to run the deepest scan it possibly could, right down to the bios of the system, the base layer, everything, like scouring a corpse with a blade.

The voice tried to say something. If it had been Maksym, maybe Alek would've listened, but this was just a bully and he was sick of it. His grandfather would never talk to him like that. Alek put the phone on flight mode, killed all the apps, opened the camera and headed for the cellar. There was an idea; there was something he could do.

You can't do anything. You've always been a nothing. Why do you ever try and do things? Why do you think you're capable? Go to one class – take one lesson – hype yourself up to the point of truly believing it, but you'll fail, you sad pathetic virgin. You loser. You silver-spoon husk.

Alek gritted his teeth, kept walking. It was always there, a background noise, but he wouldn't let it win. He opened the cellar door and descended into the gloom. It reeked of piss... and shit, too. The tall, lean, mean man turned and stared into the light.

Alek watched it all through the phone screen. He hadn't started recording yet.

"Please, man," he moaned. "Just let us out. We ain't saying shit."

"Alek." Jack tried to look all meaningful. "We took some stuff last night, all right? Some pills. We shouldn't have. I'm sorry. Really. I am. I'm so, so sorry. Sincerely, Alek. You deserve respect and…" He was crying. "And I'm going to give it to you from now on. I promise I will. Okay? Please?"

After a pause, Alek said, "Did you know Mia was secretly recording me? Did you know she was going to upload it with Natasha? To ruin my name? My credibility?"

"No, but that was wrong," Jack blubbered. "I'll make her stop. Let me go. I promise she'll never upload another video."

Just tell him what he needs to hear… When Alek was given divine access to Jack's thoughts, a note of hope actually touched him. Perhaps this was his Prince Ivan moment and like that long-dead Ukrainian, Alek would emerge stronger, more capable.

"You're lying to me."

Make him believe you. "I'm not. I swear."

"I can hear you, Jack. I can hear your thoughts. You're lying to me."

"I promise—"

"No, no, Jack. I can hear every little thought in your head. I know you're just telling me what you think you need to, to be free, but I'm not letting you go yet. So just… stop."

"Plea—"

"I said stop!" Alek roared, and then the other man started crying, actually sobbing.

"I don't want to die," Jack whispered, fighting off more tears of his own.

"I can't kill you, so relax."

Are you sure about that? Wouldn't it be unbelievably easy? Look at their fragile skulls. Perhaps it would make Maksym come back. He always loved bloodshed…

"Why?"

"Shut up, man," the other one barked.

Alek ignored him, then realised something. "Wait... where are your gags?"

"We managed to push them out with our tongues. But we didn't scream." The man was shivering. "We didn't make a noise. It's just so hard to breathe. I've got blocked sinuses, man."

Had they screamed? Alek couldn't remember. It would be a very brazen lie if they had. But no police had arrived. Even after the video, there were no journalists or paparazzi outside his door; this was still mostly contained to the internet community, which was good.

"I can't kill you," Alek went on, "unless you've done something which would render your removal a relief to my consciousness. So, Jack, let me ask you, did you ever join in with dear Daddy during the diddling?"

"What the *fuck?*" The old Jack came back, the tough guy. "No."

Alek knelt a few feet from Jack, still aiming the phone torch at him. It was far easier to process everything through the screen. Jack's thoughts flurried. *I wouldn't hurt her. Not Mia. Not little Mia.*

"But you never stopped him," Alek pointed out.

He swallowed, a weird dry bloodshot look to his eyes, as though his body had run out of tears. "I wish I did."

"No, come on, let's not accept that so easily. Let's explore it."

Because I loved my dad. I loved him more than I hated what he did to my sister.

"You loved your father that much, did you?"

"I hated that man."

Alek grinded his teeth. "I've already told you about lying."

"But—"

"I've fucking told you about lying!"

Jack flinched. "I loved him, Alek. It would've hurt me to hurt him."

"Did you ever hear what he did?"

"Alek, please. Please. *Please.*"

"Just answer the question."

Alek still wasn't recording; he wondered if Jack understood that. Maybe he thought Alek was recording this because he wanted to hurt Mia, but that wouldn't give him any tactical advantage. The most important thing was to get this podcast situation under control.

Can I lie to him? Jack stared at Alek, then decided he couldn't. "Yes, I did. I pretended not to. We both did, me and my mum. It became this weird thing in the house. Like, we'd have this second language. You can hear the bedroom from the living room. Mum would say, '*Cup of tea sounds good?*' and we both knew that meant, 'let's leave the room'."

"That's absolutely fascinating," Alek said honestly. "But how did you live with yourself? I have a sister, sweet Liuba, and she's the brightest point in my life. If any man ever laid a single finger on her I would absolutely annihilate him; I would kidnap him, take him someplace, and do to him what he did to my sister. I would sacrifice my virginity and self-respect to rape a man if he raped my sister."

He's going too far.

"That's your concern?" Alek laughed. "I'm going too far? There's no redemption for anybody who does that to another person. And to one's own daughter? Your diddling daddy took the easy way out, Jack.

"You miss him?" Alek grunted.

Jack flinched, almost lied, then said, "Yes."

"Pathetic."

"Yes, I'm pathetic."

But at least I'm not a schizoid.

"What?" Alek grunted.

"I'm sorry."

"You shouldn't think things like that."

"I know."

"There's nothing shameful about having a schizophrenia diagnosis," Alek told him. "People think of us how we're portrayed in the films and books, in the most extreme and exaggerated sense, but that's not the truth, Jack. The truth is, many people with that diagnosis are kinder, more empathetic, more artistic and more humane than the general population. But unfortunately for you, I am not one of them."

Alek waved a hand. "Anyway, that's not why I'm down here. I need you to record a video for me. I need ammunition. So, simply explain the situation – where you are, the danger you're in. Of course, forget what I said about not killing you. Tell Mia that, unless she does whatever I say to rectify this situation, she's sacrificing you to me. Can you do that, Jack?"

"Yes."

"Good boy."

Are you really going to kill a police officer? Does that seem like an intelligent thing to do? Do you truly think you're this powerful, Alek, to be able to get away with this – with any of this? You are a deluded, twisted, broken person.

But he was beating the officer with his own helmet, could feel the reverberations going up his arm, could hear the piggy's squeals as he told him, "You walked past three rapists and four crackheads and five perverts and six thieves to find some poor college kid who'd dropped a cigarette butt on the ground, all because you're a coward." And with each hit, there was more blood. More and more blood. "And you think this makes you impressive." Hit, hit, hit, as his head folded, and the piggy looked up and didn't even have a face, or a mouth, or an anything. Everything was melting. Reality was bleeding down the wallpaper as it stripped away, and die die die.

You've never accomplished anything. No – that was the piggy.

"You've never accomplished anything," he told the weak, unthreatening man whose only power came from the shiny uniform he wore.

Oh, Alek.

David was vaguely aware that this was pathetic. Lying on top of his quilt in bed, his dick in one hand and his mobile phone in the other, he knew he'd probably regret this tomorrow. He'd had too much to drink, but screw it, what was the point of *not* having too much to drink these days? Even his plan wasn't bringing him any joy. He'd proven his point far too easily, but he couldn't think of a way to leverage it, to enjoy it. Vicky was famous; the world was insane.

"You still there, baby?" the phone-sex woman said.

"Uh, yeah," David replied, not sure how long it had been since they'd last spoken. On the website, her photo showed a young, blonde, crack-addicted woman with dark pits for eyes and a troubled look that made the base of Dave's dick tingle. She was complete filth. "God, you're a disgusting whore."

"I'll be whatever you want me to be."

David kept stroking, but he was going soft. Too much booze. He wished he could have a real woman. He wished he could have a real life. Didn't he deserve something genuine, something more than this?

"No," David said, letting go of himself. "I mean, Krissy...

Kizzy? Whatever your name is, you *are*. A real disgusting bitch. What's wrong with you?"

"Come on now, baby..."

"Something must've happened to you. Some sort of abuse. Was it your dad, your uncle...?"

She hung up, which was downright mental. The line cost two pound a minute and she'd *hung up*. Even whores couldn't tolerate him. Jesus Christ. David stood up – he was crying, the world was blurring, and he hated himself, and he wished he was different, and he hated the world and knew it was their fault, not his – and went into the kitchen, grabbed a knife, stared down at it.

"I could've been somebody," he murmured, staring at the knife, wondering. But even the thought of it...

He needed a bloody cigarette.

Chapter 49

Seb

Seb was sitting at the kitchen table, staring at the steam rising from his third mug of coffee. Max was half-heartedly playing in the living room. Text after text was coming in: colleagues, friends, blokes he hadn't spoken to in years. They flooded in and all of them were to the same effect: if what Mia had said was true, they never wanted to speak to him again. Some went even further.

Seb massaged his forehead, reaching for the coffee. *These* messages were from people who had his phone number... He hadn't even checked his Facebook messages. He had Facebook, Instagram and LinkedIn, and he just knew each would be hellish.

The world was crashing down. His marriage was over – an *affair...*

"Daddy," Max yelled. "A policeman is outside."

Seb bolted to his feet, his mind running through a hyperdetailed replay of the night he'd collected the cocaine from Mia. He'd never meant Nat to find out. Waiting in the hallway when they were in Nat's room together, Seb had taken his chance when she went to the bathroom. But he was too slow.

Nat caught him leaving the room. He'd had to explain, or she would have thought it was something even more sinister.

The silhouette of the police officer was showing in the cloudy glass of the door. Max stood in the hallway, his games controller in his hand.

"Play your game, Max."

"Daddy."

"Just play the game."

He frowned, and Seb felt a stab of guilt. But he wasn't sure what else to do. He opened the door to find a tall young man standing in a police officer's uniform. It almost looked like a Halloween costume.

"Mr Taylor?"

"Yes." Seb swallowed. Could they arrest him, without anything on him? Was he going to have to lie to the police about the drugs? Maybe he needed a solicitor.

"Is your wife home? She's made a very serious allegation."

"What allegation?"

"Would you feel comfortable if we talked inside?" the young man asked. "My name is PC McGregor by the way."

"Sure," Seb said. "Shall I ring my wife?"

Before he could answer, and before PC McGregor could cross the threshold, there was the sound of tyres screeching in the driveway. They both turned to find Vicky pulling up aggressively to the house. When she left the car, she had a hard, determined look, even though Seb could tell she'd been crying.

"Your wife, I presume?" he addressed Seb, who nodded.

"Hi, hi," Vicky said briskly, approaching them. "Please, come inside. Would you like a cup of tea? Coffee?" She seemed manic.

"No, thank you."

The three of them went inside. Seb led the officer into the kitchen as Vicky went into the living room to check on Max. Despite everything, he felt a flutter of relief that she'd decided to say hello to their baby first. When Vicky returned, they all sat at the table.

"I've been driving around," Vicky said, picking at the table edge. Seb wanted to tell her to calm down, but he didn't want to do it in front of the police officer. "Thinking – what can I do? But it's obvious. She's taken my daughter."

"Who has?" PC McGregor asked. "Maybe you should give me some background."

"It's complicated," Vicky said.

Seb quickly cut in, "Our daughter, Natasha, she's made some serious claims about us on her social media. Now, she's gone to stay at her friend's house. They were on social media together, you see, making up... saying things." It sounded weak.

"Right, I see," McGregor said, nodding.

"Don't you need to write this down?" Vicky said. "I've just been to Mia's mother's house. The woman's kidnapped my daughter."

"What happened at her house?"

"I told Natasha to come home, and Charlotte, that's Mia's mother, wouldn't let her."

"She physically stopped you?"

"Yes. She blocked the door!"

"Were you able to speak with your daughter?"

Vicky hesitated, then said, "Yes."

"And what did she have to say about the matter?"

"She's a teenager," Vicky hissed. "She's a *child*."

"I understand that," he replied. "I'm just trying to assess whether your daughter is in any danger, or if she has run away to a friend's house because of some domestic issue. Both are stressful, I know, Mrs Taylor, but your answers will help me tailor my response correctly."

Seb had to admit, the young man seemed to have his act

together. Just talking to a police officer felt surreal. And Seb was conscious of the fact that PC McGregor clearly didn't understand the scale of this social media drama; he clearly didn't know what accusations Mia had made about the drugs.

"I spoke to her," Vicky said.

"Did she seem distressed?"

"Yes."

He sat up. "Did she seem under duress... Did you get the impression she was trying to give you any signals? Any sign she wanted to go with you, but couldn't say?"

Vicky licked her lips. "What happens if I say yes?"

"Mrs Taylor, I just need the truth."

"I just want to understand the process," Vicky said.

The young man gave Seb a look. Vicky seemed detached and anxious at the same time, a strange combination. "If you give me any reason to believe that your daughter is being held against her will, then I will have to arrange for a hostage rescue team. But since you didn't call the emergency line..."

"What? It means she's not in trouble?"

"I don't want to make any assumptions."

"She's a *child*," Vicky yelled, then slammed her hand on the table.

"Sweetheart," Seb said quickly, touching her arm.

She flinched like he was covered in sores. "She's confused. She needs to come home and be with her parents."

"I understand social media can be stressful and cause problems. But in my experience, situations like these are normally resolved within a few days. She'll soon realise she prefers being with her parents, in her own bedroom."

Vicky shook her head. "He doesn't understand."

"It's a bit... bigger than that," Seb said, struggling to find the right word. "Our daughter made a podcast episode with her friend. It's got hundreds of thousands of views. I've been receiving threats all morning."

"Threats, why?" PC McGregor said, sitting forward.

"In the podcast..." Seb paused. Millions of people would soon know – the views were only climbing – but saying it in real life felt impossible.

"They allege Seb bought cocaine from my daughter's friend," Vicky said. "They claim I forced my daughter to make videos. Neither me nor my husband would ever do *anything* like that."

Seb wanted to hug her so hard. But also, was lying to the police about what he'd done a good idea? It was too late.

PC McGregor was looking at Seb differently. Before now, he'd sensed an unspoken agreement that they were both upstanding, regular people, despite the uniform. But now the constable was looking at him like he might have to slap handcuffs on him one day. "That's a very serious allegation."

"They all want fame," Seb said, his stomach twisting as he lied. "They'll say and do anything. But I don't care about any of that. I just want my daughter to come home."

Vicky nodded. "That's all we want."

PC McGregor leaned back and finally took out his notebook. He began writing, seemingly from memory. "How do you spell Mia's surname?"

After Vicky spelled it out, he said, "And this podcast, what's it called? I'll listen during the drive over. Is it the entire episode that concerns you?"

"No, just the start," Seb told him. "The rest is about the effects of social media on teenage girls."

"Seems ironic." PC McGregor let a small smile slip.

Vicky sat up. "Our daughter is a very passionate and intelligent young lady. She's going to be an amazing podcaster one day... but not like this."

"I'm relieved, Mrs Taylor. Her being intelligent and switched-on should make this whole process go a lot easier."

The subtle jab was clear. How could she be a child incapable of thinking for herself and a mature young adult at the same time? He stood and smiled in an awkward way, looking at Seb one last time before saying, "I can see myself out. Oh, hello, young man."

Seb turned to find Max standing at the kitchen door, a lost look on his face. Seb wondered if the police officer saw him as a child being abused by his parents, as if the tears in Max's eyes were from fear. When Max smiled, Seb couldn't help but think it could easily be perceived as the smile of a child who knew, if he did anything else, there would be bad consequences.

"I want to be a policeman one day," Max said.

"I'm sure you'd make a great one."

Once the officer was gone, Vicky picked up Max and gave him a big kiss. "Want some ice cream?"

"*Now?*"

"Why not? Let's treat ourselves."

Max wriggled free. "Um, it's okay. I just want to play my game."

He went into the living room. Vicky marched over to the kettle and aggressively turned it on. Seb didn't know what to do or say. He checked his phone and saw that he had several more messages. Vicky took out her phone as the kettle boiled, while leaning against the counter.

"Oh, great," she said, seeming calmer now.

"What?"

"Another video. Me outside Mia's house. I've sent it to you." She seemed... resigned? Numb, perhaps. She turned back to the kettle.

Seb watched as Vicky yelled at the crowd, swung at the boy, then sat in the car, looking more devastated than he'd ever seen her. He went to her, opened his arms. She tried to move away from him, but he wouldn't let her, even as a little voice whispered that it had to end here. She'd been with another man. It felt so wrong. But he kept holding her.

"It's okay," he whispered.

"It's not."

"It's okay," he said again, inanely, and then just held her close to him.

She clutched on to his arms, then pulled herself in and pressed her face against his chest. When the sobs came, Seb almost forgot about everything, both of their mistakes. He just held her and smelled her hair, gently kissed the top of her head.

Vicky gently pushed him away. "I'm sorry," she whispered.

"Me too."

She paused, then said, "I was so scared of telling you."

Seb laughed, gruffly. "Me too."

"Coke, Seb?"

"Another man, Vicky?" he snapped.

She looked like she'd snap again too, but then she sighed.

"Who was it?" he asked.

"David," she murmured, shaking her head. "It was stupid. I felt alone. You were working a lot and... It's not an excuse."

"I'll have a coffee too," Seb said, walking over to the table.

The video had kept playing quietly, in the background. Now, a young man was talking to the camera. "This is Wicked Weston News, and I'm Connor, your host. Did you guys just see that? Who thinks she went too far? Imagine if she'd hit him!"

Seb clicked on their other videos. It seemed they had a track record of going around town and trying to stir up nonsense. One of their videos was titled, *Shoplifter or Predator?* It had ten views, and the thumbnail showed a blurry image of a man in a supermarket. All their videos had very few views... except for their last, which had just reached 1,000.

"David," Seb said when Vicky brought the coffees over.

She wrapped both her arms around her, looking so lost and beautiful, and nodded.

"From the pub?"

"One night, you went home early to be with Nat. I stayed behind with the girls. And then they went home and... I didn't mean for it to happen. But then it kept happening and..." She laughed in disgust. "He's not a good person. He's the reason I made that stupid video to begin with."

"What do you mean? How?" Seb consciously lowered his voice, but it was difficult.

"He'd been messaging me on Facebook for months. Saying he wanted to meet up again. He wanted it to be like 'the good old days'. But I wasn't interested. I never was, really. But then he sent me..." She looked so disgusted, Seb didn't even care that she'd cheated on him. He just wanted to defend her, to do something productive, to protect her. "A video. He took a video. In secret."

"Of you two. Together?"

Vicky nodded. "But I thought to myself – fine, he has that video, but he's not asking me for money. He's not demanding to be with me again. Instead, he asked for something so weird and specific. He wanted me to humiliate myself online by trying to become famous. To go viral, specifically. I guess it's a weird messed-up kink for him, maybe a power thing. Perhaps he was imagining I'd go down the sexual content route. I don't know. He's always been up his own arse."

"Where did you meet him?"

She hesitated, then said, "Seb, nothing's happened since."

"Where?"

"His flat," she finally said. "He wanted to lord it over me in person. He's an idiot."

"An idiot," Seb repeated. "An idiot is somebody who buys a

bag of coke from one of their daughter's teenage friends, all to impress somebody they don't give a shit about, and who doesn't give a shit about them. *That's* an idiot. Secretly recording sex with a married woman is... is..."

Seb bolted to his feet, staring down at his wife. He realised he wasn't prepared to lose her. He might have lost his daughter, but he would not be giving up on his marriage. He'd never seen her look at him like this before. She seemed almost impressed.

"His address," he growled. "Now, Vicky."

"Seb, you can't—"

"*Now!*"

He expected her to keep arguing, but she started typing on her phone. Seb's screen lit up; he saw the first line of the address. Shoving the phone in his pocket, he stormed to the door.

"Daddy?"

Seb ignored his son. He ignored the flood of messages and hate waiting for him in the virtual world. He ignored the image seared into his mind of the woman he loved more than anybody grinding and twisting nakedly with a blackmailing bully. Starting the car, he drove, and he knew he was going to do something bad.

Chapter 50

Mia

Mia kept noticing the way that Nat was looking out of the window. Mia, Nat and Terri were sitting in the dining room; Terri had dubbed it their 'command centre'. It turned out that Terri's skills as a go-between in the real world worked really well for this fame stuff, too. She was busily sorting through Mia's emails, chattering away about opportunities. But Nat didn't seem interested; she just looked out of the window, maybe thinking of her mum, maybe thinking a bunch of useless stuff that wouldn't help anybody anyway.

Maybe Nat was thinking about the police officer who had recently visited. Mia had lurked at the living room door, ear against it, listening as they asked Nat questions about her safety – if she was scared, stuff like that. Nat told them no; she was there because she *wanted* to be. But from the way she longingly gazed at the garden, and the houses and the landscape beyond it, Mia wondered if she'd passed the police a note or something. She wished Jack was here.

"You've got about fifty offers of talent managers," Terri said.

"That's your job," Mia told her. Terri flinched, and Mia

went on, "*We're* doing this for *us*. Not for some adults to take all our money and tell us what to do. Do you want the job?"

Terri bit her lip, then said, "But what if I'm no good?"

"You'll be better than any stranger we could hire. Won't she, Nat?"

"Hmm?" Nat turned to Mia.

"I was saying..." Mia thought she did a good job of hiding her annoyance. "Terri could be our talent manager."

"Is that legal?"

"Well, Mum can be the manager technically then, but Terri will really be in charge. Okay? Is that good enough for you?"

She wanted Nat to snap something back, but she was way too absent.

"I'll go ask Mum."

Mia left the room. Her mum was sitting on the sofa, staring with empty eyes at the TV. There was a half-empty bottle of wine on the table. Mum just stared and stared, almost as though she thought the TV was on. But the screen was turned off. She was just staring at her own reflection. It was so pathetic. Like *Mum* was the one who should've been acting like this!

"Mum, you're my talent manager, but not really. Terri's in charge. You just have to sign off on whatever she decides, okay?"

Mum seemed to wake up a little bit, emerging from whatever weird state she was in. "Huh? What do you mean?"

"Terri's going to be my talent manager. She's going to arrange all my interviews and stuff. But obviously, we'll need you to sign off on whatever she decides, okay? That's okay, right?" Mia's voice rose as her mum stared stupidly at her. "Or maybe you'd prefer it if we went to therapy together and talked about all the stuff that happened, all the stuff you didn't do and all the signs you ignored. Well? *Well?*"

Mum made the saddest, most self-pitying noise. "It's – it's fine," she finally said, then burst into tears.

Mia left the room, disgusted.

"You've got *so* many podcast offers," Terri said.

"What about TV?"

"Not yet. But I bet they'll come in soon. Maybe after you've done a few more podcasts."

"What should our next podcast be about, Nat?" Mia asked.

Again, Nat turned to her slowly. "Huh?"

Mia clenched her fists under the table. This bitch had tried to ruin her life. She'd tried to turn all their friends against her, the whole world, and now she didn't even have the decency to pay attention. Mia remembered when she and Nat were younger, braiding each other's hair, how important it had seemed. She couldn't imagine getting the braids just right feeling so significant now.

"Our next podcast. What should we make it about?"

"What about college?" Nat asked.

"What *about* college?"

"It starts in, like, a week."

"Newsflash. People go to college to find their dream job. We've found ours already."

Nat shrugged and the three of them sat in silence for a while. Mia texted Jack again.

> Party time's over, bro. Where are you?

But the message didn't even say *delivered*, just *sent*, which meant his phone was off. What was he doing? Jack could go off the rails sometimes, but he usually texted, at least.

"I'm going to take a bath," Mia said, quickly leaving the room.

"Mia – wait."

She turned to see Nat hurrying after her. Nat touched her hand. For some weird reason, it was easy to forget about Nat's betrayal when they touched like this. It was easy to focus on all the good times.

Nat lowered her voice. "Do you still have that video?"

"I don't want to talk about that."

Nat tightened her grip, not letting Mia pull away. "But do you?"

Mia nodded.

"Could you delete it?" Nat asked. "I've already made my choice. I recorded the video. I don't want anything to do with Mum or Dad. I even told the police I felt safe here. But this video, I feel like it's making things awkward. It's making me feel like I'm being *forced* to be here."

"If I do that, though, you could just walk out anytime you wanted."

"So I *am* being forced."

"No," Mia said quickly.

"So you'll delete it?"

Mia pulled her hand away, saying nothing, and then almost ran up the stairs. She wished Mum would hear her footsteps and chase after her, demand to know what was wrong, hold her, let her cry, let her be a little girl for once. As Mia was running the hot water, her phone vibrated. She had a text from an unknown number.

> It's Jack. I've got so much I need to tell you. Meet me at Café Nerva in the Sovereign Centre at 4pm. Please. Come by yourself, okay? I know that sounds weird, but it'll make sense when you get here. I need you. I love you.

Mia stopped running the water. She had time to get changed and quickly sneak from the house. She wouldn't tell Nat or Mum or Terri. If Jack told her to come alone, she'd trust him. She'd always trusted him, even with the big fat ugly dark secret always coming between them. But Dad was dead. There was nothing stopping them from being the best brother and sister duo ever.

Actually, she realised, as she crept back down the stairs and grabbed her trainers, maybe she should make *Jack* her talent manager. He was a better choice, thinking about it. Terri could share the role, or be his assistant or something.

Chapter 51

Seb

Seb hammered on the door, before the coward in him could come out to play. He'd always lived with that little voice, a whisper that told him he was powerless.

He slammed his fist down for what must've been the twentieth time before David opened it. It was like time had melted and the heavyset guy in front of him, with the dirty goatee and the bloodshot eyes, was the lean, witty man who'd spent almost every night at the pub. Seb knew because he and Vicky had been there at least three times a week, leaving Nat with Vicky's mum. Seb's job had been making him dog-tired, and Vicky had been going through a bout of anxiety and depression.

And this piece of *shit* took advantage of that. If he was ever going to be able to hold his wife again without feeling sick, Seb knew that was how he would have to think about it. This man twisted his woman's mind. That was the only way the husband in him could begin to accept it.

"Do you fucking remember me?" Seb said, his tone sounding ominous even to himself.

David did something so cowardly, it just made Seb burn

even hotter. He turned to run. Seb found himself shoving the door open and pushing David in the chest. David lived in one of those flats where the front door opened directly onto the stairs; he fell, made a seriously pathetic moaning noise, then began scrambling up the stairs.

Seb chased after him, wishing he was fitter. David ran through the open-plan flat. There were beer cans all over the coffee table, plus the stench of weed in the air, and porn playing on the TV in the middle of the day. They ended up in the kitchen. When David took the knife from the block and turned, Seb thought, *If I die here, then okay.*

He wasn't some badass. But push any man far enough, and that conviction will arise eventually, unless he's been broken beyond all reason.

"Are you going to stab me, hmm?" Seb said, walking slowly towards David.

The knife tip juddered from side to side, David's lips doing the same sort of strange dance, like he was trying to choose between crying or summoning the courage to use his weapon.

"Do it," Seb said, taking another step, feeling hyperaware and alive in a way he hadn't since his last physical confrontation as a twelve-year-old kid. "Do it..." His voice got louder. "Do it, do it, do it." Then he grabbed David's hand and brought the knife to his own throat, felt the tip of the blade, the coldness on it. An almost hallucinatory voice commented inanely in his head, *This is realer than the internet.* He began to shout, "Do it, do it, *do it, do it!*"

But David was too weak and pathetic Seb realised, just like himself. Both of them were cowards. Seb snapped, darted his hand out, grabbed David's wrist and wrenched it to the side. David yapped like an injured dog and dropped the knife. Quicker than he knew he could move, Seb picked it up, brought it to David's throat.

Seb wanted to kill him. That was the cold truth. It was as though his wedding band was pulsing with heat, telling him to do it. Could he? He *would* have done if the law wouldn't have sided with the blackmailer. "Explain."

David licked his lips, then he said, "It was just a game."

"A game? A *game*? If you don't explain what the *hell* you thought you were doing, I swear to God I'll bleed you out right here. I don't care anymore. Too much has happened, too much has gone wrong for me to care. And all because of *you*."

"I wanted to... to make a point."

"What point? I'm really, honestly curious."

"People will do anything for fame."

Seb felt sick as he laughed. "*That's* your point? *That's* why you blackmailed a married woman? Why you threatened to expose an affair? Why you ruined so many lives? Because 'people will do anything for fame'? Do you realise how obvious that is? You might as well tell me you did it to prove the sky is blue."

"It was... more than that."

"I'm curious. Tell me."

"I don't agree that people, in general, will do anything for fame."

"You're the one who bloody said it."

"A *lot* of people will," he went on. "But Vicky? A happily married woman with two children? I wanted to see how far a *normal* person would go. But I didn't expect any of this. How could I? Do you honestly believe I wanted any of this to happen?"

"You secretly recorded your sexual encounter with a married woman. You then used the video to blackmail her for the most pathetic reason I can think of. Do you think I should let you go, David? Do you think you deserve that?"

It was like Seb heard what he'd just said. The anger made

him throw David to the floor and dive on him, shoving the knife against his throat, his knee driving into his belly. "Where's the video?" Seb said. "*Where?*"

David was crying. "There wasn't a video. I just... I just..."

"You're a pathetic loser. Your flat reeks of piss. You're not clever. You've got no prospects. You'll never achieve anything. Your *point*, your *thesis*, is something a moron could come up with while daydreaming. You think you're blowing people's minds by saying, by *proving*, fame *is bad?*"

Seb pushed with more pressure, wishing so badly he could get away with this, wanting it in a hungry sort of way. He wanted to gut him, watch him bleed.

"Are you lying to me about the video?"

"I wouldn't do that," David said through sobs. "Me and Vicky, we were... It wasn't like that. It wasn't seedy."

Seb snapped and brought the knife down in a hard, purposeful arc towards David's hand. Luckily, David smacked it away at the last second and the blade clattered across the grimy kitchen floor. Standing, Seb knew he had to leave before he did it again and didn't miss.

"If you're lying to me... Don't stand up." David cringed away. "If you're lying to me," Seb went on, "I'm coming back here, or finding you in whatever hole you run to, and I'm finishing the job. Got it?" David cringed some more. "*Got it?*"

"Yes, yes, yes," David whined, covering his face with his hands when Seb took a step forward.

Seb made himself leave quickly. He was afraid of what would happen if he didn't.

Chapter 52

Alek

Alek waited in the corner of the café. There was a *kill yourself* tickling at the corner of his mind, and he didn't like it, but Alek was a strong man; he was a brave man. He wouldn't let it win. He was wearing a cap, pulled low, but his size still drew some looks. Alek thought the man sitting across from him might recognise him. He was a college-aged kid, with dyed green hair, a bull ring through his nose and a little leer on his face.

Grab that ring and pull hard. Tear it out, make him bleed, lap up the blood and spit it in his face. *He's going to hurt me.* The boy's thoughts thundered in the air.

"Can I help you?" Alek said.

The green-haired freak looked over his shoulder, then back at Alek. "I'm sorry?"

"You're staring at me," Alek told him.

"I didn't mean to."

Now he's trying to backtrack. Hurt. Him.

But then he got up and left, shouldering his knapsack; it was covered in futile, absurd pins. Plastered in them. Alek thought he saw a hammer and sickle, and he stood, meaning to follow the boy, because that was just unacceptable. How the *hell* had the hammer and sickle become a symbol to these young people? That hammer and sickle had hung over as many or more mass graves as the swastika, and yet, one was still acceptable.

Alek sat down again when he spotted Mia. She was wearing a hat, too. She turned, scanning the place. Her shoulders slumped when she saw Alek where her brother should've been.

Mia approached the table. "Where's Jack?"

"Sit down," he told her.

"Where is he?"

"Please don't make me ask you again."

Mia sat, pulling at the skin around her fingernails. It was already red raw and flaking away. "Did you send me that text?"

"I'm going to need you to go to the toilet. Wait in the corridor."

"Why?"

"Because otherwise I won't be able to tell you what I need to."

"I don't understand."

"Just do it, Mia. For fuck's sake."

Big man scaring little girls... But it worked, so screw it. Mia stood and walked in jittery, scared steps to the toilet. After a moment, Alek followed. He found her pacing up and down in front of the ladies'. The hallway was quiet, so Alek did his work quickly.

"Woah. Hey!"

Alek quickly patted his hands up and down her body. He grabbed her phone from her back pocket, checked it wasn't recording, then handed it back to her. "Keep that in my sight, the entire time."

"So this is what you wanted all along?" she hissed in disgust, shivering.

"What?" Alek asked.

"You just grabbed my ass."

Alek snorted. "I took your phone from your back pocket. I've got no interest in sex with anybody, Mia, least of all a child. What's wrong with you?"

I just want to be loved.

Alek sighed, then left the hallway. A moment later, Mia followed. At the table, Alek decided to stop wasting time. Making sure her phone was still in sight, he said, "If you want Jack to be okay, we're going to need to make some arrangements."

"Why wouldn't he be okay? Where is he?"

"Keep your voice down," Alek snapped. "Let's just say he made a mistake. He broke into my house. He tried to rob me. And now he's... somewhere safe."

Mia's eyes were wide. *But... but... but... Jack!* "Where is he?"

"Lower your goddamned voice, Mia."

She did, with visible effort. "What have you done?"

"Please don't become accusatory," he told her. "You started this with your vicious lies."

"You *did* make me record the podcast!"

"Don't argue with me. We're going to fix this. You're going to help me. I refuse to allow the world to believe I'm some sort of demon. I'm a good man, Mia. I've never hurt anybody who didn't deserve it." You've never hurt *anyone*. Where are the bones? Where are the bodies? What is your purpose? "So, you'll help me, yes?"

"Is Jack okay?" Mia asked, fighting off tears like the annoying brat she so often allowed herself to become.

"He's fine," Alek snapped. "Look."

Alek took out his phone, went to the photo he'd taken, and showed it to Mia. Listen to that gasp. This has all just become so, so real for her. Mia opened her mouth like she wanted to speak, but all that came out was a weird, strangled noise.

"I'll let him go," Alek told her. "I don't want to hurt him. Really. I don't. But you need to help me, Mia. You need to—"

But Mia was clearly not thinking straight. She bolted from her chair, turned, ran from the café. *Ran.* Actually *sprinted* so that the four other patrons and the girl behind the counter all watched. Alek tucked his phone away, grinding his teeth. How did she think *running* would help anything?

Alek finished his black coffee and stood, his head swimming.

"Everything all right, mate?"

This is my chance to be a hero. Alek heard the rat's thoughts, before he saw him. Turning, he found a typical Englishman standing there, a bulldog of a man, shaved head, no neck to speak of, football T-shirt, vague green and grey tattoos all over his hairy arms, a belly he seemed to wear as a point of pride.

Think how easy he would be to handle. And he has the gall to look at you with that wannabe hard-man face.

"Why wouldn't it be?" Alek walked right up to him.

"That girl, she looked pretty torn up. What did you show her on that phone?"

"Were you watching me?" Alek slowly and very gently put his hand on the man's shoulder. The bulldog allowed it to happen. "Hmm, big man? Were you?"

I can't let him do this to me. I can't let him show everyone how small I am.

"Now listen here, mate—"

Alek could've tolerated the words, but when the man aggressively chopped at Alek's hand in an attempt to violently jolt his hand loose from his shoulder, Alek reacted like the savage beast he was – the ancient man, the time-before man.

A right hook, a knee to the gut and the bulldog was stumbling away, and everyone was screaming. Reality did a shimmering thing, then Alek was outside, hurriedly walking down the street. Some panicky instinct made him send a text.

I love you so much. You're the best sister a man could dream of.

Sun glared into his eyes; sirens rang in the air. Were they coming for him? He turned, looked at the beach, the sun bouncing off the metal railings, and then the light shifted and he saw the outline of his grandfather, a silhouette walking towards the sun, as if he was trying to beckon Alek to follow him. They'd emerge in the mid-1950s, when The Father of Nations had passed, letting the rich two-harvest soil and its people finally recover. Alek would be there, smiling, playing music, eating, and Maksym would be there too. Maybe Alek would even be able to take Liuba with him.

He blinked. Maksym was gone.

Wiping tears from his eyes, Alek kept walking.

Chapter 53

Mia

Mia pulled her cap low, her chest cramping as she tried to comprehend what had just happened. She knew that her life would never be the same; everything else was shrinking in comparison to the hell she'd just been exposed to. Pulling her hoodie up too, despite the sun, she almost broke into a jog when she thought about what had happened.

It had been so *public*, sitting at the café table, but nobody took any notice of them. Mia had thought, *Well, we're not famous enough yet, then...* but Alek didn't look right. He had a sheen to his skin, a twisted glint in his eyes. Mia almost stopped walking when she thought about the moment he'd pulled out his phone and showed her the photo, the pain of it. She kept walking, though; she couldn't stop, or she knew she'd collapse to the ground and be unable to walk, to think, to function.

Finally, she reached the bus stop. She stared at the ground and stuffed her hands in her pockets, trying to be invisible. "Mia?" somebody gasped, and Mia almost told them no, not her. She'd stopped being Mia the moment she saw her brother. Dead.

She had to ring the police, didn't she? Why hadn't she done that already? What else could Alek do to her?

He'd already killed her brother.

"Mia?" the boy said again.

She looked up after a pause, feeling so far from everything. She wished Nat was here; Nat was her only friend, the only person she wanted to be close to right now. Terri was being helpful in her own way, but Mia felt as though she and Nat had been fused through this experience.

The boy was the 'cool' kind: skin-fade haircut, designer clothes. Mia would've normally tripped over herself to talk to a boy like him. He had his phone in his hand. "Can I get a selfie?"

"Sure," she said numbly.

Her brother was dead.

He waited for her to stand, but she didn't trust her legs to do that. He sat next to her, lifted his arm. "Uh, can I?"

Mia said, "Are you asking me for consent?" It was a question, but it came out flat.

She couldn't stop thinking about the emptiness in her brother's eyes, the torchlight shining on them, the trademark shaved line in his eyebrow, the twisted, fixed-in-place tilt of his lips.

"Yeah..." The boy lowered his phone. "Are you all right?"

"I'm always all right."

"I don't need a photo."

Mia shrugged, staring, trying to get herself to take out her phone and ring the police. But she was sleepwalking through sludge.

"Are you sure you're all right? Has something happened?"

"Something has happened," Mia said robotically, then shivered. She hadn't realised how cold she was. Once she started shivering, she couldn't stop.

"Mia? Uh..." She felt a light jacket drape over her shoulders. She cuddled it closer around her, and then she was suddenly crying, big gulping sobs.

"What happened?" the boy kept asking, over and over.

"Police," she managed to say.

"You want me to ring the police?"

"He... He... *He killed my brother.*"

She screamed the last part, keeling over, thinking of all the times with Jack: all the smiles, even all the times when she'd come downstairs *after* and he'd been sitting in the kitchen, a hot chocolate waiting for her, and she'd loved him for the gesture and hated him because it meant he knew.

"Explain," the boy said, then to somebody else Mia couldn't see, "I don't know. She said to ring the police."

A woman knelt in front of her, took her hand. Her skin was crinkly and warm. "Let's take some nice deep breaths. Can you do that? Nice and slow."

Mia tried, but it was like all the air just kept being sucked into her, inflating her with more air, and none would come out. But the old lady just kept whispering, waiting, and Mia's breathing finally slowed. Her head felt like it was splitting right down the middle.

"What happened?" the lady asked.

"Alek sent me a message. It said I had to meet him, or he'd hurt my brother. So, I went and... and he showed me a photo of my brother's... *dead... body.*" She forced past the agony. "But he was talking like my brother was still alive. It was like... like he didn't know he'd killed him."

Mia was certain he was dead. The photo had been so brutal, the flash showing in gruesome detail her brother's corpse, the paleness of his skin, the savage cuts all over his body, his cold dead eyes. That was the part that sealed it. Earlier, she'd thought her mum's eyes were dead as she stared at the turned-off TV. But now, she knew she had been wrong. Now, she knew what dead eyes really looked like.

Chapter 54

Alek

You are not worth anything. You are incapable of love.

Alek ran into his house, slammed the door. Liuba was ringing him. But he didn't want to speak to anybody. He was tired of the voices. He was tired of the game. But he couldn't let *them* win. He had to get more than just a photo of Jack. Mia simply didn't understand the severity of the situation.

Maybe you should fuck her until she gets it.

Alek roared, slammed his hand against the side of his head. The voice – it wasn't Maksym – the voice – where was his grandfather? – the voice was putting ugly images into his head, ugly sounds. But the voice was a liar because Alek would never, ever hurt anybody in that manner. Alek would honestly rather slowly bleed out over the course of several days, while somebody tortured Liuba in front of him, than cross that line.

Keep telling yourself that. We both know you're jealous of her dear dead Daddy and all the fun he got to have.

"No, no, no."

A flit – reality was bleeding, and then Alek's knuckles hurt. He'd smashed his television to pieces; small shards of glass clung to his knuckles. His head raced, he wanted to die, and he was desperate to live.

A child can be trained to do almost anything, Alek. Anything a sick man could desire. You could even make her pretend to enjoy it; you could even twist her poor deranged mind into believing, in some fatal and heedless way, that she actually *is* enjoying it.

Alek was panting heavily as he went into the kitchen. He needed the voice to stop. His phone kept ringing. Sweet Liuba, but he couldn't say anything; he couldn't do anything. He drank a *lot* of whisky, the sort of gulps a man took of water after a long jog in the sunshine. It seemed to help a little bit.

When he was able to think somewhat clearly, Alek went to the cellar. The door was still busted. Switching on the light caused silhouettes to dance across his vision, but Alek knew he couldn't follow them until he'd done his work. He took the steps slowly, then stared across the cellar at the...

You did this.

At the...

You were always a monster.

"This wasn't me," Alek whispered, rubbing his cheeks when tears decided to appear. "This wasn't *me*."

They reeked of death. They were covered in blood and cuts and bruises and death. They were not alive. They did not have any breath left in them. They did not hear or see or smell or think or exist. But Alek didn't – this wasn't him. Who did it? Who killed these men?

And they were there: the journals. Maksym's journals.

He stumbled across the room, tears pouring freely now, but he didn't sob. He just let them fall down his face and over his lips so that he could taste the salt and the pain. Opening the journals, he saw words and then no words, and then words, and no words. They were pushing through the page like blood, the ink was bleeding, and Alek didn't know what to do, what it meant. Why wouldn't the words stay still?

You know why. Oh, how desperately you needed to be special. How hungrily you felt that desire to *mean* something, Alek, but you've never meant anything to anybody, and you never will.

Sirens. Alek heard sirens.

He dropped the journal, rushed up the stairs, looked out of the window.

Police cars were driving down the street right at Alek's house. There were two cars and a van following behind. What the fuck? The fat bulldog at the café had called the police; he must've told them some lie to make them react so quickly.

You've never been as clever as you think you are.

Alek grabbed his phone and went to his Instagram page. When he went live, viewers instantly started flooding in.

"I'm being persecuted," he yelled into the phone as he grabbed the biggest knife from the block in the kitchen. "Is this you, Vicky? I'll fucking end you. I'll end all of you!"

He rushed for the back door, struggling to hold the camera steady. Slipping through the rear entrance, he skirted along the side of his house and ran away from the sirens, telling his viewers that this wasn't his fault. But it was hard to talk because there were more tears. And he was sobbing now. And he was running. And life was twisting painfully.

A text appeared on the screen. Liuba.

End the live!

"The State is persecuting an innocent man!" Alek yelled, ducking his head and breaking into a jog. "I've done nothing except fight for the dignity of the forgotten and oppressed. Vicky, Mia, you're my enemies – know that, remember that. Even if these officials and their dogs tear me limb from limb, we'll still be fighting. We'll never stop fighting."

Alek ran.

Chapter 55

Vicky

Vicky was watching Max on the trampoline like she had countless times before, but nothing about it felt natural or genuine. She felt like, not only was *she* going through the motions, but he was too. Max would smile and do star jumps, but any time he grinned over at her, she saw the questions in his eyes: when was Nat coming home? Why were Mummy and Daddy so stressed and taut and terrified?

After the phone call with Nat, Vicky had expected... something. She wasn't sure what, exactly. But she knew her daughter, and despite the mistakes she'd made, she knew there was love in her little girl even if the world was chewing them up and spitting them all out. The fame. The game of it. She knew Nat would always love her, the same way she'd always love Nat. But what was Vicky supposed to do? Storm over there again, make another scene?

"It's happening again," Seb said quietly, appearing at the back door.

His eyes were wide, dark circles, bloodshot. Vicky knew she didn't look much better. Neither of them had slept last night. They'd lain awake, side by side, not talking, staring at their phones, scrolling, reading about what terrible parents and people they were. There was a sick kind of addiction to the virtual self-flagellation. She began to wonder whether if she read enough, she'd start to believe she was what they said she was.

"What is?" she asked tiredly.

"A police car is outside."

"A police car?" Vicky snapped. "What if something happened to Nat?"

Seb sighed, shaking his head. "We're in this together, yeah?" Clearly, he thought it was more fame crap, more *games*.

She stood, went to him. They hadn't even really spoken about the affair, the reasons for it. But Seb flinched when she hugged him. The doorbell rang again; they ignored it. Finally, he wrapped his arms around her. Max climbed down from the trampoline and ran over to them, joining the hug.

"Why don't you make Max a sandwich," Vicky said, her voice too dull to make the question sound like one.

"Chocolate spread, big man?"

Max was the bravest of them all. He clearly sensed their moods, but he smiled and nodded anyway.

Vicky went to the front door. It was the same officer from before, PC McGregor, with another officer standing at his side. Behind him, in the street, Vicky saw more cars pulling up: news vans. *News vans.* She blinked, rubbing her eyes, wondering if she was seeing things. There were four vans, people with *real* cameras, *huge* monstrosities, nothing like the mob that had hounded her outside Mia's house.

"Mrs Taylor," PC McGregor said. "Can we come inside? I'm afraid it's urgent."

"Sure," she murmured. "What are *they* doing here?"

"They're bloodhounds," the other officer said.

"This is my colleague, PC Sharma."

The lady smiled tightly. She had a tough, sinewy look to her.

"Is my daughter okay?" Vicky said. "Come in, come in."

McGregor didn't seem aggressive. It was more like... protective? Was that the right word? Vicky led them into the kitchen. "It's nothing like that, Miss."

"More police!" Max said brightly... though it seemed a little forced. Her son was making the biggest effort out of all of them.

"I'm sorry," Vicky said, looking at PC Sharma.

She laughed, shaking her head. "Nothing to apologise for. It's nice to see somebody smile at the sight of an officer."

"*I'm* going to be one," Max said proudly.

PC Sharma smiled. "I'm sure you are."

PC McGregor cleared his throat. "Mrs Taylor?"

"Oh, yes." Vicky glanced at Seb.

"Come on, champ."

Seb seemed relieved to be able to scoop Max into his arms, holding the plate in the other, and carry him from the room.

"Does he need to be here?" Vicky asked, hoping this wasn't about the cocaine buying. It was surreal. Between that and the affair, Vicky finally felt like she understood what wedding vows were for – though she'd broken hers, of course.

The constables shook their heads. PC McGregor motioned to the table. "Let's sit down, Vicky." They all sat at the table, and then he went on, "There's no easy way to say this, but we have reason to believe that Aleksander Bodar is responsible for a very serious assault, possibly worse than that. He is currently being chased by police and livestreaming himself. He mentioned your name, hence the news vans, and hence us being here. His livestream is allowing us to track him, but we need to be on the safe side."

Vicky struggled to process it all, her head swimming. "He's... killed someone?"

It seemed so much more real than everything else that had happened so far, the videos and the backstabbing and the betrayals. A murder?

"Who?" she asked. "Or can't you say?"

"We have reason to believe it is Jack, Mia's brother."

Vicky bolted to her feet. "My daughter is with her!"

"There are officers at their residence too, ma'am," PC Sharma said. "Your daughter is safe."

"You know that for a fact?" Vicky said. "You've spoken to her?"

"My colleagues have," she replied. "Alek is nowhere near her."

"I need to ring her anyway."

"Of course."

Vicky grabbed her mobile and pressed *call*. It rang one and a half times, but that felt like a very long time. Like an eternity. When Nat finally answered, Vicky gulped in a breath as though she'd just emerged from water.

"Nat?"

"I'm here, Mum. It's okay."

In the background, Mia almost yelled, *"Okay?"*

"I meant *I'm* okay," Nat said. "Mum, I love you. But I have to go. I need to be here for Mia."

"But you're safe."

"I'm safe."

"I love you, sweetness. I love you so, so, so much. And that will never change."

"Never?" Nat's voice almost broke.

"Never," Vicky said firmly. After she hung up, Vicky said, "What now?"

"We wait," PC Sharma said. "We ignore the vultures outside."

"How do I find the livestream?"

The officers exchanged a look. "I'm not sure that's a good idea," PC McGregor said.

"With all due respect, this is my home, and I can watch whatever I want."

Vicky had to see, with her own eyes, that he was nowhere near her daughter. She didn't have to look very far for the link. She searched 'Alek livestream' and it was the first result. The viewer count was at 20,000 *live* viewers and climbing.

Alek jogged, breathing heavily into the camera, sirens in the background. She could hear seagulls and somebody yelling for him to stop. "They won't get me," Alek panted. "They can't get me. Won't let them. Never let them. Grandfather? Maksym?"

Comments flooded in.

LOL. Is this real?

Bloke sounds like a proper nutcase.

Fake. Big YAWN.

Hahaha this is so staged.

Guys I think it might be real...

Show those pigs!

We don't even know what he did...

Bacon is as bacon does.

That all happened within the space of perhaps three seconds, and then there was another wave of comments, then another.

"I think he's running towards the sea," Vicky said.

PC McGregor nodded. "We'll have our hands on him soon."

Chapter 56

Alek

Alek could hear his own voice mixing with the other voice and the yelling of the police officers. He was a big and fast man, and as he ran down the promenade and up a set of steps that led to a higher porting – yes, this is your place, this is where you belong – he knew he couldn't let them get their hands on him.

Look what happened to your people, Alek. When the people in uniforms come, you better have a way out. Or they'll give you one.

"Alek Bodar!" somebody yelled from below.

Ignore them.

Alek turned and saw there were several police officers standing at the bottom of the stone steps. He was on a platform that overlooked the Old Pier and gave him a vantage point of the rocks below. The tide was in despite the sun, wind whipping, waves crashing beneath him and glistening in the light.

"Please – we just want to make sure you're okay." This came from a female police officer. Look, Alek: they've made her look like Liuba to soften you up. Alek blinked, and it was true. The female police officer had his sister's features.

They're trying to trick you.

Alek turned to the waves and stared at his phone. He had just reached 100,000 live viewers. The man in the phone looked nothing like Alek. He looked weak and scared.

"Remember me," Alek yelled, and then he tossed the phone over the wall.

Quickly, he climbed up and people started yelling, telling him to come down. But he had a better chance in the water. Looking across the sun-kissed sea, he studied Steep Holm. It was an island the Vikings had once used as a docking station, like a humpback whale made of rock and grass lounging on the surface of the water. Alek was a big man; Alek was a strong and fit man.

You could swim that easily. You can do anything. It will take them a long time to reach you. They'll have to call the Coastguard. That will give you time to build defences. Perhaps you can find a cave on the island. Yes, Alek. This is a good idea. You can do this. You can make it work. All you have to do is jump.

"Alek! Please! We just want to keep you safe!"

Like the people in unforms would tell him the truth. How could Alek trust them?

Jump – you can swim – jump – you're a powerful person – jump and... Ah, ha, ha, good boy.

The water rushed up to meet him, but the police had somehow arranged this too. They'd made sure the water *just* covered the tip of a jagged rock. Alek felt it crush into the side of his body. He tried to breathe, but salt water rushed into his mouth. There was pain, but it was far away, and then...

Makysm?

Yes.

Is that really you?

Yes.

Am I dying?

Yes.

If you're here, it means I did everything right. We can change the world. We can save everybody. No more summers spent walking barefoot and bloated across the broken soil, no more winters spent huddling without a fire, slowly realising a loved one is no longer breathing, lacking the energy to move them. The earth is too cold to dig anyway, and even if it wasn't, who has the energy for that? No more lying there, smelling a corpse, waiting to become one. No more hammers and no more sickles and no more starvation. Yes, Maksym?

No. You lost your way. All you cared about was fame. But it doesn't matter. You were never going to change the world.

More and more water rushed into Alek's mouth. On some level, he was aware that he was attempting to swim, but his body felt utterly mangled. His limbs wouldn't work.

I was, he told his grandfather.

You're a freak who stared at blank journals, Alek. I never wrote a diary about what happened, and we rarely talked when I was alive, just a few words here and there, a grunted admission that I lived through those times. And what did you do? You made it yours. You claimed it. You did the exact thing you apparently hated Vicky for. You hallucinating husk. You're not a righteous avenger. You were never going to change the world.

You wanted your own grandfather to be a cannibal. You are not a strong man. You are not a clever man. You are not even a man.

Alek felt like he was crying, but he wasn't sure. Maybe it was the ocean. He wanted to scream, but the ocean claimed that too.

You're a disappointment, Maksym said, as the world began to fade.

Chapter 57

Nat

Nat was lying awake in bed next to Mia, scrolling on her phone, her belly twisting in agony every time she read a comment that implied somehow *Mum* was responsible for Jack and his friend's deaths – just like *Mum* was responsible for Alek's mad dash along the prom and his jump into the sea.

Let's just use logic here, folks. She's a fame-hungry psycho. If she'd never made her pathetic little video to begin with, none of this would've happened.

Her own daughter wants nothing to do with her. What more is there to say?

Exactly!

There were a few comments talking about how it was possible for a daughter to run away from their parents and for the parents still to be good people, but they were shouted down almost immediately.

The truth was, Nat missed home. She missed her room. She even missed Max nagging her to play his video game with him. But Mia had the degrading, insulting video.

Turning off her phone, Nat rolled over and tried to sleep. When Mia wriggled up and pushed against her back, Nat tried to ignore it. But then Mia slipped her arm around for a hug. It was way more intimate than how they'd hugged before.

"Do you think they're still out there?" Mia whispered.

By *they*, Mia was talking about the news vans. They had assembled outside Mia's house as soon as Alek went live. After his jump into the ocean, he hit his head on the rocks and had to be rushed to the hospital. The last Nat had heard, he was currently in a coma. But she didn't care about what happened to him, the nutcase. He'd killed two people and he would've killed Mum, or maybe even Nat herself, if he'd had the chance.

"Nat?" Mia went on, and Nat kept trying to pretend she was asleep. Mia huffed and rolled away. Nat thought she'd got away with it, but then Mia kept talking. "I know you're awake, Nat. But it's fine if you want to pretend. I just want you to remember something, okay?" Mia touched Nat's shoulder, slipped her hand under her nightie and touched her bare skin. It was very unwelcome and one-sided. "I've got that special video of you. So you can act however you want. You can sulk or whatever. You can make *my* brother's..." She coughed back a sob. "About you. But you're never leaving me. Never. We're going to do this together. Like we planned."

Nat said nothing. She wasn't actually sure Mia knew she was awake; maybe it was a test. Nat waited as Mia began to watch TikTok on her phone. As Nat lay there, it all started to seem so silly and immature. Maybe it was because she could only hear the music from the videos, the same five or so songs on repeat. Nat was getting sick of it all. People hated her mother. There were threats... all because of her.

Finally, after *hours*, Mia fell asleep. Nat still waited another half an hour, just in case Mia was faking, then slowly turned over. She moved as though she was underwater. She knew that, if this went wrong, Mia would have a complete meltdown.

Taking Mia's phone, Nat turned on the screen, waited for

face recognition to reject her, then opened the phone with the four-digit passcode. She'd had plenty of chances to watch Mia type it in over the past few days. Nat then rolled over, turning the brightness down, and quickly went to Mia's gallery.

There were selfies, some artistic black-and-white shots... and right there, the sick video. Nat deleted it, then deleted it from the trash bin, then scoured Mia's phone for backup software. She deleted it from the Cloud and also from another backup app. What if Mia had a hard copy, though? What if Terri had a copy too?

Nat thought about it for a moment, but there was nothing she could do. She couldn't stay here. Turning over, she found Mia staring right at her, her eyes wide, hurt, making Nat feel insanely guilty for a moment.

"What did you just do?"

There was no point lying. "Deleted the video."

Mia gasped, sitting up and snatching her phone. "I-I made backups," she said. "So don't think—"

"It's over," Nat said.

"So you don't want it anymore, you boring bitch? You just want to be normal? I thought we had a dream. The red carpet. The cameras."

Mia looked and sounded sick. In a twisted way, Nat was almost grateful. It was like Mia was giving her a real look at what this fame business meant.

"I can't let my mum's name get dragged through the mud anymore," Nat said. "I need to go home."

"And tell the press what?"

"I don't know. I don't care."

"You *have* to care," Mia said fiercely, taking Nat's hands and squeezing them hard. "Don't mess this up for me. I've got a chance here."

"Mia," Nat said softly. "Jack is—"

"Jack's dead. Dad's dead. I was five, Nat, *five*, when Dad first did it. Five! Do you fucking hear me? Do you fucking understand? I was in my room playing with Barbies, literally fucking Barbies..." Mia was crying, and suddenly, Nat loved her friend again more than ever. It was all so tangled. "Then he told me to come downstairs. He was drunk. Whisky *stinks*. There was a video on the TV..."

"It's okay," Nat whispered. "You don't have to tell me."

"You know what happened. Sometimes, when I'm at a party or whatever, I look at a little girl and I think, how? How did he do that? They're so *small*, Nat. So tiny."

Mia broke down, and Nat wrapped her arms around her friend, letting her cry.

"I don't have anything else," Mia told her. "Please don't ruin it. Don't tell anybody about the video. Just say you were confused. You thought it would go viral. But you've changed your mind, or something. And I'll leave you out of everything else, too. Please?" Mia sobbed again. It was heartbreaking. "*Please?*"

Not even a minute after describing the first time her dad had put her through hell, *this* was what Mia was begging for. Mia began to say it over and over... *Please please please please...*

"Okay," Nat finally said.

"We can be best friends until the sun comes up," Mia whispered, and despite everything, warmth moved through Nat.

Chapter 58

Seb

Seb couldn't stop noticing the way Vicky anxiously massaged her hands together, as though she was trying to push away all the pain and the tension and the knowledge that their lives would never be the same. They were in the kitchen, talking with the publicist they'd hired, over video call. Max was with Vicky's mother; it was easier to keep him away from the news vans parked out front.

The publicist was a slick man apparently called Maverick, though the name seemed as fake as his shiny teeth. It had been Seb's idea to consult somebody so they could better handle the fallout from all this madness. People online were saying that *Vicky* was responsible for what that lunatic did.

Seb's phone was open next to the laptop, showing a live view of his house from one of the cameras outside. It was surreal seeing the front of his house, curtains closed, knowing tens or even maybe hundreds of thousands of people were watching.

"We need to avoid making any concrete statements," Maverick said. "This is about how people *feel* about you, anyway, so the truth of any matter isn't particularly relevant. We need one image stuck in everybody's head – the two of you, looking sombre, serious, expressing empathy in the most believable way possible. Are we on the same page?"

Seb felt disgusted with the man. The confrontation with David had triggered some violence in him, some weird primal thing, and he wished Maverick was here in person so he could spit in his face. Reaching over, he took his wife's hand, gave it a supportive squeeze. She shot him a look, eyes registering shock, then nodded a small thanks and held him just as tightly.

"Shall we discuss what you're going to wear?" Maverick went on. "And Vicky – do you usually wear make-up?"

"She doesn't need it," Seb snapped, part of him still wanting to let her go when he imagined her and David writhing around together. But Seb already knew he wasn't going to leave his wife. It made him feel both empowered to make the decision, and like the cuckolded loser so many people would no doubt brand him.

"Well, we can discuss options."

Seb was about to snap at him again, but then Vicky made a noise that took Seb back years, well over a decade. He'd been dancing around the room with Nat in his arms, swinging her up and down. She'd been giggling like crazy... and then Seb had slipped, fell. Vicky had gasped like all the air had been sucked from her lungs. Even when Nat was clearly okay – Seb managed to fall onto the sofa, catching her – Vicky had still looked terrified.

Seb glanced at her now; she was staring at his phone. Seb looked too. It was Nat attempting to walk through the cameras, but the mob was hounding her. Their daughter looked so small and vulnerable as they yelled questions at her. Vicky bolted to the front door. Seb quickly followed, ignoring Maverick's voice as he told them to be careful, like he thought he was suddenly their boss, the prick.

Outside, Nat was surrounded by four or five news-type

cameras, with more people with mobile phones, all of them yelling at her. Vicky, wearing her comfortable house hoodie and an old pair of leggings, barefoot, her hair wildly trailing behind her, looked like the fiercest mother bear who'd ever lived. Pride flooded Seb as she raised her voice.

"Get away from my daughter! All of you! Now!"

Seb jogged after her. Two men were literally blocking Nat in on two sides, aggressively shoving their mobile phones into her face. Seb darted forward, aware of the cameras, and glared at one of the bastards. Just like when he'd held that knife, he felt ready to do it, to kill. That's what this had made him, ever since he bought that bag, used a child for his own pathetic gain. It had turned him into somebody else, someone less optimistic, less naïve.

"Lay one fucking finger on her," Seb growled, but that was all it took.

The men took a step back and Nat ran right for the house, her head ducked, crying like it was causing her physical pain. Vicky ran after her. Seb was about to go inside too, but then one of the cameramen said, "Is she here to deliver some coke, Seb?"

Seb turned, fists clenched. It seemed like there were a thousand camera lenses aimed at him. Vicky had talked about her fear of cameras so many times, sometimes with rage and sometimes with quiet acceptance. Seb had never understood, but he did now. The fear pissed him off. It was like all the lenses were part of one many-eyed monster.

"You're all sick," Seb told them. "I've made mistakes. I never pretended to be a perfect man. But two people are dead and you're here, doing this. If there's a hell, you're all going there. Hopefully soon."

Seb ignored their yelling as he walked back towards the house, being careful to move with purposeful slow steps. He wouldn't let those assholes see him running.

Inside, Nat and Vicky were intertwined on the floor, both of them crying, both of them saying the same thing over and over, almost in unison. "I'm sorry, I'm sorry, I'm sorry..."

From the hallway, Seb could hear Maverick through the laptop speakers. "Seb! I'm watching the stream. Seb! Can you hear me? That wasn't a very good idea."

Seb walked into the kitchen. Maverick smiled so that his white teeth threatened to break the screen's brightness setting. "Okay, Seb, let's cool off and discuss damage-control—"

Slamming the laptop closed, Seb went to be with his wife and daughter.

Epilogue

Alek

Three Years Later

Oh, my sweet Alek, look where you've ended up. But it could've been worse. I know you don't like the pills or, indeed, the occasional injection when you become a little too rambunctious, but I think we can both agree, this is far more preferable than having your murderous, insane self out in the real world, affecting real-world things.

But I know how clever you are; I know you listen to the nurses, and you feed me the morsels they gift. And it's not as though you're blind, my dear boy, my dear grandson. I'm sorry for leaving you, but I never stopped loving you.

Even now, as you sit in a wheelchair despite being able to walk, as you stare catatonic out the window at the same tree you've been staring at ever since they moved you here eighteen months ago, as your sluggish, slow mind tries to process each leaf at a time, in sequence.

I thought you may like to know: Mia has started an online

prostitution account. I'm not sure of the official name; she uploads photos of herself to perverted, demented men online. None of hers are *nude*, however, which seems to make everybody feel better about the whole thing. The day Mia turned nineteen, guess how many subscribers this depressed, drug-addicted – oh, yes, and that; she's been seen in public completely incapable of reasonable thought or action – troubled young woman had? *Fifty thousand.* Her first photo was 'leaked'. Black and white, artsy, Mia in a bikini sitting on a cold bathroom floor with her knees tucked to her chest.

This was you, Alek; you took her brother and her father from her. The brother with your blackout rage and the father with the truth. The father, fine, but why the brother? Oh, you didn't mean to. I get it. But you did, Alek. It was always in you. That anger. That hate.

Don't feel bad for her, though. Fifty thousand lonely, borderline paedophilic men, all of whom are paying ten dollars per month for her *content*. Well – you do the maths, my boy.

This was a game, sweet Alek, a fame game, and she won. Mia – the smallest, the most scared, the most fragile, the most *used* – she won.

Are you even conscious of when Liuba visits you, the two of you sitting awkwardly in the visitor's room? Liuba always looks shell-shocked, her hair greasy, she's lost and confused. Hating you, yet still loving you. Do you even see her?

Oh, what's this? Another visitor? This is interesting. If you knew about this before, I suppose you decided not to give it to me, Alek. Are you hiding things from me? Are you still capable of that?

They wheel you in and there she is, the woman who started this all. Vicky looks good, doesn't she? She looks far better than your usual visitor, anyway. A little thinner, sure, but not unhealthy. She looks like a determined, tough woman. I can feel that waking something in you, my dear boy, waking some sort of twisted resentment. Did you want to break her?

"Can he understand me?" she says.

If you were ever going to break your catatonic state, Aleksandr, it would be now...

"He can, but he pretends not to." That's a staff member. What a cruel thing to say. Go on, Alek. Leap up from that chair and hurt him.

Vicky folds her hands, oh-so civilised. "Alek, hello. It's... nice to see you." She clearly didn't mean to pick that word. "I didn't know if this was a good idea, but I wanted you to know... I don't know. I just see how Michelle is. How much she's suffering. She said something to me a few months ago... *He's sitting in that chair, hating himself.*"

Liuba is the sweetest, kindest person who's ever lived. She ascribes the noblest and most honourable characteristics to you. And if you never had them to begin with? Who cares.

"So I want you to know," Vicky went on, "what you did ruined many, many lives. But it didn't ruin mine. It didn't ruin my family. It didn't ruin my marriage. We've been through so much, all of us, but we've moved house now. We live on a farm. Well – it *was* a farm once, and we're making it that way again. It was difficult at first, ditching our devices. We've got one family computer in the living room, that's it.

"It was hardest for Nat. No friends. No phone. For the first couple of months, Alek, it was like I'd unplugged her power source. I thought she might end up in a place like this... well, a non-criminal one."

She *is* nervous, isn't she. But she seems different. Stronger somehow. "But then one day, I looked out the front window, and I saw Nat with one of our neighbour's children. They were climbing a tree and Nat fell, and then she started rolling around on the ground.

"I was terrified, obviously. So I ran, and you know what I heard? She wasn't hurt. She was rolling around in the grass laughing. And that's when I knew we'd made the right choice."

Ah, she's leaving, that's good – no more guilty talk. No more stress. Just the window. Just staring. Just emptiness. But what's this? She stops, turns back, frowns. "But next month, we might be evicted. It's not exactly easy to earn a living." Vicky is changing into somebody else, warping demonically as she returns to you, sweet Alek, and leans down, my boy, and stares at you in such a way I see the optimism was a social-media-like pose.

"Michelle told me something when she was drunk a few weeks ago. She said she'd noticed you not taking your medication. But she was happy for you. You seemed so purposeful, so happy, so *you*. So... not numb. She hates herself for it, Alek. She hates herself for letting you loose. She was always singing your praises, always gave you every chance. But look at you now." Did she just spit? In this supposedly sterile place? "*Look at you now!*"

THE END

Also by NJ Moss

All Your Fault

Her Final Victim

My Dead Husband

The Husband Trap

The Second Wife

Through Her Eyes

Ruin Her Life

The Twins

Nowhere to Run

Acknowledgements

Thanks as usual to everybody in the Bloodhound family, and especially my editor, Rachel, for her excellent work and insights!

A note from the publisher

Thank you for reading this book. If you enjoyed it please do consider leaving a review on Amazon to help others find it too.

We hate typos. All of our books have been rigorously edited and proofread, but sometimes mistakes do slip through. If you have spotted a typo, please do let us know and we can get it amended within hours.

info@bloodhoundbooks.com